AF095155

THE GLASS HEART
···
THE SLEEPING CITY
···
MARTY HOLLAND

Stark House Press • Eureka California

THE GLASS HEART / THE SLEEPING CITY

Published by Stark House Press
1315 H Street
Eureka, CA 95501, USA
griffinskye3@sbcglobal.net
www.starkhousepress.com

THE GLASS HEART
Published and copyright © 1946 by Julian Messner, Inc, New York.
Reprinted in paperback as *Her Private Passions*, Avon, copyright © 1947, 1948. Copyright renewed January 25, 1974 by Marty Holland.

THE SLEEPING CITY
Copyright © 1952 by Marty Holland and published in
Thrilling Detective, Fall 1952.

Reprinted by permission of Suzanne Estella Tarvin. All rights reserved under International and Pan-American Copyright Conventions.

ISBN: 979-8-88601-053-4

Cover design by Jeff Vorzimmer, ¡caliente!design, Austin, Texas
Book design by Mark Shepard, shepgraphics.com
Proofreading by Bill Kelly

PUBLISHER'S NOTE:
This is a work of fiction. Names, characters, places and incidents are either the products of the author's imagination or used fictionally, and any resemblance to actual persons, living or dead, events or locales, is entirely coincidental.
Without limiting the rights under copyright reserved above, no part of this publication may be reproduced, stored, or introduced into a retrieval system or transmitted in any form or by any means (electronic, mechanical, photocopying, recording or otherwise) without the prior written permission of both the copyright owner and the above publisher of the book.

First Stark House Press Edition: October 2023

THE GLASS HEART

Down on his luck, Curt snatches an overcoat and is chased by the police into a Beverly Hills neighborhood where he meets Mrs. Virginia Block. Virginia is expecting a new handyman to show up, and Curt quickly snags the position. He doesn't realize that this seemingly sweet old woman is a rich miser, and finds himself working for pennies as her gardener, her chauffeur, and whatever else she needs to maintain her huge house. Then Lynn, as aspiring actress, moves in, and things don't seem so bad there after all. But it isn't until Curt discovers Mrs. Block's secret that he finds out what kind of a goldmine he's sitting on. All he has to do is figure out is how to work it... and then stay alive.

THE SLEEPING CITY

Officer Wade Reed is given his mission, to pose as a member of the Les Ties gang and infiltrate a local mob. As Jim Cox, he is an out-of-town gunman who has been hired to help with a heist set up by Louie Thompson, an old-style prohibition hoodlum who's planning a comeback. It's Wade's job to find out the details and report back to the Gangster Squad. One false move from Jim Cox, and Wade's fiancée Betty will have to find a new husband. But Wade doesn't figure on Thompson's girl Madge. At first she seems like a real tough cookie. But once she gets under Wade's skin, he begins to have his doubts about the mission. Can he protect Madge and still stop the heist?

Marty Holland Bibliography

Novels
Fallen Angel (Dutton, 1945; revised & updated as *Blonde Baggage*, Avon, 1949; Novel Library, 1950)
The Glass Heart (Julian Messner, 1946; reprinted as *Her Private Passions*, Avon, 1948)
Fast Woman (Diversey, 1949)
Darling of Paris (Avon, 1949)
Baby Godiva (2011; published posthumously)

Novellas
Terror for Two (*Scarab Mystery Magazine*, January 1951)
The Sleeping City (*Thrilling Detective*, Fall 1952)

Short stories
Lady With a Torch (*Thrilling Love*, Oct 1943; as by Mary Holland)
Night Watchman (*The Shadow*, March 1943)
Rain, Rain, Go Away (*The Shadow*, April 1943)
D.O.A.—East River (*Street & Smith's Detective Story Magazine*, March 1944)

Screenplays
The File on Thelma Jordan (1950; original story)

7
THE GLASS HEART
By Marty Holland

121
THE SLEEPING CITY
By Marty Holland

THE GLASS HEART
MARTY HOLLAND

Chapter One

It was one of those ritzy hash joints in Beverly Hills, away from the hoi polloi. Fancy lace tablecloths, demitasses, and waitresses in pink organdy outfits. One of those places. I was sitting up at the counter, sipping coffee, puffing on a cigarette, soaking in the warmth of the room, and glancing now and then through the draped window at the rain outside. It was raining like hell. No ordinary downpour: heavy, splotchy drops—the way it rains in California.

I was watching the rain, and people hurrying past on the sidewalk, and people inside—sprinkled throughout the room. A blowzy matron at one corner sat with another dame in nurse's getup, and a couple of kids. The fat one kept griping about the servant problem, how she couldn't find a decent cook for the kids.

I was sitting there listening to that when the door swung wide open and the sucker came in. He brought a gust of raw wind, scraped his shoes on the mat, and threw his overcoat on the rack. Over my motheaten slicker. Then he was seated up at the counter beside me, calling the waitress by her first name. He was a big flabby guy in tweeds with a Hollywood scarf, a loud voice, and a three-carat flasher on his little finger.

My eyes just naturally went back to the coat rack. He'd hung up a brand-new camel's hair. Must've set him back two hundred at least. And I figured it'd bring twenty-five bucks. The idea wasn't exactly new; I'd been making a living at it for a couple of months now. You'd be surprised how elementary it is to pick up a guy's overcoat—by mistake of course.

So I reached for my hat and got to my feet. At the cashier's cage I left my check and a dime for the java. I sauntered over to the coat rack and picked up my suitcase. I looked back at the counter just once.

A moment later I was out the door, shooting up the boulevard, with the camel's hair under my arm.

The next second all hell broke loose. The cashier was screaming behind me. There were footsteps, garbled groans from the sucker—waddling up the street in the rain after me. I recognized the voice all right:

"Hey—*bub!*"

I shifted into a fast fox trot.

"*Christ Almighty! My topcoat!*"

I crossed the street quick. Then I was running. Down Santa Monica Boulevard—like nothing flat. I beat it down a side street. A colored maid, carrying a bag of groceries, kept ogling me. I slowed down till I got past her. Then I glanced back.

In the distance was the police car. Beverly Hills is the best police-patrolled city in the U. S. *Why hadn't I thought about that?* Evidently cops had just been cruising past the restaurant. I could see the sucker jabbering, with one foot on the police car running board—pointing in my direction. I didn't feel very good about it. I guess I began to sprint.

Ahead there was the wet shiny sidewalk, tall shivering silhouettes of trees in the dusk. I ducked in at the corner house—an immense two-story stucco—and ran back past some shrubbery, through a moss-covered archway. Vines, hanging loose from the side of the house, hid me from the street. I opened a wrought-iron gate and closed it behind me and kept moving.

Suddenly I'd crashed into something human. A shrill little scream pierced the air. I saw the old woman who'd been bent over. She bolted up now, holding a battered pie tin in her hand.

"*Goodness!*" she whimpered. "You—frightened me half to *death!*"

I halted and pulled my hat down over my forehead and grinned, trying to figure where to move next.

"Well—*my!*" She was still panting and holding one hand over the region of her heart. "You made me spill Blackie's dinner!"

I saw the doghouse then and her rain-soaked, sad little black cocker spaniel.

"And goodness, you're late."

I turned back to her, wondering what she meant. She was standing under the arbor now, out of the rain, massaging the cold from her arms. Through the corner of my eye I saw the police car pass by, slow. Cautiously I darted over beside her, to where the vine-covered pergola hid me from the cops' view. I figured I was safe here. Best to stall. Best not to risk the street for a while.

"It's past six-thirty," she said irritably. "The agency said you'd be here at six."

"Oh? They did?" I was keeping the conversation moving, with my eyes still glued through the patch of leaves to the street. *Who was the old bag taking me for?*

"As long as you've worked for Judge Brewster, your references are just fine. I'll explain the job—"

I glanced over and nodded, with my mind still on those patrolmen out front. Lucky it was raining, or they'd be out of the car now, making a search on foot.

"You'll make things hum around here. It's your job to keep the place in order. If something needs repair, you'll fix it." She was waving an arm out to the rear.

I gave the grounds a quick once-over. The backyard covered about a half-acre, enclosed in a high brick wall that shone wet and rusty-orange. There were a lot of fruit trees in the rear and a big old garage with broken windows. Vines hung loose all over the roof and down the side of the back gate.

"The sprinklers must be turned on once a week," she said brusquely, "except, of course, when it's raining." She squinted up. "You'll be expected to drive me occasionally. But you won't to have to wear a uniform. And you can just put on old trousers to do the gardening and general work." She pursed her lips together, then smacked them open. "Know anything about mechanics?"

"Mechanics? Oh, oh—sure."

"I have two automobiles. And I can tell you they go on the blink often enough."

I was beginning to get my breath now, and a load of this old goat. She was frail, wan-faced, with spindly bantam legs in lisle stockings. She wore a faded brown print dress pinned with a brooch at her neck. There was a twisted straw belt around her waist. Her hair was a mat of gray against the pallor of her skin. But it was her eyes I noticed mostly: they had a peculiar stare. Small, light, gray beady, shifting eyes that looked everywhere but at you.

"I suppose," she went on, "you'll want to discuss salary."

"Salary? Yeah—"

She put her hands where her hips used to be. "Twenty dollars a week and board and room. It's a good room, with a private bath."

"Twenty bucks a *week?*"

"That's the salary! It's equivalent to a hundred dollars a week when you consider the high cost of living—the way people are frantic for a bed to sleep."

"Lady, listen—" I started, then didn't say anymore. For one second I'd forgotten about the cops cruising by out front. It didn't matter what the salary was. It was a place to park for the night—gratis. In the early morning I'd clear out.

"You can take it or leave it!"

"I'll take it, lady," I said.

She laughed, a girlish little laugh—as if she were delighted. She held the screen door open for me. I was barely inside the back porch when she said:

"Right here's your room."

She opened a door between a big refrigerator and two washtubs and switched on the light. I moved over and peered inside. I got a little sick: cracked, shredded taffeta drapes hung at the windows. There was a muddy red carpet, for the greater part worn through. An old wicker chair sat by the bed, and beside it was an end table with stacks of dust-covered magazines.

The bed was the predominating feature because it practically filled the room. Obsolete, broken-down, archaic. Its headboard nearly reached the ceiling. On it were two carved figures lying down. You could barely make out a guy and a girl with wreaths of flowers around their heads. And she had long, flowing hair. A woodsy atmosphere. Grecian, I guess. I tried to figure if they were naked or whether the bed was so old their clothes had worn off. Anyway, they looked nude to me.

The old dame came in with "That bed's an antique. A fine old piece."

"Yeah. Anybody can see that." My eyes traveled up to the spider webs in the corner of the ceiling.

"The room's dusty, I know," she said apologetically. "But I've been living out at the ranch, and this whole house has been locked up all summer."

"It's plenty dusty all right, lady."

"I'm having a woman in tomorrow. It'll be clean as a pin."

"Ma'am," I said, "that's the way I like things. Clean." I threw my new overcoat on the bed and set the suitcase down.

"My! You came all prepared to stay."

I put on a sheepish grin. "Guess I did at that."

I went out on the back porch and looked around. The kitchen was dusty too. As if it hadn't been mopped up for months. She saw my eyes travel up to the pile of dirty dishes and rusted silverware in the sink.

"I'm baching it," she said with an embarrassed little laugh. "The servant problem, you know!" She brushed past me, into the kitchen. "Come on inside. I'll get your name."

I followed her through the kitchen and on into a sun parlor. It had a cement floor which once had been painted red, but now the paint was cracked and a faded splotchy henna. It had long dirt-streaked windows, potted green plants, and variations of cacti in big orange flowerpots sitting all around on the floor. Wicker table and chairs. She swung a door open. We went on into the living room.

The living room was worth talking about. First I noticed the mirrors. Antique. Framed all around in ten inches of gold with more gold filigree at the top. There were four of these museum pieces. They stood on the floor and reached the ceiling. That was reaching—a circus company could have set up their trapeze act in the room.

It was all dark woodwork. There was a fireplace, smelling of must and mold and burnt wood. It was getting dark outside. Shadows stretched across the room, reflecting their dark and wavering silhouettes in the mirrors.

Above the mantel was a portrait in oil of a stuffy-looking old gent. At this moment the old woman switched on the lights. The portrait in oil lit up. For a second I wondered if I wasn't in the lobby of Grauman's Chinese. My gaze roamed to the pictures on the side walls: a seascape, a desert scene, a Mona Lisa.

A bay window at the front had faded drapery all across, preventing you from looking out to the street. Through the French doors directly opposite was a flagstone patio. You could hear the rain beating against the panes and on the dirty rain-soaked canvas thrown over the garden furniture.

A baby grand stood at one side. Over its top hung a red Spanish shawl. Two flower-print rugs which didn't match met in the middle of the room. A burgundy divan sat where the rugs came together, facing the hearth. At the other end, a stairway led up from the entrance hall and beyond that was the dining room, filled with massive furniture.

The old woman waved me to the couch. "Please be seated—while I find my notebook."

I sat and folded my hands—like teacher's pet. My eyes wandered over to the bookcase. There was *Robinson Crusoe, Gentlemen Prefer Blondes, Bad Girl* by Vina Delmar, a few F. Scott Fitzgerald novels. There was also *Penal Code of California, 1941,* and further over I noticed some nice leather-bound medical journals.

The old lady was sorting through the junk in her desk. So I got up and roamed over to the piano. I began tapping a finger over the keys. The notes echoed hollowly while my eyes darted about the room.

"Real nice place you got here," I said. "Must be worth around thirty thousand."

"Thirty thousand dollars?" She was peering through her pince-nez at the papers in her hand with her profile toward me. But I saw her nose go up. "I had an offer from a realtor yesterday—forty thousand. But I wouldn't sell for a penny under fifty-five."

"Fifty-five grand?" The words slipped out.

She nodded matter-of-factly. "As far as that goes, I wouldn't sell for any price. Now, what was your name?" She had the book open and the pencil poised.

I folded my hands again. "My name is Curt," I said, sickly-sweet. "Curt Blair."

"Kurt?" she asked "K-u-r-t?"

"Spelled with a C. You can blame my father, ma'am. He thought up the name Curtis." I grinned meekly, like a lamb.

She was writing it down. "Why there's nothing at all wrong with that name. It's perfectly good."

"Yes, ma'am, I guess it is at that," I said. Anything to please her.

She turned to me abruptly. "I'll take your card of introduction—"

"Card?"

"Yes, the one the agency gave you."

"Oh, *that*." I fumbled around in my pockets. Finally I lowered my eyes as if I'd done something awful. "I must've lost it."

She studied me for a moment, her fingers pulling at the loose skin around her throat. Then: "How long were you employed by Judge Brewster?"

"Five years, ma'am." Pretty cute, I thought. The brain was working.

"And before that you worked for—"

"Before? Before the judge, you mean?"

"Yes, yes," she replied wearily.

"I worked for a very important gentleman, ma'am." I was fishing in mid-air.

My eyes stopped on the bookcase. I read two names from the novels. "Scott Delmar," I said.

She thought for a moment. "Never heard of him."

"Oh, he's a famous writer."

She nodded abstractedly and wrote down the name. I relaxed a little. I noticed a little candy dish sitting on the piano scarf, filled with chocolates. I waited until she wasn't looking and grabbed up a fistful. I shoveled them in. I saw the sheet music, open on the piano rack. Schubert's *Serenade*. My fingers just naturally slid down and began tickling the ivories. When I glanced over at her she was staring at me with an annoyed expression. I snapped my hands up quick.

"I—I'm sorry, ma'am. I should have asked you, but you see, I have a weakness for pianos."

"Go ahead," she said with a tolerant half smile.

"Yes, ma'am."

My fingers were stiff. Hell, I hadn't touched a keyboard in years. I was half through the piece when she said in an astonished voice: "Where in the world did you learn to play so beautifully!"

I grinned. "You can blame my father for that, too. All I can remember when I was a kid is him grabbing me by the ear and dragging me off to different piano teachers."

"Continue," she said.

So I kept on playing. Schubert's *Serenade*. Acting unconcerned. But

I was jittery over that guy from the agency. Why hadn't he showed up—and what was I going to say if he did? I expected the doorbell to buzz any minute, and I'd be out on my can again, in the rain again, dodging cops, going from hotel to hotel again trying to find a room. I was trying to figure a way I could get to the door first if the guy did show, when she looked up with those swivel eyes.

"I'm Mrs. Virginia Block," she said through the music. "And it's going to be nice having you here, Curtis. Such a strong, sturdy young man in the house." She smiled wearily. "I must confess it's rather tiresome sometimes—being alone."

The chocolates stuck in my throat. "You're all alone?"

"Yes, indeed. Ever since—" Her gaze strayed up to the oil painting above the mantel. "—since Henry left."

I did another take on Henry. The light shooting up from the little lamp below the frame accentuated his thick bull neck, made his bald head shine like nickel.

"That's my husband," she continued with a tremolo in her voice. "My son, Jeffery, he's living up in Salt Lake City with his wife." Her eyes shifted down to the carpet. "So you see I'm quite alone."

My notes hit a discord. "That sure is too bad."

"Although," she said, "I have little time to think of my loneliness. The ranch takes up a great deal of my spare time."

"You own a ranch?" She was watching, so with my right hand still playing the melody I reached over with my left and picked up the last chocolate. I held up my little finger and nibbled at it daintily. She went on:

"Oh, yes. I have one hundred acres of walnuts. That's why I shut this place up all summer. I've been living out in the valley at my ranch. I'll want you to drive me there occasionally. And also to my beach house."

Ranch house—beach house—Christ!

She got up and moved toward me and handed me two keys. "These are for the back and front door." She opened her mouth to say something else. But suddenly she stopped and gazed toward the window. Outside, the dog, her cocker spaniel, was whining. She hurried over and opened the window.

"Be quiet, Blackie!" she yelled. "You must be quiet!"

"It's my fault maybe," I said, "for spilling his dinner. Maybe he wants more."

She closed the window. "Goodness, no! The little mutt eats his head off."

I eyed the empty candy dish. "Come to think of it, ma'am, I'm a little hungry myself."

She looked at me sort of aggravatedly, but her voice was dulcet. "Well, goodness—why didn't you say so? You'll find plenty of things to cook in the cupboard!"

"Oh, did you want me to cook your supper, ma'am?"

"Gracious, no! I have dinner over every evening by six!" Her mouth twitched. "You'll find canned soups, vegetables—anything you want in the kitchen. You just go in there and fix yourself up something."

"Yes, ma'am."

Through the corner of my eye I could see her studying me. With a pleased grin on her face, as if she'd made a good bargain. As if she were thinking: twenty bucks a week and he cooks his own meals ... I sure hooked myself a wee minnow!

"I'm going upstairs and read a while," she said. "I probably won't be back down." She thought a moment. "Let's see—the front door is locked." She hurried over to the window, closed it, and turned the latch. She turned to me. "You'll be sure to lock the back door?"

"Yes, ma'am."

She walked over to the stairway. "Oh, yes—I've rented one of the side bedrooms upstairs to a lady. If she comes—" She broke off. "Oh, dear, I'm becoming quite forgetful. The lady telephoned saying she wouldn't be here until tomorrow." She started up the steps, then: "Curt, I can't stress too strongly that things must be locked day and night..."

"I'll sure remember that."

"You'll probably want to retire early yourself, since you have work ahead of you early in the morning."

"Yeah. I feel like going right to bed."

She nodded and hurried on up the stairs. She was a wiry little thing. She didn't go up the steps slow—like most old people. With lithe little bounces she practically took two steps at a time.

I went out into the kitchen. I flung open a cupboard door, grabbed up a can of soup. I took a can of corn, too, and some Spam. I opened the bottom cupboard door and brought up a pan. There was a little spray gun in there with the words, *Dy-E-Ze—Insect Killer.*

I heated the soup and corn and fried the Spam and sliced some bread. There was coffee in the silex already made. I heard the old lady's footsteps upstairs while I ate. And I bawled her out for keeping such a dirty joint—only she didn't hear me, of course. The dinner tasted all right. But I didn't like the unwashed dishes and skillets in the sink or the looks of the mice tracks in all the cupboards and drawers.

But, hell, I thought, it isn't raining inside here. There's a roof over my head. No cops. Chow's on the house. It was sweet—a natural—I didn't have a gripe to my name.

After dinner, I could still hear her footsteps over me. Her bedroom, I figured, was right above the kitchen. I made a quick survey of the lower floor. The only thing I hadn't seen downstairs was the dining room. I went in.

There was nothing in sight worth a tinker's dam except furniture of course. I opened drawers looking for silverware. I found it: rusty, worn. Worth about a buck—the whole lot. Ash trays of brass. I stepped back from the buffet. It was then that a shrill little buzzing pierced the air. I jerked up straight.

My right foot had stepped on some kind of an electrical appliance near the head of the table. I hurried back into the kitchen, with my heart in my mouth, wondering if she'd heard the buzzer and knew I'd been snooping around.

I went into my room. I rifled the camel's hair pockets. There was a dandy pair of gloves rolled up in a ball, a soiled handkerchief, and a little leather cigarette case. I flipped it open. Two cigarettes left. I put the stuff in my dresser drawer and hung the overcoat up in my closet.

I opened my suitcase, yanked out my old leather jacket, and threw some clean underwear on the towel rack in the bathroom so I could find it easily in the morning. I sat on the bed and picked up a magazine. *True Detective, December, 1940.* I tossed it aside. I was still uneasy about that guy from the agency. What had happened to him? I plunked myself on the bed and thought about that.

Jesus, that room was depressing! Damp—cold as a morgue. I sat there shivering under the flicker of amber light from the old dust-covered chandelier, thinking about everything—for a long time. I looked at the cobwebs in the corner and breathed in that odious smell of must all around me. Through the dirt-streaked panes I could see the palm trees shivering outside. And the rain kept beating down in a strange uneven rhythm. I kept sitting there thinking and listening to the noises, the creaking sounds an old house makes at night.

It wasn't until later, when I was in bed—lights out—that I really began to get ideas, that I began to sum up the whole deal.

An old dame—apparently her husband had left her. She had a son, married, living in Salt Lake City. She was alone—in a house worth fifty-five grand. Two cars. A hundred acres of walnuts. A valley ranch home. A beach house.

The next thing I was out of bed, strutting back and forth on the carpet like the cock-of-the-walk, thinking the whole situation out. I got so excited my hands were shaking and my lips were trembling and that little inner voice was screaming:

You small-time bastard! This is what you've been dreaming about!

On those freight cars—building castles in the air. Eating those rotten dime hamburgers. Sleeping in two-bit flophouses. Wondering how clean sheets would feel. Counting dimes—and trying to imagine what a couple hundred bucks would do for you. Lifting overcoats, wallets in a crowd ...
  Christ sake! You've struck it, kid!

Chapter Two

It was later, maybe twenty minutes later, when I heard the front door buzzer. I held my breath and listened for footsteps upstairs. I heard nothing. I threw on my old leather jacket and stepped into my shoes. At the door I stopped, wondering if I should answer it. If it was the guy from the agency—

The bell rang again, longer. And I was making tracks through the kitchen, the sunroom. At the stairway I stopped and listened for any sound from upstairs. I threw open the front door.

Before me on the porch stood a pimply-faced guy with horn-rimmed glasses and a streak of oil across his face. He was rain-soaked. The water kept dripping off him.

"Sorry I'm late," he began limply in a thin little voice. "I'm Basil Lake. Craft Agency sent me." He pointed out to the street, to an old jalopy parked in front. "Something went wrong with my car, I—"

He didn't finish. Because I was pushing him on down the steps. "People are asleep here," I rasped. "We better go outside to talk."

I'd made up mind to one thing: this was strictly my setup. And nobody else was going to muscle in.

I took him by the arm and hurried him out to the street, through the downpour. We got in his old Chevvy '33 sport roadster, with two spotlights and a lot of extra gadgets. A fox tail tied to the rearview mirror hung down between us, and there were beads of rain glistening on it.

A street lamp shone down on our faces, and the rain made a tinny, hollow sound on the car roof. Basil pulled the wet collar of his coat up around his neck and his teeth began to chatter. I looked back at the house, to the second story. Everything was dark. I turned to Basil.

"Sure is lucky for you you didn't wake up my aunt—rolling up here this way at ten o'clock!"

He looked hurt. "I'm awfully sorry. I left the house at six-thirty. I'd just hit Western Avenue when the darned motor went kaflunk. And the service station at the corner was closed. I had to work on the distributor myself. Rain or no."

"That sure is too bad."

He leaned forward in the seat and looked past me at the house. "Maybe I'd better come back tomorrow and see this Mrs. Block."

"Won't be necessary," I said with authority. "I handle the servant hiring for my aunt."

"Oh, you do?"

"That's right. I'll tell you about the job and if you want to start work in the morning it'll be okay with us."

He gave me an ingratiating smile. "It's nice of you to interview me this late."

"No trouble. Did the agency explain the job?"

He nodded. "The way I see it, you need a handyman around the place."

"Yeah. Sort of a jack-of-all-trades. It's a lucky thing you know how to fix motors 'cause my aunt has two cars she wants overhauled."

"Well," he said weakly, "I'm not so very good at that. I kind of play around with this old Chevvy. I'm really not a—"

"You mean to say you're not a first-class, A-1 mechanic?" I put a dark frown on my face.

He hesitated. "Well, no sir, can't say that I am."

"Don't know how my aunt's going to go for that." I said grimly.

He looked over at me. "Mrs. Wimple, at Craft, didn't mention that part. She said all I had to do was keep up the garden and the lawn and the like. I had no idea you wanted a *mechanic!*"

I stared straight ahead. "But she told you about the termites of course."

"Termites?" He sat up.

I sighed, exasperated. "I can see that that Mrs. Wimple didn't tell you much at all. You see, about half of this foundation is overrun with termites. You'll probably have to spend a week or two under the house to—"

His mouth flew open. "You mean I'm to spend a week or two *under* the house?"

"You think we want those termites running rampant all over the place?"

"Oh, no sir," he replied meekly. "Of course not."

It sure was hard to keep from laughing. But I kept a deadpan on my kisser. "Now, the termites are up in one rafter of the left wing, on the south side. You might even have to take out the lumber clear to the roof, put in new wood, and plaster over again."

He scratched his head. "*Plaster?* Funny—Mrs. Wimple didn't say anything about that."

I turned around in my seat. "You mean to tell me you don't know anything about termites either?"

"Well—no, sir, I don't. But it seems to me that people always have a regular man come out and do that kind of work?"

"You don't know my aunt! She doesn't go for a lot of riffraff milling around the grounds. She wants one good man who can do everything." I lowered my voice to a confidential tone. "But, hell—don't let that stop you, Basil. You can maybe talk to a regular termite man and study up how to outsmart those termites."

He swallowed hard. "Think so?"

"Sure." I paused. "So you can start to work in the morning. And, course you know the salary?"

"I know you get room and board. But it seems to me that with all that specialty work the salary Mrs. Wimple quoted must be a mistake. She said it was twenty dollars a week."

"That's right. Remember you get that *every* week!"

"For that money," he said, "you'd expect a soft job, almost a sinecure."

"There's nothing hard about it. But I did forget to mention—sometimes you've got to stay up nights with my aunt. When she's sick and—"

"It seems to me," he interrupted, "that's a great number of duties for one job."

"You'll get used to it. I haven't touched everything. You got to feed the dog once a day, do the marketing, and—"

"Marketing?" He was getting pale around the gills.

"Yeah. And you only have to do the housework on the maid's day off. And, oh yes—when my aunt's sick, or when she stays in bed all day like she does most of the time, you got to cook her meals and take them up to her on a tray."

"I can't cook!" he blurted.

I had him scared half to death by now. "Don't let that part bother you. You'll learn. Then, at other times, she'll expect you to go out to her ranch and pick walnuts."

"Pick walnuts?" His eyes were bulging. He couldn't get the rest of the words out fast enough: "Listen, I—I didn't tell you, but I have a job. With Judge Brewster, see?" He laughed nervously. "I have one, see? But I—I sort of thought I needed a change. I wanted to improve myself—"

"Sure. Well, you'll improve on this one all right. You'll be stronger than an ox in no time."

His voice wavered. "No, sir—after thinking it over, I believe I'll remain where I am."

"Better think it over careful. Don't be too hasty and turn down something you'll regret later."

He already had the motor started. "Thank you very much, sir. But I don't think I'm the man for the position."

I had one foot out the door of his car.

I walked to the house, and the Chevvy shot out from the curb in a gust of smoke, with connecting rods rattling and the muffler banging.

Lucky thing I'd left the front door open. I sneaked in the house. And when I reached the kitchen I stood listening for the old lady's footsteps. Everything was silent upstairs. So I figured she was fast asleep and had heard nothing. I went into my room and threw off my jacket and shoes and got back into bed.

It was then that I started laughing.

Poor Basil!

Chapter Three

I was awakened by a faint tapping on the door. I opened my eyes and saw that it was still kind of dark outside. For a second I wondered where I was.

"Curtis—"

It sounded like Mrs. Block's voice. But I wasn't sure. I bolted out of bed, wondering what was up, thinking maybe the old lady had found out about Basil—or maybe the cops had caught up with me. I jerked my overcoat down from the closet and shoved it under the bed. I threw on my jacket. Then I was at the door, listening, with my heart fluttering like a humming bird.

"Curtis."

"Yeah?"

"It's seven-thirty!"

"Oh, is it?"

"Time to go to work!"

I yanked the door open. It was Mrs. Block, all right. All done up in a straw basket hat, a red sweater, navy-blue slacks, black galoshes, and white garden gloves. She held up some little packets of vegetable seeds in one hand, a hoe in the other.

"I've been up since six," she snapped. "My! If you want to accomplish anything this day you'd better get a move on. It isn't healthy to sleep so long."

I gave her a sloppy smile. "No, ma'am, it sure isn't. I usually get up at six myself."

"Hurry and fix your breakfast!"

She hurried on out the back door. I sat on the bed wondering if I'd heard right. Was she kidding? Ordering me around at seven-thirty A.M.!

I thought about her some more under the shower. I was still sore. But then, I reasoned, you had to consider she was old and kind of childish and maybe hadn't meant to snap my head off. I got out of the tub and dried off and got dressed and breezed into the kitchen.

There was a colored maid in there cleaning up the dishes. Young, with an upswing hair-do. Big black eyes. And you couldn't overlook the streamlined chassis.

"Hiya, honey child," I said. "What's your name?"

"Jasmine," she drawled. She smiled, showing healthy white molars. She went on washing the dishes while I fixed breakfast. There was coffee made and some dried-out toast in the oven. I fried myself a couple of eggs and sat down at the table. The maid was drying dishes now, putting them up in the cupboard.

"You new here?" I asked.

"I sho' am. And I ain't nevah seen sich a filthy kitchen!"

I laughed. "You can say that again."

She stopped working and looked at me. "How she 'spect me to clean this whole house in one day? Why, I cain't even git this heah kitchen in ordah!"

"She asked you to clean it all in one day, honey child?"

"That sho' is right. The only thing I kin do is dust ovah things."

"Yeah. That's about all."

She frowned. "It sho' is gonna git cleaned in one day, howevah, 'cause I ain't showin' up tomorrow—or evah again heah. No, suh, I gits seven dollahs a day when I works. The kind of money she pays sho' is depressin'."

"Yeah," I said. "I'm underpaid myself around here."

"Curt, are you planting the beet seeds half an inch under the soil?"

"Sure. Sure, I'm measuring each one."

"All right. Bring me the rake. You'll find it in the cellar."

It'd been going on like that all morning. We'd planted beets, carrots, lettuce, and radishes. And I was beginning to feel like Luther Burbank.

I went over to the side of the house, to the cellar entrance, and opened up the two doors that swung outward on a slant. I walked down about eight steps. My feet hit cement. Then I was moving along and brushing cobwebs from my face.

It was dark in here. And there was a strong, septic odor of must and dampness, as if the cellar hadn't been opened for years.

I noticed trash all around: a workbench in one corner with old lumber piled up against it, a battered trunk, worn lampshades, a studio couch—everything gray with dust. You could hear water dripping from somewhere. It seemed to come from behind the back side wall, like one of the plumbing pipes was leaking under the house. I supposed that Mrs. Block would be after me next to fix it. Anyway, I found the rake and took it back outside, to the rear of the garage where she was.

"Now, Curt, before you clean up the leaves out front, you can start mowing the lawns. The backyard first."

"Lawns?" I said weakly. "Oh, sure—"

Poor Basil—Who was I kidding?

I went into the garage to look for the mower. It was the first time I'd been in here. I saw her two cars: a black Packard sedan '38, which needed paint, and a little blue Pontiac coupe '39, with dimpled fenders and worn upholstery.

The garage was tidy too—a galaxy of junk. About everything you could imagine, including a stepladder, old tires and tubes. Nothing worth a damn!

I dragged the lawn mower outside and got it going all right. It had rusty blades. No cinch to maneuver. And the grass was still damp from the rain. So you can see how I sweated for the next two hours. And she was right behind me most of the time—bossing. If she wasn't ordering me around, I could hear her inside directing the colored girl.

The lawn was all mowed, and I was sitting on the grass wiping the perspiration from my forehead when Mrs. Block was beside me again, juggling some wood boxes.

"Now, Curt, you can get the stepladder. I want all the avocados picked—green or ripe."

"Sure, sure."

"And be most careful how you handle them. I can't market them if they're injured."

"Yes, ma'am."

I spent the rest of that morning up on the ladder, reaching high. It was a hell of a fruitful crop—ten lugs. She helped me carry the boxes to the garage. I was taking one at a time, but I looked over and saw her with three boxes in her arms—filled with avocados.

She wasn't one of those fuddy-duddy grandmothers. She wasn't old lace and tea and crumpets by the fireside, I'll say that for her. She had Amazon strength!

She helped me pile all the boxes in the back of the Packard. Then, outside, she was on my tail again, pointing up to the roof of the garage.

"See how those Bougainvillea vines have grown loose? You can trim them up short. Goodness, you're a fine worker, Curt. My! When Henry was here he helped me do all this. He was always so—"

"You want the vines trimmed first? What next, lady, what next!" I was plenty irritable by this time.

"Then you can start on the hedges. You'll find the big garden shears in the toolbox in the garage."

Poor Basil—hell!

I was hot in the head now and I was swearing under my breath. But I managed levelly: "Isn't it chow time yet?"

"Chow?" She screwed up her face. "Oh, yes. Yes, indeed. I'll have Jasmine fix lunch. You can go right ahead on those Bougainvillea vines."

"Here you are, Curt. Four nice avocado sandwiches."

"Avocado?" I gave her a look and flopped down in a chair at the kitchen table. "I was hoping it was a good beef stew. That's just about my favorite dish."

"Well, goodness," she said, "there's a big bag of walnuts on the back porch. Eat all you like. The vitamin content is equivalent to meat."

"Thanks," I said drily.

She poured me a glass of milk. I watched it curdle up on the sides of the glass. Stale.

"If you don't mind, Mrs. Block, I'll take java."

I ate half of one of the sandwiches with one gulp. Then she was puttering around me, heating up the coffee, bringing me salt and pepper and mayonnaise, fussing like a mother hen with one chick. She poured me a cup of coffee and took the milk herself and sat opposite me with her plate piled up with sandwiches.

I sat there stuffing down that fluff and listening to the footsteps of the maid upstairs and thinking about how last night I'd been so excited over this setup. And how today I'd suddenly lost my enthusiasm. I'd struck oil all right, only it turned out to be a duster. It was this Virginia Block who was reaping.

I'd put out about fifty bucks worth of labor for her already. I decided it was time for a change. And now was the moment to pitch. She was such a homely old wren, it was hard for me to begin, but I got going all right.

I sat there staring at her with a dreamy stare in my eyes while she gulped down her food. Pretty soon she noticed my expression.

"Why, what's the matter, Curt—aren't you hungry?"

"Would—you mind turning your head—the way you did just then, for just a moment?"

"Turn my head?"

I nodded. "So that streak of sunlight catches your hair again?"

She was feeling around on her head. "What's wrong with my hair?"

"Wrong?" I said in a caressing tone. "Nothing's wrong. It's just that—the way you looked then, with the sun on your hair—you reminded me a lot of someone."

"I do?" She went on munching her sandwich.

I put a treble in my voice. "Of—Nancy."

"Nancy?" She drank down half her milk. "Who's Nancy?"

"Just a little gal—one of the best." I shook my head and laughed, then continued with a touch of nostalgia. "The good times we used to have, Nancy and I—"

She took a big bite of her sandwich. "I remind you of *her?*"

"Yeah." I scrutinized her closely. "I wondered what it was so familiar about you. Nancy's eyes, Nancy's nose, the same little laugh. Why, hell—for a minute I was back in Nashville!"

She gobbled down her food. "Why don't you go back there and find her?"

I sobered. "She eloped with that guy. That Air Corps looey."

"Oh, she did? Nancy eloped? Well, you shouldn't have trouble finding another girl."

"That's kind of you to say so, ma'am. But in the meantime, it's—tough being alone in the world."

"Humph! There must be something wrong with you. A nice-looking chap shouldn't be lonely. If you were my age—"

"*Your* age?" I laughed scoffingly and took a swig of coffee. You—*old?* At forty you're only beginning to live."

"*Forty?*" She blinked over at me. "Why, I—I'm *fifty*, Curt!"

I almost choked on my coffee. The old bag looked all of sixty to me. "Just the same, ma'am, you're very active. The way you get things accomplished is close to miraculous."

"Humph! With my responsibilities I've never had time to sit back and take things easy. It's being busy that has kept me young!"

I coughed. "It sure has."

She was on her feet now, brushing the crumbs from her lap. She started clearing the table. I got up quick and helped her carry dishes over to the sink. She seemed surprised that I wanted to help.

"My!" she said. "I don't know what more a girl could want." She glanced up coquettishly. "Tall, dark, handsome—"

I was standing close to her. I wondered whether to grab her and kiss her—or let it go for the moment. My lips brushed her hair.

"Goodness!" she snapped. "Put the sugar and creamer away!"

I kept standing there by the sink, beside her. I looked down at that prune-wrinkled face, those thin, pinched lips. A cold shiver went all through me. My stomach started churning—and I knew that if I didn't get it over with fast my lunch was going to come up.

"Ma'am—did I ever tell you—"

She moved away. (Playing hard to get, I guess.)

"My!" she said. "I'll have to be going out to the ranch. And I must stay out there tonight. You see, I have my men harvesting. If I'm not out there watching, my help steal me blind."

It was then that the front doorbell rang. She stopped still, her eyes shifting suspiciously.

"I wonder if that's the new roomer—" She turned abruptly and left the room.

I slumped down in the closest chair, feeling limp.

Saved by the bell!

In a moment she was back. Glassy-eyed this time, with her forefinger over her lips, making a shushing sound. "It's the process server," she whispered.

"Process server?"

She shushed me again, then hurried out. I followed her into the living room. The doorbell rang again, louder and longer. She stood at the big front window now, peering out through a crack in the drapery. I went over beside her and peeked out.

A tall, hawk-faced guy stood on the front porch. He was wearing an overcoat, the collar turned up, and his hat was pushed down over his forehead. His hand moved up to the bell. The buzzer screamed again. He shifted his weight and waited. Finally he moved back down the walk. I watched him get into a black coupe and drive away.

When I looked back at the old lady she was chuckling to herself.

"I fooled him," she snickered. "I always fool those process servers!"

"Somebody suing you?"

"Trying to. You have no idea how the multitude try to take advantage of a woman alone. I think it's the decorating company this time. They painted my bedroom walls and charged me double what the job was worth. I paid them half what they asked. And now they're trying to force the balance from me. Trying to squeeze a few dollars more from a defenseless old woman."

"That right?"

She nodded. "You must remember, Curt, I'm never at home to anyone until you check with me."

"I'll sure remember." I walked away from her, back through the kitchen to my bedroom.

I sat on the bed thinking—*what was I doing here?* Was it worth it? You only had to put two and two together to see she was a tightwad, eating avocado sandwiches, walnuts in place of meat, dodging process servers, refusing to pay her bills. And the work she expected out of me for twenty bucks a week! It wouldn't be easy to lay hands on that mazuma. Maybe I'd best just pack up and scram, collect the buck or two she owed me and blow. Otherwise it meant a big build-up to get her soft on me. And I could picture myself working my head off in the meantime. She wanted a human dynamo! Besides, I couldn't go through with that romance deal. I really couldn't.

I made up my mind. I pulled open dresser drawers and threw my stuff in the suitcase. It was then that the front doorbell rang again. I went on packing, wondering whether to go in and tell her I was leaving, or instead make a clean exit out of the back door.

But, hell, she owed me a few bucks. I decided to find her and collect.

She was in the entrance hall by the stairway looking up. I caught a glimpse of something feminine going up the steps. The front door was standing open and there were two suitcases on the porch. A taxi was parked out front and the driver was lugging a small wardrobe trunk up the walk. He set it on the porch, alongside the suitcase, and stood waiting for his dough.

Then I was staring. Because now the something feminine was coming down the stairs. Legs filmed in sheer tan stockings. And I could see the tops held up by pink garters, the cream skin above that. I made a mental note of the hips: tight in a black linen dress. Long gams with high thighs.

The waist was small and above that her breasts were big. Not too big—nice and neatly rounded.

She walked down those stairs like Queen Lil—with a stagy, theatrical swing. The contours were okay and she knew it. I got a closeup: blue-green eyes, sultry, thick lashes. Cimmerian hair, hanging straight down past her shoulders and curling under at the ends. I saw the dark trace of circles under her eyes, as if she'd had a bad night. I saw her profile. Somehow it reminded me of that Grecian gal on my bed.

And that wasn't a bad thought.

I felt as if I were drowning and struggling for breath. From a million miles off I heard the old lady's voice:

"Don't just stand there, Curt. Can't you help the lady with her luggage?"

"Yeah. Yeah, sure." I was all hands picking it up.

Chapter Four

I took the suitcases up, two in one hand, and her little portable phonograph in the other. She stayed downstairs, giving the driver his dough and talking to Mrs. Block. When I got back down she was opening her purse again, pulling out bills. I saw the old lady's eyes gleam at the sight of those greenbacks.

"Ten, twenty, thirty—" the little brunette began in a husky voice. She stopped and looked up. "Is it agreeable if I pay you every two weeks?"

I got a load of the overacted, starchy way she had of talking, the phony accent. Then Mrs. Block looked as if she'd been robbed. Her voice grew excited:

"Every two weeks? Certainly not! I must have a full month's rent in advance!"

Those big green peepers gazed back down at the money, like this little brunette didn't want to part with her dough. But she put on a smile and began counting again, handing it over.

"Forty, fifty—" She stopped. "It's all I have with me. I'll give you the ten dollar balance—" She hesitated. "—tomorrow."

I stood staring. Sixty bucks she was paying for that room. I couldn't believe it. With Mrs. Block swimming in dough and charging this kid that kind of money! I watched the old lady fondling the greenbacks, her eyes shining. Then she was talking, her voice calm again:

"That will be quite all right. I'll give you a receipt when you pay the balance tomorrow." She smiled crookedly. "You said your name was Lynn. Lynn York. What an odd little name." She nodded in my direction. "And this is my new gardener, Curt Blair. I don't know quite what I'd do without him. Such a splendid yard man—"

I said: "It's sort of a hobby. You see, I don't usually do that kind of work. But I figure—"

The little frill arched up one brow and interrupted:

"Thank you, my good man, for bothering with my luggage."

She stood there smugly, like a goddamn Queen—as if she expected me to get down on my knees and bow three times. She was even more upstage with those artificial airs. I looked at her with a smirk on my kisser. Then I turned and walked away and went back into my room.

She wasn't fooling me with that "my good man" puritanical patter. Hell, those circles under her eyes weren't from good sound sleep.

Anyway, I was automatically throwing my clothes back in the drawers and cussing myself at the same time. What was it about the dame that sent my fever up? Chemistry? Or whatever you call it. This one really had it, whatever it was.

The next thing I knew Mrs. Block was at my door, holding a big red-plush book in her hand.

"Pssst," she whispered. "May I come in?"

I felt weak again.

"I want to show you something, Curt."

The old lady was inside now, sitting on my bed. She opened the book. I saw what it was, all right—the family album.

"Here I am," she breathed excitedly and pointed, "when I was twenty-five!"

It was a wedding picture. She had on a white shiny dress with lace high around her throat and a little veil all over her hair. She really did look cute. She leaned closer. Then with childlike eagerness:

"Do I look like Nancy there?"

"You sure do! The dead image!"

Suddenly her smile faded into a frown. "And here's Henry, right there beside me, when we were married."

It was a younger version of the same face as in the oil portrait over the mantel. He was chubby, with a little mustache and his hair was slicked straight down on the sides. He had his arm around her and on one fat finger he wore a round ring. A peculiar design: a big disk of silver, or nickel, and a very small black stone set in the center.

"How fine he looked then," she said remorsefully.

"Yeah. He must have been some guy."

Her head jerked up. "Why do you say 'must have been?'"

"Ma'am, you said yourself he isn't around anymore. You said he'd skipped." I wondered how long she was going to keep this up. I could hear the phonograph playing faint from upstairs— "A Little on the Lonely Side".

It put a chill through me, the plaintive ring of that song. I got all goose pimply just listening to it and thinking about her up there playing it. It was hard to get my mind back on what the old lady was drooling about.

"Yes, Henry has left," she was saying. "But I don't like the way you said it. As if—Henry is no more on this earth!" Her eyes clouded. "It was only two years ago in August that he—disappeared."

"He disappeared?"

"Yes, indeed. I never could understand it. Even there toward the last, he—*adored* me."

"I sure can understand that," I said drily.

"And then—one night—he was gone. My son and I were frantic. Frantic indeed, I can tell you. We called the police. They checked everywhere."

"You never did locate him?"

"Never!" She wrinkled her forehead and her voice was whiny suddenly. "It's like what I told the gentleman from the Missing Persons Bureau. I said, 'My Henry is somewhere. Somewhere, poor soul! Perhaps suffering with amnesia, wandering the streets in aimless directions, or—'" She closed her eyes and shuddered. "—or in the hands of cruel people!"

"That's a bad deal for you all right." I got up and moved over to the dresser and got out my comb. I stood there slicking back my hair, hoping she'd leave. But she only sniveled up at me.

"I've never given up hope of seeing him again!" She flipped the pages over. "Oh, I can't bear to think of him. Poor soul, poor soul—"

The next minute she was up beside me, shoving the book in my face. "And here's our son. Here's Jeffrey." She sighed self-pityingly. "Jeff left me too."

I glanced down at the picture of Jeffrey. He was good-looking with high cheekbones and black wavy hair.

"The image of his father," she murmured.

"He's got your light eyes."

"I'm only his stepmother," she said. "So there can't be a resemblance. Henry and I have no children of our own." She was studying the picture. "Do you think Jeff cared enough for family tradition to comply with my wishes? No, he chose to forsake the woman who had brought him up, the woman who devoted her life, denied herself, to be his mother—to marry a cheap little gold-digger. Nothing but a Jezebel!"

I yawned while she flipped over another page.

"Here she is!" She spat out the words. "Here's Natalie Ford, the *creature* Jeff married!"

I saw the photograph. In technicolor. Creature was the word for Natalie all right—long reddish hair with almond-shaped eyes and luscious full red lips.

"This woman was out here from Salt Lake City, entertaining at a night club on the Sunset Strip." She leaned closer and whispered, "It was a vulgar type of dance she did, in harem pantaloons, with practically no clothes at all. An East Indian nautch business."

"It was?" My ears perked up.

She nodded. "Oh, she beguiled Jeffrey quickly enough, dragged him into the quagmire," she added dramatically. "All she married him for was his money, knowing he'd inherit his father's fortune." She pursed her lips. "They took me out to Hollywood Park one day. Do you know how much of my son's money she lost in *one* race?"

"I can't imagine."

"Thirty-two dollars!" she cackled. Her eyes narrowed. "So you can see how she'd throw my hard-earned capital to the four winds."

"That's—terrible."

"But Henry kept indulging them. He couldn't seem to see through her. He was actually fond of the hussy, if you can imagine liking a woman of that caliber!"

"I sure can't."

"Nor I, goodness knows. But Henry was so—" She searched for the word. "—cosmopolitan. He permitted Jeff to bring her here to live in our home. Then the moment Henry left, Jeff was after me for his money. Some sum or other Henry had promised him. I saw that she was behind it, with all her conniving ways. She put him up to it!"

"Oh, she did?"

"Indeed, yes. Unquestionably. And when the two of them realized finally that I wasn't going to be the soft mark, when they woke up to the fact that they weren't going to squeeze another cent from me, they packed up and went off to live in her apartment in Salt Lake City, leaving me alone and friendless."

"That sure is too bad."

She caught her breath. "I know I did the right thing. The son of Henry Block, of Block Borax Mines, Incorporated, married to a common little trollop is more than—" She broke off and sighed.

"Borax, eh? There must be good dough in that."

She puckered her mouth. "It isn't as lucrative as you might think. My royalty checks are getting smaller and smaller."

"Oh—the business is all yours?"

"Indeed not. It's half Henry's. I'm a co-partner."

"Then—a—since Henry left, all his assets are subject to your control?"

She nodded. "And luckily our bank account called for either signature. Fortunately, too, the two houses and the ranch were in my name. Otherwise, I would have been out in the cold."

"Yeah."

She went on: "Now Jeffrey and Natalie are both sitting around waiting for me to die so that they can inherit my money, the money I saved all my life, scrimped and denied myself for. But I tell you, Curt, I can stand on my own two feet and defy them!"

"You sure can, all right."

She glanced at the clock on the dresser. "Goodness! I must be getting out to the ranch." She smiled and wiggled her forefinger. "We've quite forgotten the hedges."

At the door she paused. "You can take your time as long as you get them all trimmed this afternoon. And—oh, yes, I won't be back until tomorrow around noon. So in the morning bright and early I want you to clean out the garage."

"Sure thing."

She left the room. And I beat it outside for a breath of fresh air. Then I remembered the hedges. I picked up the big garden shears and started to work on the shrubbery.

About fifteen minutes later she came out again, the old dame, all dressed up in black and white. With a bunch of artificial red roses on the front of her hat. The outfit was for my benefit, I knew that. I was acting like some kind of a shrub artist. I'd just stand back from the hedge, measuring it with my eye, then I'd run over and snap off a leaf.

Next thing she was right up beside me, with those roses on her hat bobbing in my face.

"Curt," she said sweetly. "I want you to know it's nice having you here."

"Thanks."

She flashed me a roguish smile, "And Curt," she said a little breathlessly, "you may call me Virginia."

I had to grit my teeth hard to keep a straight face. "Thanks—Virginia."

I went on with the hedge work. Pretty soon there was a loud roar of exhaust in the garage, a motor racing, a streak of smoke, gears shifting. She backed the old Packard out recklessly and waved goodbye with gay abandon. She shot off down the street.

I threw the shears down and flopped on my can on the grass. And that's where I intended to remain. But just then, through the hedge, I saw an old truck pull up with its back end filled with garden hose, tools, and the like.

An old sleepy-eyed gent, with a long beard, wearing a checked shirt and Levis, got out and walked over toward me. He looked like Rip Van Winkle. Now he peered over the hedge.

"Mrs. Block home?"

I told him she'd just driven off. He edged up closer and held up a piece of paper.

"What's she intendin' to do 'bout this bill?"

"Sure I don't know, mister. What kind of bill?"

"She owes me six months' gardening service. She slipped off three months ago on a vacation or somethin'—and I see the house is open again." He eyed me. "Now I want my money. Forty-eight dollars. Maybe she used to cuff them damn Japs, but not me! No sir—little Harry Albright gets paid!"

"Don't look at me," I said. "I have nothing to do with it."

"Well, ain't you her son she talks so much about?"

I grinned. "I only work here."

"You work here?" He chuckled humorlessly. "Better get your salary in advance. I ain't never seen more of a deadbeat than that Mrs. Block!" He sobered. "Now if it ain't paid soon I'm takin' her to court. You can tell her that."

"Sure. I'll tell her, mister."

"And I mean business."

"I'll pass the word."

"No more foolin' around. I'm goin' to collect my money somehow. Get me?"

"I get you."

"If it ain't paid within a week there's goin' to be hell a-poppin'! Understand?"

"I got ears," I said.

He eyed me again for a long second, then marched back to the truck. And I was making a bee-line for the house with every muscle inside me aching. I wasn't used to that shrub-trimming, mowing, picking fruit stuff. I went into my bedroom and flopped on the bed. I looked up and saw the colored girl, Jasmine, standing in my doorway.

"Do y'll know what's happened to Mrs. Block?"

"She's gone," I replied wearily, "gone, gone."

"I jist don't know what to tell these people on the telephone. They wants to talk to huh. It's Craft Employment Agency."

"Just tell them—" I jumped up quick and hurried into the front room. At the desk I picked up the receiver.

It was Mrs. Wimple. I told her that Mrs. Block wasn't home and she said she'd call back later. I said, "I'm the new hired hand, so you don't need to call back later, because the job's been taken." She said, "Oh, the position has been filled?" and I said, "Yeah." She said, "But Mr. Lake told me—" I said, "Never mind what Mr. Lake told you—the job's taken. And Mrs. Block said to tell you she'll get in touch with you if she ever needs you again."

And that was that. I stood there for a moment thinking how lucky it was that I got that call—and not Mrs. Block. I hadn't figured on the agency checking like that.

Then Jasmine came in, with her hat and coat on, and said she was leaving and where was her money? I told her I was no clairvoyant, that I didn't know where her money was. She was ruffled. She wrote down her name and address and said she expected the day's salary in tomorrow morning's mail and no foolin'.

She left and I went into the kitchen and fixed myself a bite to eat. After that I went back in my bedroom and flopped again, so tired I couldn't think. But I kept hearing Blackie whimpering and I kept hearing those footsteps upstairs. And I could see that figure. I could hear her, this new roomer, singing in that low throaty voice:

I keep thinking of you only—and wishing you were by my side.

I felt my eyes closing. And I guess I fell asleep before she finished the song.

But I woke up in about an hour and everything was quiet. I got up and took off my clothes. In bed again, I picked up a magazine and flipped it open. My eyes focused on a dame and guy in evening dress, the two of them wrapped in a clinch. Below it read: *Keep Lovely to Love.*

My fingers felt the stubble of whiskers on my face. Then all at once I heard her again, moving around upstairs. I lay there motionless and it dawned on me suddenly that I was alone with her—in this big house.

I got up and shaved.

While I was in the bathroom she walked right overhead. My hand shook so bad the electric razor nicked the side of my nose. When I was back in bed—lights out—I kept listening. I kept hearing those little footsteps! Wood creaking under her weight. I wondered what she was wearing now. I kept wondering. I guess I went to sleep again thinking about that.

I woke up once more and saw the clock: one in the morning. The screwy part was that I could still hear her footsteps. Once I swore I heard the sound of high heels clicking down the wood stairway. It wasn't my imagination because all at once there was a tapping on my door.

"Curt—"

My heart was all choked up in my mouth. It was this Lynn, all right, her voice strained and low. I leaped out of bed and jabbed my arms in my new overcoat and opened the door.

Chapter Five

She stood there with anxiety printed all over her face. For a moment I couldn't see for looking. She had on a blue satin robe with long blue silk fringe that shone like star sapphires in the streak of moonlight.

She stared for a moment, breathing hard, with her nostrils quivering—like a high-spirited filly that's just finished the mile-and-a-half. Then:

"What goes on in this house!"

"Goes on? What d'ya—"

"Is it haunted or something? What *are* those noises?"

"Noises?"

She swallowed hard. She was really scared, this kid, and I suppose that was why she'd shed that highfaluting way of talking.

"Y-yes. I fell asleep—with the floor lamp on. I woke up later and got out of bed to turn it off. That's when they started."

"They?"

"The noises. Like—like I don't know what. It was after I turned the lamp off. And look here—" She lifted the fringe and showed me her small, shapely legs. "What's this?" she panted. "These red marks. Something keeps biting my ankles."

I took my time looking them over. Sure enough, her skin was covered with little red puffed places. I knew now why Mrs. Block kept that flit gun in the kitchen cupboard, that *Dy-E-Ze* insect killer. I made a quick diagnosis.

"Looks to me as if you've been well bitten by fleas."

"Fleas?" she gave a little cry. "*Fleas* in my *bed!*"

"It sure looks that way to me."

"Oh, m'Gawd!"

"Maybe I'd better go up and see."

"God, yes! Yes, *please* do."

I followed her through the kitchen, into the living room, and up the stairway—close behind her. Too close. I could smell the perfume she wore. Heavy and heady. As if you were surrounded by a garden of Paradise!

We went into her bedroom. I saw a black brassiere and under slip lying in a heap on the floor. The light was on. She switched it off.

"Listen," she said tensely. "See if you can hear it."

We stood there in the dark. I guess I was only two feet away from her. She moved closer.

"Listen," she whispered.

I listened. The room was so still all I could hear was my own heart pounding like a drum. But in a few seconds you could hear the noises all right. I knew what it was. You could hear them racing across the floor, making a running jump. You could hear their bodies fall.

"Hear it?" Her voice trembled. Her fingers clutched my arm. "What is it?"

I didn't answer right away. I liked being alone with her in here, with those long fingernails of hers digging my arm—and only a streak of moonlight across the twin beds.

"Curt, what *is it?* Is the place haunted or something?" She shuddered and switched on the light.

The glare blinded me for a second. I found my voice: "You got any food stuff on the dresser?"

"A box of cookies."

"That's where the trouble lies."

Her mouth opened, then closed.

"You see," I explained, "rats smell food and go for it."

"Rats?" Her face paled. "Not—*rats?*"

"Yeah."

All at once she was pacing back and forth in the room, with that long blue fringe trailing after her. "What else! What now!" She whirled around. "If it isn't being kicked from hotel to hotel, it's *rats!*"

"That's what the noises are, all right."

She was swinging her head around so that that long hair of hers flung from side to side. "I thought tonight—just for *one* night—I'd have a good night's sleep!"

I said: "Don't let those rats bother you." I picked up the box of cookies and put them in my overcoat pocket. "You won't have any more trouble now. You see, they smelled this food."

She put her hands on her hips. "How about the fleas?"

"Oh, the fleas." I guess my mind was on other things. I'd forgotten about the fleas.

She was shouting. "I can't sleep in a place where there's rats and fleas! It's—*unhealthy!* They carry all sorts of contagious germs. I demand a refund! I want my rent back! Every bit of the fifty bucks! I want it immediately! The room was misrepresented. That's what it was—*misrepresentation!*"

"Lady, I'm not the landlord."

She flung her hair at me again. "Where is she? Where is the old crow?"

I told her—spending the night at the ranch.

Her shoulders slumped. "I guess I couldn't find a hotel room this late even if I *could* get my rent back tonight. There aren't any. This goddamn housing situation is enough to—" She sat on the bed. "You don't know how it is to be out on your can."

"Oh, no?"

"You've got a bed, your two-bit job here." She was on her feet again. She walked over to the window, then went into her act again—that aloof way she had of talking. "You've never heard those officious hotel clerks say, 'So sorry, Miss, you'll have to vacate by one.' 'So sorry, Miss, the room has been reserved for a Navy Commander.' 'So sorry, Miss, you may have the room for five days only. So sorry, OPA regulations.'"

"It's rough, all right."

Her voice lowered. "And damned expensive! Do you know that two months ago I had five hundred bucks—*cash?* I thought at least with that money I'd be able to locate an apartment and settle down and find a job. Instead I've spent it on hotel rooms, and time looking for hotel rooms."

"You from out of town?"

She nodded. "Frisco." She went over to the dresser and picked up a cigarette. She tapped it hard against her thumb nail and lit it. She inhaled and blew the smoke out in a thick stream. "This isn't getting me anywhere," she said under her breath. "Rats, fleas— Guess I'll have to stick it out for the night."

"Yeah."

"I'll clear out of here fast tomorrow." She looked over at the beds and winced. "Isn't there *anything* you can do about them?"

"Them?"

"The *fleas!*"

I thought of the flit gun. "Sure," I said. "Sure thing." I beat it out the door.

In no time at all I was back up, spraying in every corner. I even lifted up the sheets in her bed and sprayed down at the foot, too.

"I can stand the smell of that stinking stuff better than I can stand fleas," she said. Then she went on raving some more about the condition of the room, saying that she was moving out tomorrow and getting her dough back.

"No need of that," I told her. "There'll be no more rats and no more fleas."

Those big peepers glared at me. "You couldn't pay me to stay in this dump. It's really a laugh. Here I was, thinking I was moving into a class spot. I put this ad in the paper saying I wanted a room in a private home. And Mrs. Block answered it. When she gave out with the address I nearly collapsed. 848 Lilac Drive. A prime address in Beverly Hills. North of the tracks—"

"Yeah, it's—"

"So I came out and looked the place over." She laughed, deep in her throat. "I must've had stardust in my eyes. I sat there in the living room talking to the old woman. Everything was dusty, but she said it'd been locked up all summer. When I moved in, I expected to see it all shined up." She paused. "I thought I could pretend this house was mine." Her eyes came up hesitantly. "You might think it's funny I want to pretend something like that."

"I know what you mean."

She was wistful. "I always wanted to live in a big dump like this. I didn't dream it had—vermin. It all goes to show you can't judge a book by its cover."

"No, you sure can't. But Mrs. Block is having it cleaned. There was a colored girl here today."

"I don't care if she gets twenty-five maids to clean it. I don't like this rat hole. I'm getting my rent back tomorrow." She stubbed out the cigarette. "A lot it means to you. Well—good night."

I got up and started for the door.

"Oh, Curt—"

I turned around. Her mouth was slightly parted and only her lips were smiling. "Thank you," she said huskily. "Thank you very much."

"That's all right." I reached the door, then thought of something. "If they bother you anymore be sure and call me. You can just yell, and I'll be up in a flash."

Then it was on again, full blast—that grandiloquent tone: "I will. You're terribly sweet. I don't know quite how I'd have managed without you."

I was already going down the steps. I hit the living room and the kitchen. I went into my room and got back into bed. But I could still smell her perfume. And I could visualize her standing in my doorway in that blue negligee. And I kept thinking I heard her voice. So I'd get up and go to the bottom of the stairs and listen, then figure she hadn't been calling me at all. It was only in my mind—the thought of my wanting her to call me.

I kept that routine up until daylight. So you can understand why I didn't get much sleep the rest of that night at all.

Chapter Six

The next day I was still in bed when I heard the old Packard pull into the garage. I saw the clock—twelve bells. I'd been sleeping that long! I jumped up quick and began to throw on my clothes. My bedroom door was open and I could see through the back porch screen. The old woman came in the back gate and stood looking at her avocado tree.

I was dressed and in the kitchen when she came in. I was slicing the loaf of rye and trying to look wide awake.

"I see you're fixing lunch," she said.

"Yeah."

"I had mine."

She stood by the sink looking out of the window, kind of staring—as if she wasn't thinking about me, how I wasn't cleaning out the garage the way she'd told me to do, but something else.

"Everything go all right at the ranch?" I asked. She didn't answer, so I repeated the same question.

Her thin lips pinched hard. "Trouble, trouble, trouble. No end of expense. You don't know, Curt, I—" She broke off, faltered. "And now this little York girl—"

"What's wrong?"

Her voice was high pitched. "I wonder if it ever occurs to her that there is a balance of ten dollars for the rent of the room."

"I wouldn't know."

She stood watching me eat, talking about her ranch and Lynn and the ten bucks. I finally got in about the gardener—how Rip Van Winkle dropped past and how he was hot for his dough.

"Humph! He'll never get one cent from me, the deaf old reprobate! He chopped down my best red hibiscus, when I distinctly told him to take out the white oleander."

She kept on babbling about her white oleander, then she'd go back to Lynn and the ten bucks. I didn't say anything more. I let her rave on. Pretty soon she caught on that I wasn't in a sympathetic mood. She flounced out of the room.

I heard it then: the hurricane in the front room. She and Lynn going round for round. Lynn demanding her fifty bucks back. And there was no stagy patter this time; she was calling a spade a spade.

I went outside, over to Blackie, and sat down. I could still hear the arguing going on inside. It was a hazy garble.

"Hi, pooch," I said.

Blackie was scratching himself like fury.

"You got fleas, dog?"

Suddenly I felt a bite on my leg. It occurred to me that Blackie had probably slept in Lynn's room, before Mrs. Block had decided to rent it—and that explained the fleas in the room. I got up and went back in the house and picked up the flit gun. I brought it back out and gave Blackie the works. He didn't mind it at all. He seemed to enjoy the flit bath. He was goofy about the attention.

I remembered how he whined at night. He sure looked sluggish. His fur wasn't bright and shiny, yet he was a young dog. I noticed the food in his pan: a creamy, gummy substance. I picked some of it up and rubbed it through my fingers. It looked like some kind of ordinary meal to me. I remembered the Spam in the icebox. So I went in and sliced off a hunk.

I could hear the arguing—words flying fast and furious. I didn't know who was winning. Anyway, I took the Spam back out.

"Here you are, boy."

He took it all right, with one snap that almost included my fingers. As though he hadn't seen meat in months. I wondered why the old dame was feeding him that mealy-looking stuff. Then I concluded that he was sick and she was putting him on some kind of a diet. Probably had a special veterinarian for him, like some of those Beverly Hills dames.

Sure was a cute mutt, though, even if he was scrawny without too much pep. He kept looking up at me with those big sad eyes, begging for more Spam.

"No can do, Blackie. The old woman'd raise hell if she knew I'd fed you that much."

I heard a door slam. Now there were footsteps in the kitchen.

"I'm telling you once more," Lynn was saying evenly, "if you don't refund my money immediately, I'll take my case to court!"

Then Mrs. Block was talking, unruffled. "Don't be nonsensical. If you say there are rats, I'll set traps. If you say there are fleas, I'll spray your room. That'll get them right away."

"You don't seem to understand," Lynn said. "I'm not interested in ridding your house of this vermin. I want a refund. Now! This whole place is unhealthy! It should be reported to the board of health!"

"Humph! My dear, I have nothing further to discuss. I'm not returning one cent to you. As a matter of fact I expect the ten dollar balance before this day is through. That's a perfectly good room, but of course if you wish to vacate now that's your privilege."

I got sore listening to that. I felt the blood creeping up hot in my face.

The old lady was even a worse skinflint than I had her pictured.

"Oh, you—you—" Lynn's voice broke off. Then she was out the back door. She flopped down on the steps.

I whistled softly. She saw me—and got up and came over. I motioned for her not to say anything, because Mrs. Block might be listening. I beat it down the steps to the cellar and gestured for Lynn to come down. She did. And we stood at the cellar entrance.

"I heard everything," I told her. "All you've got to do is go see the City Attorney. It'll only cost you two bucks to file suit."

"I haven't the two dollars," she said gloomily.

"I can loan it to you."

She brightened. "Would you?"

"Sure. I'll be your witness. It isn't fair for her to gyp you like that."

"The dirty old miser!"

"That's the word for her, all right."

She looked at me. "You come with me, Curt. We'll both go see the City Attorney."

"Well, I—" I was thinking about Beverly Hills cops. But they didn't see my face that night I lifted the overcoat. As long as I kept away from that restaurant I was okay. Besides, who was going to prove it wasn't mine? Possession is nine-tenths of the law. "Sure," I said. "I'll go. Damn right! The city hall's only five blocks. We'll walk. You wait right here till I shave and get on a clean shirt!"

We ambled up the walk to the side of the City Hall. Then up the steps and into the outer office of the Police Department. There was a long counter inside the door, to our right. Lynn went over to one of the cops and explained that she wanted to see the City Attorney.

"Right down the hall, miss," this cop said. "The second office."

We hurried on down the hall. In a minute we saw the lettering on the door: CITY ATTORNEY. And underneath that: ASSISTANT CITY ATTORNEY.

I opened the door. We went inside and over to another long counter. A pretty little redhead smiled up. Then Lynn was explaining how she rented this room at 848 Lilac Drive and discovered rats and fleas.

The desk girl was shocked. She said she thought it was perfectly disgraceful that such a condition actually existed—in Beverly Hills! On *North* Lilac Drive! And she said that Lynn should certainly be able to get her rent back. And that the City Attorney wasn't in right now, but we could certainly speak to Mr. Slater, the Assistant City Attorney.

So it wasn't two minutes before she ushered us into a small office down at the end of the room. And behind the desk was Mr. Slater. A nice gent, around forty, with thinning brown hair and a mustache. He told us to be seated and asked what he could do for us.

Then Lynn was talking. It was on again too—the accent: "I've been so terribly inconvenienced. You see the health department should be notified. Rats and fleas—as if *anyone* could tolerate them. All over the whole house. And you can see the *secretion* everywhere. In the dresser drawers in my bedroom, even on the telephone desk downstairs." She said she simply demanded her money back.

Mr. Slater sat back, toying with a pencil, with sort of an amused expression. But he was trying hard not to show it. He said:

"Your landlord owns the property there?"

Lynn hesitated and looked over at me.

I said: "She owns it all right."

"What's the name?"

"Block," I told him. "Mrs. Virginia Block."

He pursed his lips and said in a calm low voice: "*Her* again. That woman has caused a great deal of trouble in this city. Every merchant has sued her at one time or another." He shook his head. "Nobody ever got to first base." He paused and leaned forward. "Of course, you can sue her—if you want to gamble two dollars."

Lynn's eyes widened. "Gamble?"

He nodded. "She's a sly one. An expert at dodging process servers. In your case, you could serve the papers on her yourself since you're living there in the house."

"I suppose I could," Lynn said doubtfully.

"Yes," he said, "that part could be done. But I don't know if I'd fool around with Mrs. Block."

Lynn opened her mouth to say something, but Mr. Slater went on:

"She has all her money in a fictitious name. In my position, I say this reluctantly." He took a deep breath and continued: "There's little advantage in starting this suit." He thought for a moment. "After getting a judgment, we could call for a supplemental examination of her accounts. But that would be costly in time and money, of course." He shook his head again. "My advice is for you to drop it. I don't think you'd get very far. She'd wear you down with postponements and delays, even if she chose to fight your suit."

"She can keep my fifty dollars?" Lynn asked.

He nodded. "I'm sorry to say that's about the size of it. That is, unless you're prepared for a long, drawn-out civil action. It's unfortunate that we must tolerate a woman of her type in this community."

The wind was out of Lynn's sails. She turned to me. "Guess it's my loss."

"Yeah," I said.

We both got up and thanked Mr. Slater. Then we were outside again, walking down toward Lilac Drive.

"Well—that's that!" She was laughing. "It's funny."

"It is?" I wondered what she saw funny in it.

"Don't I get myself into the damnedest situations?"

"Do you?" I paused. "By the way, haven't you lost something?"

She stopped and looked back on the sidewalk.

"Your accent?"

She laughed and we walked on.

"I guess," she said, "I picked up a few broad A's in Boston."

"You been to Boston?"

She shook her head and laughed again.

I said: "Why do you try to be phony like that?"

She wasn't laughing now; her face was sour. "What makes you so damn matter-of-fact, so serious?"

"I am?"

Her nose went up. "You remind me of a man without a sense of humor."

"That's bad."

"It certainly is. When things get the roughest you've got to see the humorous side. If you don't, you've got to cry. And I've cried enough for one lifetime."

"I see what you mean."

"No, you don't," she said in that sultry voice, "but let it go."

We walked on. Thoughts whirled through my brain. When I looked back at her she gave me a half smile.

"You win," she said. "It isn't funny—that old bat keeping my hard-earned cash!"

"There's a solution," I said. "I just figured it out."

"Suppose you tell *me*."

"Okay. She rented you that room for sixty bucks. Right? And there's twin beds. So what prevents you from renting out one of the beds—for thirty bucks a month?"

"You mean—"

"Find some dame to share it with you. What can the old lady do but scream her head off. She won't have you legally evicted; she wants nothing to do with the law."

Her eyes lighted. "Why, Curt—you're ingenious. As far as that goes. I could rent the whole room—and get my money back!"

"Sure. But you don't want to do that. Thirty bucks a month is cheap enough rent these days."

"I guess you're right. I'll keep the room until I find a suitable job. When we get home I'll look in the advertising section—I've got today's papers. You'd be surprised how many people advertise for living quarters. And there are a lot of girls desperate for any place to live."

"Yeah. Just don't tell Mrs. Block I put you up to it."

"I won't."

We walked on. I noticed that she was studying me, hesitantly. Finally she took a deep breath and said:

"Do you s'pose you could still loan me that two dollars, anyway?"

"You want to file suit?"

"No, it's just that—" Her voice-trailed off.

"Let's have it, baby. Let's have it."

"Well, I—I gave the old woman my last fifty dollars. This morning I—I sneaked in the kitchen and fried myself an egg and—"

"You got no dough? You want to buy food with the two bucks?"

"Yes. But I'll pay it back to you," she added quickly. "Just as soon as I get working."

Oh, brother! I'd heard that song before! But I'm strictly Simple Simon when it comes to dames. I've always been a sucker that way. I can't say no to a pretty dame! I just automatically dug deep in my pocket and pulled out my life's savings—four bucks. I peeled her off two.

"It's very sweet of you," she said.

"You fix yourself anything you want to eat in the kitchen. It was your understanding when you rented that room the price included meals."

She looked puzzled. "It didn't. Mrs. Block said I couldn't have kitchen privileges."

"You open those cans in the cupboard and eat!" I said exasperated. "So what can she do about it!"

"Oh, I see. But that won't be necessary, I hope. I'm going to see about a job tomorrow. I could go out to dinner with friends tonight, but I—I'd rather not."

"Friends? You mean a guy?"

"Yes," she replied. "A guy. But I can't stand him near me, and he—well, he's hard to get along with."

I laughed. "The kind that expects an eye for an eye?"

She smiled. "You guessed it. I'd sooner be on my own. You see, the only reason I came down here from Frisco is because I want to attend Creighton Hall."

"Attend what?"

"Creighton Hall," she repeated. "It's a dramatic school on Wilshire Boulevard. I want to study to be an actress. That's why I have to be particular in the job I take. The hours have to be just right, so I can make classes. And the pay's got to be good, so I can afford the lessons. Maybe I'll get a night job, maybe a showgirl somewhere."

"You tall enough to be a showgirl?"

"You think I'm too short?"

"No. Just right." I paused. "What do you want to be an actress for?"

"Why? Why does anybody want to be anything? I got the fever. That's about the only way I can explain it. I got the fever."

"I got a kind of fever, too," I said.

"To be an actor?"

"No. Christ, no!"

"Then what have you got the fever for?"

"If I told you, you'd have nothing more to do with me."

She laughed. "Don't be so sure."

We were approaching the house now, coming in from the side street. I told Lynn to go on around and in the front way. I'd sneak in through the back gate. She said she'd look in the papers and find a roommate, and she left me.

I beat it in through the back gate and picked up the hedge shears. Then I was over beside Blackie, working on a little shrub tree.

It was about a half hour later when the back door opened and Lynn came back out. She hurried over to me.

"Well, it's done," she whispered excitedly. "I called a dozen people—finally found one girl who was being evicted today. She said she wanted to be as close to Sawtelle as possible. And when she found out the room was in Beverly Hills, she snapped it right up. We're only two miles from Sawtelle."

"Yeah. What does the dame want in Sawtelle?"

She shrugged. "I didn't ask her. She's moving in at five today."

"Did Mrs. Block hear you calling up?"

"No. I used the downstairs 'phone. She's up in her bedroom reading."

"Then now's your chance. Go on in and fix yourself a bite to eat."

She gave me a smile. "I will—in a second. I just want to thank you for everything."

"That's all right." I was snapping hell out of the shrub tree, wishing she'd go. It bothered me, her standing here watching me do this kind of work. I sure was clumsy at it. The shears weren't any too sharp either. I remembered that big three-cornered file down in the cellar. I walked away from her and down the steps, hoping she'd be gone by the time I came back up. But the next thing I knew she was down in the cellar with me. She looked around and shivered.

"What a quaint little place."

"Yeah." I went on crashing the file against the blades.

"Is this your office?"

"Not exactly."

She slanted her head. "What's that noise? Like water dripping."

"Probably the plumbing—leaking under the house."

"It gives me the creeps."

There was a silence; her voice came lower:

"What are you doing around here anyway?"

"What does it look like? I'm the general repair man. I'm the gardener."

"Oh, yeah? You're no gardener. I saw the way you were mutilating the shrubbery." She paused, looked around again. "Exactly what *are* you doing around here? Feathering your nest?"

"Can't you see I got a job?"

"I see more than you think. You're hanging around here for something—and I know what it is."

"You're pretty chintzy."

"You're wasting your time. You'll never get a nickel out of the old woman."

"I found that out, all right."

She was over close to me now. "Then why *are* you staying? What's the enticement? There are plenty of *good* jobs."

I stopped working. I lit a cigarette. My fingers shook when I took a drag. "I like the scenery."

"No, you don't. You've got big ideas. What's the attraction here? Why are you still staying on, slaving over those goddamn hedges, when you know it's no deal upstairs?"

"Get out of here! Beat it!" My lips were trembling and my blood was all hot in my face.

She didn't budge.

I said: "You better watch your step. You know what happens to little females who follow matter-of-fact guys into dark cellars!"

"I haven't the slightest idea. What happens?"

It hadn't occurred to me until now that she wanted to play hopscotch.

I looked at her—standing there with that black hair of hers hanging straight down on the sides. Those scarlet lips parted in a smile, like that Mona Lisa upstairs. For a second she was a picture like no picture you've ever seen! I pulled the cigarette from my mouth, dropped it, stomped it out. My eyes came up slow.

"You really want to know why I'm still around?"

She nodded.

I grabbed her.

I crushed my mouth hard on hers. Through the corner of my eye I saw the studio couch. I picked her up and carried her over to it and laid her down. The dust flew high and thick. She was choking and holding her throat and squirming up to a sitting position.

"Curt—"

I couldn't see her for the dust. But I pulled her over close. I kissed her again, quick, to keep her from saying anything. I held her closer. She was sucking air into her lungs.

"Curt, I—"

"Listen, baby—" I was looking straight into those aquamarine eyes. "Hell—what do you think I been hanging around here for! I've been nuts about you ever since—"

She found her voice:

"Don't waste so much time talking," she said.

Chapter Seven

I didn't see her anymore that afternoon. But while was fixing my dinner I heard the doorbell ring. And I heard Lynn talking and the footsteps going up the stairs. A few minutes later you could hear voices, the free-for-all. The old woman was squawking loud and fast, so I knew that the new roomer had moved in.

It was about fifteen minutes later when Mrs. Block came knocking at my door.

"Curt, I must speak to you!"

She came in with a warrior's countenance. She sat on the bed. Those gray little eyes strayed up and focused. "The nerve! The insolence! That girl! Upsetting me so dreadfully!"

"What's up?" I knew what was up, all right.

She touched her temples and caught her breath. "I was benevolent enough to rent the room to this brazen little Miss York because I knew the housing situation was so critical. And now to have her display her appreciation in such an antagonistic manner is more than I can—"

"What's she done?"

Her voice rose to a high pitch. "She has permitted a girlfriend of hers to move in with her—bag and baggage, mind you. That's what she's done! And she gave me some silly-sally excuse that the girl was only going to remain for a few days. But I know what happens in this instance—it's a few days, then it's a few days more, and the next thing the friend is living here." Her eyes went down to the floor. "The room was rented to one person only. Bringing in another person makes the contract null and void. I told her she had three days to vacate, from this date."

"That was the thing to do all right."

She gave me a superior smile. "I'll show Miss York how far she can go with me! I can't have two persons occupying the room." She took a deep breath. "This is my first experience renting to a young girl. Heaven knows I'll choose my next tenant carefully. It will be a gentleman, like the last one I had, who worked all day and was out of the house. Not a foolish girl who washes her underthings every night and is glued to the telephone all day long." She sighed. "Well, we all live and learn."

"We sure do."

"Oh, when Henry was here things were so much *easier*. It all goes to show how people take advantage of a poor woman—alone."

I was fed up suddenly. "Why don't you let both the girls stay?"

She was aghast. "Why—why—the rent would be a hundred and twenty dollars for two! Goodness—I couldn't permit all that running of the hot water, burning of electricity, clean sheets and pillow slips for two beds, double linen. Humph! My home isn't a charity organization!"

"It sure isn't."

She heaved a big sigh. "Oh, dear, when Henry was—" She broke off. She looked up and touched my arm. "I must dismiss all this unpleasantry from my mind. I want you to drive me to the theater, Curt. I'll see the early show."

"Well, I—I'm—"

"I'll be ready in a few minutes. You get the Packard out front."

"Yes, ma'am."

I waited for her in the car. She came out in about a half hour, dressed up again. In a ratty black fur coat that reeked of moth balls, and a hat with a peacock feather sticking straight up and a thick black veil hanging clear down over her face.

I hopped out and opened the back seat door for her. Then I was chauffeuring her down to Wilshire Boulevard.

I pulled up out in front of the Beverly Theatre. It was just opening, and people were lined up waiting to get their tickets.

"Curt," the old lady's voice came over, "you may attend the movie with me." She said it as if it were part of my job.

"Well, I—"

"Over across the street is a parking place."

"Yes, ma'am."

I parked, and we walked back to the theater. I hurried over and looked at the coming attractions on the billboards. At the cashier's cage, she lifted the veil and opened her purse and squinted inside. She plunked out the dough for the seats.

Before we reached the doorman she said:

"I'll deduct fifty cents for your ticket from your salary check. That will make us even."

I nodded. We went inside. An usherette showed us to our seats.

Mrs. Block had on some perfume that smelled like a mixture of vanilla and turpentine. This mixed with the stench of moth balls. I could scarcely stand it. I got up and went out to the can. When I got back I couldn't find her. Finally the usherette came up and said:

"Your mother moved over to the center."

I found her and plunked down and sat for a while. Nothing much was happening on the screen. I sat there thinking about Lynn, wondering what she was doing and how I was going to keep the old lady from kicking her out. When the perfume and moth balls got obnoxious again, I got up and went back out to the lobby and drank some water and smoked a cigarette. Hell, I never have been able to sit still in one spot. Jumpy nerves, I guess you'd call it. Boredom jitters.

After a while I went back in and saw the rest of the picture out.

Back outside, she said:

"Curt, in the morning bright and early, I want you to drive me out to the ranch."

"Sure, sure."

When we got back to the house I went straight to my room and went to bed. I'd had enough of her for one evening.

The next morning early I drove her out to her ranch in the San Fernando Valley. She said she didn't want to go over Coldwater Canyon, so we went through Hollywood, out Cahuenga, along the Freeway, and turned off at Mountain View. Then as far as you could see there was walnut acreage.

"This is my land," she said. "All this, right on up as far as—" She squinted ahead. "—to the last fence mark."

"Must bring you a lot of dough."

She shrugged. "An average harvesting amounts to around two thousand an acre."

I was multiplying one hundred by two thousand—and feeling sick. *What was wrong with me?* It was a shame that I wasn't cashing in on some of that velvet!

"'Course," she went on, "that isn't every year. Last September the hot spell hit at budding time. The crop brought less than half the usual amount because of the blight."

"Blight?"

"Yes. It begins with a black spot on the hull and enlarges. It becomes black, mushy pulp. The bacteria go to work inside the kernel and the nuts are impossible to hull. Inside the kernel is shriveled and dry."

I couldn't help thinking she was describing herself—the wet-rot of the soul.

"Then," she went on, "the upkeep of the trees is quite an expense in itself."

I said: "There can't be much expense to growing walnuts."

She gestured to the guys at work in the grove. "You think these men work for nothing? I suppose you think it costs nothing to keep the trees in order—spraying and all."

"You have to spray them?"

"Goodness, yes! With lead arsenate. It keeps the red spiders out. They can defoliate a tree in no time."

"Red spiders, eh?"

"Yes. They're cousins to the aphis on rose bushes."

"Cousins, eh?"

She nodded. "A sucking insect. But with proper dusting you can hold them down. Then I have to look out for the codling moth. It's the same kind of worm that gets in apples. And of course there's the husk fly, but we're not bothered much with that here in the valley."

We passed another group of men with ladders, shaking poles; other were gathering up the fallen walnuts from the ground and putting them into buckets and big manila hemp bags.

Suddenly she gesticulated. "Here we are. Turn left on this road."

I turned in. You could see the ranch house now. Half hidden in the grove. I pulled up alongside a big shed. The house itself was a low rambling farmhouse structure with a red roof and a brown dried-out patch of lawn.

Mrs. Block got out and hurried into the shed. I followed. There were two guys inside standing by a huge bin; they looked over at us and nodded.

Then she was escorting me around tourist guide fashion, showing me this and that and explaining how everything worked. She said that the bin, the dehydrator, held two thousand pounds of walnuts and the heat was kept at 110 degrees Fahrenheit, that the drying process took twenty-four to thirty hours. The nuts were then run through the machine huller, where steel blades snatched the hulls like magic. She explained that she belonged to the Growers' Association, but they did no harvesting at all. She had to see to it herself that the crop was harvested, dried, hulled, and delivered.

I listened to her, yawning and nodding. About all I can say for that day is: I Sure Learned About Walnuts.

It wasn't until dusk, when I was driving her home, that I got in what I wanted to say:

"Virginia, you serious about kicking that girl out?"

"Certainly!"

I said casually: "Why don't you let her stay? She isn't—"

Her eyes narrowed. "I didn't know you were interested in that young lady."

"Interested?" I laughed. "It isn't that—it's only that she's in a spot."

She turned and looked at me.

"Lynn's a nice kid," I went on, "when you get to know her."

"I see. You've gotten to know her."

My face was hot. "No, but—"

"Curt, you will bear in mind that you are not employed as my business manager."

"Sure, but—"

"If that young lady's welfare means more to you than your position, you can leave anytime."

"Forget the whole thing," I said. "Just forget it!"

We didn't talk anymore all the way home. And even when we reached the house, she just got out with her nose way up in the air and marched over the lawn and in the back door. She was griped! Because I was taking an interest in Lynn. And she didn't like it. Not one bit.

In my bedroom, I pulled off my necktie and picked up one of the detective magazines. I looked up and saw Lynn standing in my doorway. She was wearing a white silk dress that did a lot for her figure, and some fancy white sandals. Her legs were bare and there was a shiny little chain on one ankle.

"Hello, Pied Piper," she said in that deep, soft voice.

Chapter Eight

"Pied Piper?" I laughed. "Hey—where do you get that?"

"You called the rats away."

She was inside now, standing before the dresser mirror. "Is it all right for me to come in like this?"

"Why not?"

"I thought maybe this room was reserved for the old woman."

The grin faded from my face. "That isn't funny."

She moved over beside me. "I'm sorry. I didn't mean that—really. But you left with her last night—and all today." She curled her lower lip. "I never thought I'd be jealous of an old hag like that."

"Quit kidding."

"I'm not kidding."

"Hell, it's only part of my job."

Her eyes came up, green and wide and shiny, like a jungle cat's. "You must think a lot of that job."

"You know better than that."

She walked over to the window and looked out and didn't say anything.

"Locate any work yet?" I asked.

She shook her head. "I have an appointment to see the manager of the Vanities Club in the morning." She paused. "I only wish I had some new clothes." She looked down the street. "Wouldn't it be nice to be able to run into Saks and buy up anything you wanted."

"Yeah."

"These wealthy woman can do that."

"Your clothes are okay."

"No. I haven't anything decent." She picked up a cigarette from the pack on the dresser. I got up and lighted it for her. She inhaled a drag and draped herself on the bed. Then:

"Your idea of having a girl move in with me isn't so good."

"How's that?"

"She's really a queer one."

"Yeah? What's the lowdown?"

"She prays."

"She *what?*"

"Prays. You know—"

"So what? A lot of people do that."

"But she makes a regular ritual out of it. She gets down on her knees beside the bed, like a little kid. Gawd—she's got religion!"

"I'll be damned!"

"She's one of those tent evangelists."

"Salvation Nell?"

She nodded. "She gives lectures—calls it modern religion. She's got a new setup in Sawtelle. I didn't half listen to her. Her name's Elise Monteith. She had a picture of this Army Chaplain on the dresser, the boyfriend. She talks to him in her prayers, as though he was there in the room."

"She does sound plenty odd."

"I can't understand it. Because she showed me the telegram from the War Department saying that this chaplain was killed in action in the South Pacific."

"He's dead?"

"That's how the telegram reads. But Elise says she refuses to believe it. And there she kneels praying, looking at his picture, calling his name. Talking to him as if he were alive." She shook her head. "She's one sad bag. And it's going to be a shock to her when the boyfriend doesn't show up."

"Yeah."

"Anyway, she paid me thirty dollars, and I gave the old woman the ten I owed her. But you should have heard her scream when she saw Elise moving in."

"I heard."

Her voice faded. "So I have my verbal notice to vacate."

"You're not going anywhere," I said. "You're staying here until you're damn good and ready to leave."

She smiled sarcastically and arched one brow. "Where do you get all the authority? You been winning the old woman over today? Is that what you've been doing?"

I swung one arm down and jerked her up to her feet. "Shut up! You think I *like* bowing and scraping to the old scarecrow? You think it's fun sitting next to her in a movie like I did last night?

"Curt, you're—"

"—Driving her around today, yessing her. Listening to that asinine drool about walnuts!"

"You don't have to get sore!"

"You think I'm content to be her pet flunky—do you?"

"No, but—"

"I've got ambitions!" I pulled her closer. "Jesus, you're a dumb little lamb!"

"Curt, you're hurting me."

"Dumb," I said. "But nice curves."

"Ouch."

"What I'm doing I'm doing for you, baby. So we can both stay on here till I figure out what's the best thing for us."

"Us? *Us*, darling?" Her arms went up around my neck. "Well, aren't you sweet! I guess I am awfully dumb. I had no idea you were doing it for me." Her eyes were bright. "Oh, Curt, darling—"

I pushed her away. "Beat it. The old lady'll catch us. She'll run the both of us out."

She looked hurt. "I wanted to talk to you."

"Okay. I'll meet you down in the cellar."

"Gawd! It's dark down here."

"Yeah."

"And there's that noise again—like running water. Hear it Curt?"
"Yeah, yeah."
"I can't stand it. Why don't you fix it?"
"I will, baby. Tomorrow."

Chapter Nine

Late the next afternoon I was cleaning out the garage when I saw Mrs. Block come out the back door. She stood squinting at the sky. There was a vacuum in the air, a stillness—rain would start pouring any minute. She retreated back in the house and came out again wearing galoshes and carrying an umbrella.

When she reached the garage I asked, friendly:

"Going out to the ranch?"

She brushed past me and got in the Packard and started the motor without saying a word. I guess in her mind we were having a lover's quarrel—about Lynn. And she was jealous. Anyway, she wasn't speaking.

When she was gone I remembered that dripping in the cellar. So I went down there to try and figure exactly where it was coming from. I decided that it was to the north. I went outside and found a vent.

I crawled in under the house, till I found a plumbing connection. It was dry and perfectly okay. Yet I could still hear water dripping. I crawled back out and went down into the cellar again. I noticed the partition—new wood. It had probably been put up rather recently. The dripping seemed to come from behind it.

I picked up a hammer and chisel. Then I was busy pulling out nails and swearing under my breath. Each board held about fifty nails, as though some amateur carpenter had made a pastime out of hammering them in.

It was almost dark outside when I finally pulled out a space big enough to slide through. I moved inside. Behind the partition the floor was still cement—for about five feet. Evidently the cellar had been larger at one time, and Mrs. Block had had part of it closed off. The cement wall at the far end didn't go clear to the top, and you could see under the house.

My eyes focused on a drainpipe, half hidden by the junk. Under it was a little pool of water. An evil-smelling vapor fumed up from the stagnant pool.

There were a lot of boxes piled up all around. I stepped up on one and peered over the wall. At first all I could see was more junk, broken vases, mildewed shoeboxes, a pair of broken bookends, an old-fashioned wood hat-block.

I stepped down off the box and decided that the best thing to do was to dig a little outlet somewhere, so that the water could run outside. But first I decided to fix the leaking pipe.

It was one those elbows that turned under at the bottom. I went back through the partition over to the toolbox and picked up a spade and a monkey wrench. I figured I had to dig down in the dirt below the elbow to get a space big enough so that I could work under the pipe. I crawled up over the wall.

In a cramped position, I started digging. My spade hit rotten wood. It splintered and cracked. I dug right through it. Then I was looking at something—something shiny. I cringed, with cold shivers running all up and down my spine.

I was looking at a hand—a human hand—like no hand you've ever seen. It was only the skeleton! My stomach began to contract. The something shiny was a big disk ring with a small black stone set in the center. It was the same as in the wedding picture the old lady had shown me, but now the ring hung loose on a bony finger. And I knew the identity of this corpse all right! My lips formed the word:

Henry.

For a terrible second I kept staring inside that crude wood coffin, with my knees buckling and sweat forming on my forehead. I slid down the wall and made tracks through the partition, thinking maybe I was going to faint any minute. I threw the boards back up.

Then I was in my bedroom, with a cold clammy sweat all over me. I brushed the dirt off my trousers, with my hands still shaking like the palsy. I flung open the dresser drawer and pulled out one of the pints of whisky I'd been saving for a special occasion.

This was a special occasion.

I lifted the bottle to my lips. It rattled against my teeth. I gulped down half the pint. I sat on the bed, trying to erase the picture from my mind—Henry entombed in that old wood coffin! I got scared, thinking maybe I'd never forget it! I took another drink. The St. Vitus in my hands was steadier. Somewhere in my mind there were the words: *the old woman, the old woman, the old woman.* They danced a jig through my brain, over and over. Then slowly thoughts began to form.

The salary she was paying me for all the work I did—the way Rip Van Winkle couldn't collect his dough—the City Attorney telling what a deadbeat she was—she had two old wrecks for cars when she could afford Cadillacs—the room she rented to Lynn for sixty bucks when she didn't even need the dough

The way she peddled those avocados off her tree for the few extra bucks they'd bring—and scrimping and saving on food—the gleam in her eyes when she handled dough—the way she'd expected that colored maid to clean the whole house in one day and then skipped off without paying her—

Lynn had her tabbed. Miser. A groveling old miser! But she was a hellcat, too—the old woman. I thought of the song and dance she'd given me about Henry. He'd disappeared, all right. He took a long trip, he did, from the house to the cellar.

I remembered what the old woman had said about her stepson, Jeffrey, how she'd refused him the money Henry had promised him. *That was why she'd killed Henry! She'd made her mind that Jeff wasn't going to get that dough!*

Maybe she'd carried him down to the cellar herself!

She could carry five men! She was that strong. And she'd probably hauled in the big pine box herself, dumped the old man in his coffin and dug his grave. Then she'd called in a carpenter to put up the new partition, so that Henry could have his own private tomb.

And Blackie—it occurred to me that it probably was corn meal she was feeding him. Because she didn't want to lay out a half buck now and then for dog food. No wonder that poor pup whined and his fur was—

I got boiling mad thinking about that dog. Henry be damned! I took another swig of whisky before I made tracks into the kitchen. I opened cupboard doors and grabbed a can of Spam. I opened it and took it out to Blackie. He lapped it up in five seconds flat.

"And more tomorrow, pal," I said.

I went back inside the house and finished the bottle. After that I paced back and forth on the carpet, with new thoughts forming. I'd struck oil—and it was no duster! I knew exactly what my plan would be. All I needed now was the old woman to come home!

I went out to the garage and got in her Pontiac and waited, thinking things out—the things I was going to say to her and how I was going to say them. I guess I sat waiting out there a good hour, thinking like crazy!

I wondered about Lynn. I hadn't heard the phonograph or her moving around upstairs. She should be back by now. She'd gone to see the manager of the Vanities Club, but that was this afternoon. *Where was Lynn?*

Good thing she was gone, though. My plan was secret. Strictly secret—between the old woman and me. You can't let too many people in on a good plan.

It occurred to me suddenly that my hands were icy and my forehead was burning hot. I got out of the car and closed the garage doors and hurried back to the house.

Thunder rumbled low and exploded with a crash. A tiny streak of lightning flashed blue. The air was dry, and there was a peculiar amber glare in the sky.

I went into my bedroom and brought out a new pint. I sat on the bed sipping at it. The whisky was raw and hot in my throat. Raindrops began to fall gently on the panes. The air in the room was musty and damp. A plane droning overhead muffled the sound of the rain, and through it came the whirr of wet automobile tires on the street. A fly buzzed against the window. A woman in the neighborhood started calling her cat, "Here, kitty, kitty, kitty, kitty." She kept repeating it over and over. And finally there was silence. I heard the rain again, gaining momentum—strings of silver in the growing darkness.

Then suddenly I heard the Packard pull in. I rushed to the door and flung it open. I was flying high! I remember I was seated back on the bed when the screen door opened and slammed shut. I heard her shoes creaking. She'd come in.

I grabbed up a magazine and pretended to read. But from the corner of my eye I could see her standing in my doorway. I turned a page. She still didn't say anything.

I looked up. She was gripping her umbrella cane. I watched the beads of rain fall from it to the floor, making spots where they hit.

She moved over toward me.

Chapter Ten

"I want to have words with you, Curt."

"Sure, lady, sure."

"I must say I'm rather disappointed. You've done a slipshod job cleaning out the garage. Furthermore, there is something I neglected to tell you. While putting the avocado boxes in the back seat of my car you tore the upholstery. It's a costly job to have that fixed, and it might require complete new upholstering. It won't be necessary to tell you that the repair bill will be deducted from your salary—" Her eyes flashed. "—or salaries, shall we say?"

I grinned.

She took a step closer and sniffed the air. Her voice rang accusingly: "You've been drinking! There's one thing I won't tolerate in my help.

That's alcoholism. If this situation continues, I'll be forced to give you notice."

I flung one leg over the side of the bed. "You can't expect too much from a guy for twenty bucks a week. Maybe if you raised my pay—"

"*Raise?* Humph!" She smiled contemptuously.

"To, say—five hundred, or even one grand per week."

She sputtered a little moan of incredulity. She bent over and started peeling off her galoshes. The rain beat a steady tattoo against the windows.

"You must be out of your mind!"

I shook my head. "You see—I ran into an old friend of yours today."

"Old friend?" She blinked. "Old friend? You mean the process server?"

"I don't mean the process server."

"Who, then?"

I got up and went over to the dresser. I lit a cigarette. "Somebody you wouldn't want anybody to know I met." I kept my voice low. "Or you wouldn't want the cops to know I met him either."

The galoshes fell to the floor, but her voice remained calm. "Police? What *are* you trying to say?"

"You see, I fixed a leak under the house. *Under* the house—understand? And that's where I ran across your old friend."

Her hand grasped the umbrella tighter. For just one second she tottered. Then she froze. "You're drunk! Dead *drunk!* I can tell by that smirk on your face. And—you're making up things," she protested weakly. She slumped down on the bed, her body limp.

"So—" I took a slow drag off my cigarette. "—I thought maybe you'd like to know Henry didn't leave your house at all. He was here all this time."

"You're talking in riddles," she gasped.

"Think so?" I got up. "Okay, Virginia—have it your own way."

I left her standing there. I went into the kitchen. I stayed close to the door, listening. Because this was still part of my plan. The floor squeaked under her footsteps. The back door opened and closed. She'd gone out—just as I'd expected. I waited a second longer, then beat it outside.

A peal of thunder crashed. I hurried over to the cellar steps and down. I stopped in the doorway.

She was there—holding a lighted match in her hand. It illuminated her face, accentuating her eyes. She held the small flame inside the partition. A low moan escaped her lips.

"I was talking in riddles, eh?"

She whirled around, her eyes wild. They looked reddish in the dark. The match went out. The room was pitch black. Her words came in spasms:

"*Sneak!* Destroying my property. Where did you get permission to tear down my house?"

I stood motionless in the doorway. "It was strictly by accident, Virginia. You see, I was fixing the plumbing."

Through the gloom her voice came closer and dropped to a dead whisper: "Who knows? Who else knows?"

"Nobody, Virginia. Only me."

Her voice relaxed a shade. "What—makes you so sure it's Henry?"

"The ring," I said. "The same one your husband wore in that wedding picture. You remember showing me that picture, don't you, Virginia?"

"Yes, yes," she gasped.

A forked streak of lightning flashed. Through the glare I saw her face closer, her eyes glassy—the pupils too large, too bright. Then darkness closed in the room.

"Who could have done this thing!" she sobbed. "Poor, poor Henry! All these, years I've searched for him, not knowing some fiend had buried him here in the cellar, killed him. Some monster has killed him—*murdered* him!"

"Murder is the word, all right."

"Who could have done it! Who *could* have—"

"We'd better call the cops," I said.

"Police?" Her voice was barely audible. "Well, well, I—you—you haven't notified the police?"

"Not yet, Virginia."

She was stalling, for time. "You—you think it's really Henry—and you—you think someone actually did murder him?"

"Yeah. That's what I think. I think you even built that pine coffin yourself, dug out this shallow grave and—"

"You—think—I—" Her voice choked.

"Yeah. You. And you even nailed up this partition yourself to shut him off."

Her voice shook. "A woman *my age* couldn't be capable of all that, carrying his body in here—"

"You might be able to convince the jury."

"You're mad!"

"If you didn't kill him," I said. "Then how'd you know where to find his body? That's about all the proof anybody needs."

She groaned. Then she was talking a mile a minute. "Upstairs, Curt. Upstairs you mentioned a raise in pay. I—how much is it? I'll give it to you. What is it you want? How much is it? You're intending to blackmail me, is that it?"

"Blackmail?" I dropped my cigarette and stepped on the burning coals. "I don't like that word. But I'll take a raise in pay."

She sucked in her breath. "Well—"

"A thousand a week."

"A thous—" She couldn't get the rest of the word out. "I—I—" Her eyes flickered up through the darkness. "You can't demand that much. Why I—I'm just a poor old—" She broke off.

Silence enveloped the room, a deafening silence. Then all at once you could hear the trickle of water from the pipe—over Henry's grave. I saw the silhouette of her body slumped against the wall. I heard her heavy breathing. I could almost hear her mind ticking—a hundred thoughts spinning in her brain. Suddenly her voice gushed out:

"All right. All right. I'm willing." She hurried over to the opening in the partition and pointed inside. She was waving her hands like fury. "You must go back in there! You must shovel the dirt back over. Nail those boards back up! *Make it look as if it hasn't been touched!*"

I didn't budge.

"Don't stand there!" Her voice was stark panic. "Get busy, Curt! *Get busy!*"

"You forgot something, Virginia. Do we have a deal or don't we?"

"Yes, of course."

"A grand every week?"

"Every week. Hurry. Hurry! Put the dirt back over. Here's the spade—"

I took the spade. Outside, Blackie gave out with a coyote wail.

"I'll go out," she said, "and stand watch. *Hurry!*" She brushed past me out the door.

I stood trembling. I dragged the spade with me—through the opening of the partition. I didn't dare to think. I climbed up on the box and shifted my weight up and over. I didn't dare to look. Up to this point I'd been fine. I wasn't fine any longer. All the blood in my body was in my head, and my ears kept ringing. The spade in my hand kept knifing into the loose dirt. Up and over, *up and over!* A crazy wild tune kept running through my mind: the *Danse Macabre*. I kept pounding the earth down with the flat bottom of the spade. The old woman's words kept screaming at me: "*Make it look as if it hasn't been touched!*" Then suddenly without rhyme or reason I threw the spade with all my might. It crashed below on the cement floor.

I lay down on my stomach and began smoothing the dirt over with my hands. And all at once there was the soft pit-a-pat of footsteps, shoes creaking. My eyes darted down over the cement wall. My heart started thumping in slow heavy strokes.

She was standing there—the old woman. I saw her figure outlined in the half light. I saw her craggy profile. I watched her stoop and pick up something. When she straightened I saw the object in her hand—the spade. She hoisted it up over her shoulder.

"What the hell—" I managed.

"It's only me, Curt." She came closer. Both of her fists were gripped on the spade handle. It occurred to me suddenly why she was there: *Dead men don't talk!*

I alone knew that she had murdered her husband. She was going to fix that right here and now!

My hand groped for some object of defense. I felt the damp shoe boxes, the old hat block. My fingers rested on the broken vase.

"Everything going all right?" she whispered from below.

"Yeah." I strained my eyes, my every muscle, watching, waiting. Sweat began to form on my forehead. The ringing in my ears grew louder. I went weak. On my feet I'd have been able to cope with her. But I wasn't on my feet. I was trapped in a space four feet long. I couldn't even rise to a sitting position.

Is this the way a rat feels in a cage looking out the wide-open door at a cat?

"Pat the dirt down well," she said.

I patted with my left hand. My right grasped the broken vase tighter. Any second the spade was going to fly—and I was going to be ready!

"Make it look as if it hasn't been touched."

I kept on pounding down the dirt. But I was watching her every move. I saw the spade upraised in her grasp. At that moment I let the vase go with all my strength. It missed her, hit the cement floor and shattered into bits. But the crash had unsteadied her aim. The spade hit the old wood hat block. I stared at it.

It was split in half!

That's the way my head would have looked!

I jumped down off the ledge. I fumbled along the cement and found the spade and grabbed it up.

"For Christ's sake," I blurted. "What were you trying to do?"

"Are you injured—badly?" her voice whined. "Oh, Curt, I didn't mean to hurt you. I was trying to help. I was trying to help pound down the dirt."

"Yeah. You're a dear old lady. Only trying to help."

I left her standing there. I beat it through the partition and up the cellar steps. I hit the air and felt better. I thought of the hat block. Had the old lady been successful, I'd be a dead duck right now. I'd be lying alongside Henry.

In a minute she came up the steps. She hurried on past me, outside.

Oblivious of the downpour. I followed her in the house. I noticed that her hair was wet and matted. She put one hand up and touched my arm.

"I'll bring you the money," she said.

I went into my bedroom and sat down in a cold sweat. In a few minutes she came in, holding an old leather wallet. She closed the door and pulled down the shades and stood with her back to the window. She began peeling off bills—twenties, fifties, hundreds. My eyes bulged from their sockets.

"A week's salary," she said miserably. "One thousand dollars."

I counted the dough over. I looked up and caught her expression—revulsion and hatred—as though she wanted to scream, parting with that dough. Then suddenly she laughed. It sent chills through me. Because it was the laugh of a crazy woman.

"This is our secret," she said.

"Why'd you bump him off?"

"I didn't say I did."

"You don't have to say it. A few minutes ago in the cellar you proved the things you're capable of. Henry was about ready to give Jeff the dough he'd promised him. Isn't that why you let him have it?"

She put a martyr look on her face, all self-pity. "Let me tell you something," she wheezed. "Let me tell you something."

"I'm listening."

She screwed up her face. "You see—I married a pauper when I married Henry. He was even in poor health. A severe lung infection. I was always urging him to go to a dry climate to live. Finally I borrowed five hundred dollars and bought an acre of land in the Mojave desert. While sinking for water, we discovered borax. We sold the mine on a royalty basis. Henry never worked after that."

"What are you getting at?"

She clenched her fists at her side. "Without my foresight and planning, Henry Block would never have accumulated the fortune he did. The money is *mine!*"

"Just as I thought."

Her eyes were wild again. "But I didn't say I killed him. I've only told you I'd raise your salary."

"That's okay with me."

She moved closer. "You're to forget everything!"

"Yeah. Down in the cellar you almost made sure of that."

"No, no, Curt. You're wrong. The spade slipped. I was so nervous." Her eyes came up. "But no one must ever know. Just us! We're partners!"

I winced.

"Yes, we are—we're partners. No one else must ever know." "Yeah."

"*No one else must ever know!*" Her eyes burned hot and sullen. She watched me a moment longer, then turned and left the room.

I stood looking after her, with the greenbacks in my hands doing a shimmy dance and my insides rocking. One thing was clear: the old woman had no intention of letting me get away with blackmail. She'd paid me the grand, sure, to keep me from visiting the cops, but only until she could think of a safe sure way to paint me out of the picture. She had murder in her blood, and I was suddenly a very bad insurance risk. I knew about Henry, and a double indemnity would cost me a million bucks from here on in.

The only thing for me to do would be to go in for real dough. A thousand a week was pin money. Time was of the essence. I had to angle a way to shake some real sugar out of her. And I had to stick around until I got it—that much I knew. I hitched up my belt. I knew it all right, that I'd stick till I hit the old girl for the jackpot. But the thought of having to be round her until I did didn't make me feel so good. What risks we mortals take for money, I thought. If only I'd been born with a million bucks in the first place, probably none of this would ever have happened to me.

I looked up, then I jumped. She was back—in my room, her eyes shifting. Then I heard it—the banging on the front door. I sprang to my feet.

"Who's that out front?"

Her face was gray. She slumped back against the wall, her eyes staring blankly.

"Who is it?" My heart started hammering against my chest.

"It's Jeff and Natalie," she whined.

"How d'you know?"

"I saw them—through the crack in the drapery. I looked out and saw them." Her voice lowered to a flat defeated whisper: "They've come back. To sponge, on me and argue and persecute me some more."

I exhaled a deep breath. "For Christ's sake, let them in!"

Her pupils dilated. "No. You do it, Curt. I—I'm going up to bed. I don't want to talk them. Not yet. Not tonight. You tell them," she went on hoarsely. "I'm asleep. I *can't* talk to them tonight. You tell them I'm asleep."

I followed her into the front room. At the bottom of the stairs, she clutched my arm.

"About tonight," she whispered, "you'll get your money every week." The doorbell screamed again.

"Let them in—after I get upstairs. Don't let them suspect. *Be calm,*

Curt! Be calm!"

"Yeah, sure." I said that, but my legs were buckling under. I floundered toward the door.

She scurried up the stairs. I waited a moment, then I opened the door.

Chapter Eleven

Jeff and Natalie stood on the front porch, with the rain pouring down behind them, both of them registering surprise at the sight of me. You could tell that they expected the old lady.

He held a suitcase in one hand. His eyes scrutinized me closely.

The dame was tall and I noticed she really did have nice curves. I found my voice:

"Come right on in."

They stepped inside and went on into the living room. He set the suitcase down and removed his hat. He took off his overcoat and looked around. He was dark complexioned with wavy, dark hair—a kind of mama's boy—wearing square-cut gold-rimmed glasses. He was tired looking, with a thin moody face.

She reminded me of a Harper's model: the chiseled face, the pale dead-white skin, the long body made to wear clothes.

She was Parisian elegance in dress, in an olive-green suit with brown fur on the cuffs. A matching fur hat sat on the back of her head, touching a big reddish-blonde bun on the nape of her neck. She kept admiring herself in the mirrors. I noticed her eyes—brown, calculating, and cold.

Now they both looked over at me with "who in hell are you" expressions.

"Well, well," I said friendly-like, "I can tell right away you're the son and daughter-in-law Mrs. Block talks so much about." I took a deep breath. "Your mother went to bed early. She's sound asleep."

They stood surveying me coolly; they didn't warm up at all. He said: "Who are you, may I ask?"

"Me?" I grinned. "You might call me the new hired hand if you like. Or you can call me General Fixit." I laughed and shook my head. "Your mother sure can think up enough work for me to do around here."

"Then mother's all right?" he asked crisply.

"All right? She's the most remarkable woman I've ever seen for her age." I meant every word of it.

They exchanged a look. Then this Natalie had a smirk on her face.

"I told you it was foolish, dear, didn't I? Worrying over her merely because she ignored your letters? You know perfectly well why she didn't answer them. And now she's upstairs playing possum. Well, she can't—"

He nodded wearily. "Natalie," he said, too calm, "I'm trying to talk to Mr.—"

"Blair," I told him. "Curt Blair." I smiled again and held out my hand. He ignored it. And then all of a sudden I wasn't nervous any longer. I felt like doubling up my fist and bashing in his face with it. But I held the smile.

"Your mother's rented the side front bedroom," I said. "But I guess you know your way around. You'll know where to bunk for the night."

"Oh, yes, yes," he said abstractedly. "Thank you, Blair. That will be all for now."

I stood glaring at him. I was boiling mad at the way he'd dismissed me, as though I was his goddamn butler or something. I turned and walked out, leaving them both looking after me.

In the kitchen, I stayed at the door listening. They were talking low, but their voices carried through the hushed room.

"That Blair fellow," Natalie was saying, "acts as if he owns this place!"

"Quite an odd chap."

"Where in the world did Virginia pick him up?"

"I don't know," Jeff replied tiredly. "What's the difference? It's impossible to engage anyone but morons nowadays. You know how servants take advantage of one's good nature."

"I know?" she replied sarcastically. "How would *I* know! I haven't had a maid since we were married. And if you think I'm going to continue spending my time in the kitchen the way I have, you're sadly—"

"Natalie, please— You know I'm trying my damnedest to work things out."

"In your own phlegmatic manner."

"*Please*, Natalie."

"Oh, it's the truth. You're so slow it's disgusting."

There was a silence. Then she went on:

"Are we going to continue letting the old bitch put it over on us? I suggest we get tough. Yes, *tough!*" Her tone was brittle. "I'd like to *wring* our money out of her!"

"For God's sake, Natalie!"

"I mean every word of it!" She grunted. "You're spineless. Why did we come out here if you're going to be wishy-washy? And after that loathsome train ride. I won't go through that again. We'll get plane reservations back or I refuse to budge."

"Natalie—" His voice broke. "If you don't stop—if you don't let up—if you keep on and on the way you have been, you're going to drive me to—"

"To what? Go on, say it!"

"I don't know. But we can't keep on this way."

"That's what I'm telling you. It *can't* go on like this. She isn't your real mother. She's never been a mother to you. You've told me that over and over. She's been a wicked, greedy old hellion! That's why Henry left her!"

"We've agreed on that point, Natalie. Why must you keep repeating it?"

"Well, what are you going to do?"

There was a pause.

"I'm going up to bed now," he said. "And in the morning—"

"Well, if you expect me to be nice to her, if you expect me not to tell her exactly what I—"

"Shut up, Natalie. That chap might be listening. That Blair fellow. He looks like a snooper to me. I believe he's hanging around here for no good."

I heard their footsteps. I beat it quick into my bedroom. They came into the kitchen. A few minutes later I heard them going up the stairs.

It was at night I had the nightmares. I saw the old Serpent, himself, in a scarlet-lined cape and cross-bones for a face. He was running me all over the Hot Spot with a garden spade. I woke up with a start—seeing the bones in that crude wood coffin, the horrible sight of Henry in his grave. I tried not to think, but he was in my mind vivid and clear. I rolled and tossed with the sweat pouring off me, wetting the sheets. I was glad when it began to rain even harder. Like the gates of hell breaking loose.

And I guess they had, all right.

Chapter Twelve

The next morning I had the jitters worse than ever. I had the grand in my pocket—sure. But the funny part was I didn't feel so good about it, because of Henry. I still had the indelible picture of him in my mind. And the old woman—she might be after me again. I'd better be watching my step. She was capable of anything—I'd found that out. I trusted her the way I trusted a cobra.

I thought about that while I took a shower and shaved and dressed.

When I went out into the living room, Mrs. Block was there, bent over the hearth, piling wood in the fireplace. She looked up and saw me and rose to her feet.

"Everything go all right last night?" she asked thickly.

"Yeah."

"I haven't seen them yet. They're not up yet." Her eyes moved slow, up to Henry's portrait above the mantel. *"No one must ever know."*

"There's just one thing," I said. "The two girls upstairs—they stay on."

Her mouth snapped open, then closed. "All right," she said resignedly. She bent down again and held a match to the fire.

I sat down on the piano bench, wondering what to do with myself. I looked out the window. The sky was overcast. The rain had lessened to a fine drizzle. I pecked around on the piano keys. Then I was playing soft. The music was soothing, somehow. I read the words to the piece as I played—about a dame named Butterfly, who never grew weary of waiting on a hill for a ship to come gliding into the harbor—for her guy to get off. Anyway, she kept waiting for him, certain that he'd return one fine day.

I didn't hear her coming down the stairs. That's why I was startled when I looked up and saw the face of a saint smiling at me from across the piano. It was the smile of a saint, too—with the bluest of eyes.

She wore no makeup. She didn't need it. Her complexion was all peaches and cream. She wore a little knitted blue suit, with a blue scarf that matched her eyes.

"Hello," she said. "You're Curt Blair. Lynn's told me of you."

"Yeah. And you're the new roomer."

She smiled and nodded her head in time with the music. "Isn't that 'One Fine Day' you're playing, from *Madame Butterfly?*"

I turned to the cover page. "That's what it is." When I looked up again I saw that her eyes were moist.

"It's a lovely song," she said. "And you play it so well."

"Thanks."

This was the first time I'd seen her—Lynn's new bunk partner. From Lynn's description of her, I'd expected to see a halo around Elise's head. She had a halo all right—blonde hair void of peroxide. You could tell that, somehow. It was rich and shiny, with curls that stopped short in line with her ears.

She stayed there leaning on the piano, listening to the music. Then she moved off quickly, over to the fireplace. Her movements were all very quick. I noticed the figure. Okay. Trim. Not bad. Not bad at all.

It wasn't until she spoke again, to the old lady, that I caught the reverential pathos in her voice. It was suddenly as though she were addressing a congregation. A melodious clear tone. And she had a quick, breathless way of talking.

"I can't begin to tell you," she said, "how shocked I was when Miss York told me you hadn't given your permission for me to move into your lovely home."

The old woman gave me a hostile glance, but her voice was calm. "That's quite—all right. You may stay as long as you like."

This Elise choked back a sob. "How generous of you! I'm so grateful, believe me. I do regret having to tell you that I'll be leaving—"

Mrs. Block perked up. "Oh—you're moving?"

"Yes. Yes, I am. Everything has worked out so beautifully. Reverend Gossin—that's my co-worker—has located me a lovely little flat in Sawtelle. It's only a few blocks from the church, you see? And it will be so much more convenient."

"Yes, indeed."

"I do hope you'll find time to come out and hear me."

Mrs. Block looked stumped. "Well, I—I suppose I will," she grumbled. "You just leave the address of your church on your way out."

The dame smiled. "Well, I'm scarcely moving out this minute. It will be several days before I can get possession of my new little flat." She looked over at me. "I do hope in the meanwhile we can all become good friends. Bless you both."

I did a double take on the "bless you both."

She said: "We're all part of a big happy family."

"Happy family?" I laughed. "Oh, sure."

"All of us, God-loving, spiritual people."

"Yeah." I watched the old lady, staring morosely at the fire.

"Brothers and sisters—all of us!"

Christ—I couldn't believe it! I looked at the old lady again. She was trying to keep busy, poking at the smoking fire, to avoid the dame. I went over to the hearth and put on a piece of wood and kept fumbling, hoping that Evangeline here would catch on that we weren't in the mood for a sermon.

"A fireplace—warmth," she murmured. "Good fellowship. This is truly a house of God!"

The old woman stirred the fire even harder. Sparks flew and crackled, and outside the rain began to fall, hard. Then this Elise turned easily and moved over to the window and peered out at the wet gloom.

"Isn't it wonderful—rain?" she said. "It is one of His blessings."

"Yeah."

Elise looked back. "I did want to go out to Sawtelle today. It does my heart good to stand in my new little church, visualizing its emptiness in quite a different light. Filled with my congregation. Courageous soldiers who have come back—"

"Your church is empty?"

"Yes," she replied. "We've just bought the building. It's my very first church. Before, you see, I was the Reverend's assistant."

"Oh," I said drily.

She glanced at the window again and shrugged. "But I suppose it's quite impossible for me to get out there today. The buses run infrequently—and there's no telling how long I'd have to wait in the rain."

I'd had enough of her. I went out into the kitchen, leaving the two of them. I heated up the coffee and fried some eggs and made some toast. I was sitting at the table when Lynn came in.

"Have you missed me?"

"Sure, baby."

"Why don't you ask me where I was last night?"

"Where were you last night?"

She picked up a slice of toast and munched on it. "I saw Mr. Marco yesterday. He's the manager of the Vanities. I got the job. Starting tomorrow night."

"Show girl, eh?"

"Well, sort of."

"What d'ya mean, sort of?"

"I have to start as a cigarette girl. He doesn't have a spot vacant in the chorus yet. But he says if I'll work as his cigarette girl—only temporarily—he'll give me a swell break in the new show."

"Show girl?"

She hesitated. "He didn't say."

"Better watch out for those guys."

She bristled. "Think I can't take care of myself?"

"Watch him," I repeated.

She poured herself a cup of coffee and sat down opposite me. She stirred cream and sugar in the cup. I said:

"How long did you talk to this Mr. Marco yesterday?"

"Just a few minutes."

"What took so long getting home?"

Her eyes were bright. "I knew I had the job, so I went on over to Creighton Hall. I had a long talk with Mrs. Hall."

"Mrs. Hall?"

"That's right. She asked me to stay for class last night. So I jumped at the chance. It was wonderful, Curt. They were casting."

"Casting, eh?"

She nodded. "And I read a part. I read the role of Ethel. They're doing *Petticoat Fever.*"

"Yeah?"

"And afterwards Mrs. Hall said I had great potentialities. She said she'd hold the part open for me in the afternoon class, since I worked nights. I didn't tell her I didn't have the money to start. She said she was sure I'd make good."

"Mrs. Hall said all this?"

She nodded again and sipped on her coffee. "If I only had fifty dollars! That's all I need to begin the lessons."

I took her by the arm and led her into my bedroom. I reached under the mattress and pulled out the dough. I kept peeling off bills and piling them up in her hands.

"You—you've given me two hundred dollars!" she said incredibly.

"Yeah."

"Curt, where did you get it?"

"Uncle Philbert," I said, "remembered me in his will."

"You're a wonderful liar, darling. Where did you get it?"

"Don't ask questions."

"But I want to know!"

"Okay," I said. "It was an old watch. My old man handed it down to me, and I kept it for years, because—hell, the old man gave it to me. But yesterday I got to thinking. It was fourteen-carat gold; I ambled down to the hock shop and—"

"Oh, darling—" She counted me out a hundred dollars and put it back in my hand. "I wouldn't think of taking it all."

"You said you needed some clothes, baby." I gave the bills back to her. "And you can start those lessons—"

She had her arms up around my neck. "You—you pawned a very valuable old heirloom for *me*, darling?"

"Yeah."

She was all choked up. "Now I can walk into Saks and order up."

"Sure. Get your coat."

"Now?" she asked eagerly. "Shall I buy them now?"

"Why not? I'll drive you up. But don't expect me to go in with you. I don't know the first thing about dresses."

"Drive?"

"I'll take the Pontiac."

"Won't the old woman raise—"

I shook my head.

She bolted for the door. Then she stopped still in her tracks and looked back. "There's something awfully screwy about this."

"Get your coat," I said.

She thought for a moment. "We'll take Elise. She wants to get out to Sawtelle."

"Knock that off," I told her, while I slid my arms into the camel's hair. "I'm not taking that dame anywhere. She gets under my skin."

"Oh, Curt, it's only a mile or two further from Saks to Sawtelle. You can drive her on out."

So that's how I took the two of them.

Chapter Thirteen

I dropped Lynn off at Saks on Wilshire. She said she didn't know how long she'd be in there shopping and that she'd take the bus back to the house. She got out and hurried along the sidewalk, through the drizzle, and into the store. Next thing I was chauffeuring Elise on out Wilshire Boulevard.

I thought of Henry and the old lady again and Jeff and Natalie. It had me all bound up in knots, and I felt lousy. Like I was in the coffin beside Henry, asking him to move over. Just to get my mind off all that I said:

"What kind of church you got? Sort of a Salvation Army idea?"

She smiled. "I merely teach our relationship to God. As you know—we are all one Universal Mind."

"Sort of a Christian Science slant?"

"In a way. We can't ignore the fact that we live in a world of thought and that everyone carves his own destiny."

"Oh, sure."

"Each of us possesses a hidden energy, a God-given power. But not all of us are conscious of it. If we think love and certainty and harmony," she went on, "instead of fear and uncertainty, we can use this power to constructive progression in life."

I cleared my throat. "Yeah," I said and gave her a look.

"It's really quite simple. Belief is all. We must believe. We must know that every man's pathway is lighted. And we must accept that fact."

"Very definitely," I said. *What the hell was she talking about?*

"But how false it is to hold a man good by fear. Fear of the devil. It is my purpose to hold a man good by entirely different methods."

"How do you mean?"

"By love," she said.

I looked over at her. She was gazing straight ahead. "Now you've got something."

"Yes," she said. "Love of mankind, truth, and kindness."

"Yeah—love." I noticed her legs. Pretty good—even in those flat brown oxfords. Pretty shapely. She glanced over. I straightened quick and turned on the windshield wiper.

I drove on, round a curve. I was conscious of her looking at me now. I kept my eyes on the road. Then I heard the horn blowing behind me. A big Cadillac shot past. I speeded up and followed close to the Cad.

First I heard the screech of brakes. I saw the Cad spin right around in front of me in the road.

"*Look out!*" Elise yelled.

And I was pressing down on the brake with all my strength, twisting the steering wheel, but I didn't know whether to zig or zag.

Luckily I zagged. You could hear the click of the fenders as I grazed the Cad. I was off the road, pulling up on the emergency brake just before I collided into a tree. When I looked back, the driver of the Cad was out of the car. He came running over to us. I opened the door and jumped out.

"Anybody hurt?" he called, even before he reached us. "I hit a bump—the pavement was wet—" He was a big flabby guy, in tweeds, with a loud scarf and—

My blood began to tingle.

It was the Sucker! The guy whose overcoat I'd lifted that night in the restaurant. And here I was, standing before him with his coat on.

"We—we're okay," I managed weakly. "Thanks." I started to get back in the Pontiac. I could feel his eyes behind me.

"Just a minute, bub."

I turned around slow.

"I never forget a face," he said, "or an overcoat."

"What d'ya—"

"Hand over my coat and there won't be any trouble."

"*Your* coat?" I could feel Elise watching me. "Go to hell!"

He grabbed the coat collar. "Hand it over, you sonofabitch! Hand it over!" His lips were turning white.

I swung. He stepped back. Then he grabbed me. I got in a hefty right to his bread basket. He puffed for one instant. Then he got sore. His fists began to fly and he landed one that let me glimpse the big dipper.

I wound up on my can in the mud with the overcoat peeled off me and blood dripping from my mouth.

"I ought to have you arrested!" he barked. "That'll teach you to pick up overcoats that don't belong to you!"

He walked off and got back in the Cad and drove off.

I got in the Pontiac and Elise brought out a little white handkerchief and began sopping up the blood on my chin.

I started the motor and drove off. But in a minute I glanced over. She was looking at me. I gazed back to the road and drove on. The windshield wiper moved back and forth—*click-swish*—*click-swish*— I was conscious of her eyes still on me. Inquisitive eyes. I felt awkward. Neither of us said a word until we reached San Clemente Boulevard.

Elise pointed. "Pull up over there by the church. And come inside and wash your face."

It was a dilapidated square frame building with a tall window and four wood steps leading up to the door. Elise turned a key in the lock. We went inside. She switched on a light.

The interior was small and damp with a stale smell of pine wood. There was one aisle down the center and rows of seats on each side. At the further end was a platform with the pulpit. We walked down the aisle, on the wood floor, our shoes making dull clicking sounds. I followed her up the three steps to the platform. She stopped and gestured to her right.

"There's a washroom," she said, "through the door to your right."

I left her and found the washroom. In the mirror above the basin I saw that my lip was ripped a little at one corner. I felt my jaw. Sore. I sopped a towel in water and washed off the blood. I tried to rub the blood off my shirt collar, but it had stained.

I thought about Lynn, and wished to Christ I'd stayed off Wilshire. The guy really landed some nifties. My lower teeth began to ache. Lucky he didn't kill me!

Yeah, lucky he hadn't killed me. That sure would have pleased the old woman. I laughed about that. I thought of Lynn again—it'd be another hour or more before she was through shopping.

I threw the towel back on the rack and went out the door, back to the platform, and made tracks down the steps and down the aisle.

"Curt, I'd like to talk to you."

Elise was beside me. Now she sat in a seat by the aisle. I hesitated—an hour to kill—I plunked down across from her. I noticed that there were big cracks in the plaster walls. The joint was really in bad shape.

"So this is your church," I said, looking around. "It's real nice."

"Curt, I—"

"Okay. So I stole the overcoat. It was one of those things. I was broke and I was hungry and the coat looked good."

I thought: what am I making excuses for? I don't owe this dame a dime! If she thinks I'm going to sit here listening to a sermon, she's nuts! I looked over at her. She was smiling.

"Did anyone ever tell you," she said, "that you're a wonderful looking person? Yes, you are. A fine physique, splendid posture, strong arms, a handsome head and face—"

"Yeah. Me and Gable, we—"

"No, I mean it. But life hasn't been easy sledding for you. I can tell by your eyes. You've had a great deal of heartache." She paused. "Your only trouble is that you're lost."

"Oh, I am?"

"Yes. You're a wandering soul. There are many like you, searching, groping souls."

I laughed. "I always wondered what I was. A groping soul, eh?" That was kind of good. It was like having your fortune told.

"Groping for that which is beyond you."

I held the smile. "You sum things up pretty well."

"There is a *rightful* way to gain."

"Yeah."

"For the moment, we might think we've put it over on the other fellow when we unlawfully take something which doesn't belong to us. But we always pay later."

"How d'you figure?"

She was very serious. "Did you ever stop to think—we are what we give out. If we give love and goodness to our fellow man, we receive the same. If we give deception and treachery, we can't exist peacefully. Because unhappiness ricochets back to us. It's what we *give*—"

"Oh, sure." This dame really had the lingo!

"You're a very strong person, Curt. Larceny is for the *weak*. Surely you're above all that."

"Yeah. Don't know why I never thought of it that way."

"If you're dissatisfied with your position in life—you have two strong arms. You have an alert mind. Why not use them in the *right* way to accomplish good. And don't reach for the moon. We must count our blessings each day."

"Yeah."

"There's a little poem," she went on, "by Robert Service—I'd like to recite it."

"Sure. Go ahead." I was egging her on. This was better than a movie!

She began slowly in that cool voice:

> For I think that Thought is all;
> Truth's a minion of the mind;
> Love's ideal comes at call;
> As ye seek so shall ye find.

But ye must not seek too far;
Things are never what they seem:
Let a star be just a star,
And a woman but a dream.

She finished. There was an awkward silence. I said: "That's pretty good, all right."

"It's only a portion of the whole poem. It—it's—"

I couldn't believe my eyes. She was crying, her face twisted, lips quivering, and tears were falling off her face.

"Forgive me," she said softly. "I can never recite that poem without—" She wiped the tears away and took a deep breath. "You see, a very dear friend of mine taught it to me. He was in the Army. I received word that he was—" Her lips trembled. "—killed. We—we'd planned so much together, we—" Her voice faded.

I watched the lovely curve of her mouth. "Looks to me," I said, "as if you're the one that needs help."

She smiled. "It does, doesn't it." She wet her lips. "You see, even at times I let *doubt* come into my mind. You see how destructive a power doubt is?"

I didn't know what else to do, so I nodded.

"I really *know* that Philip is all right. He *isn't* dead! Even if I receive fifty letters from the War Department saying so, he *isn't* dead! He's alive!" She went on passionately, "And he's coming back to me! I think it with every breath I take! I cling to that ray of hope!"

"How long has this Philip been gone?"

"Two years," she replied tonelessly.

She was biting her lip again. I wondered what kind of guy a dame could wait two years for. Must be okay! She probably hadn't even noticed another guy—and two years is a long time. She must have read my mind because she added quickly:

"If it weren't for my work—in the church, I would be very lonely without him. I try not to think of anything other than my work."

"It helps."

She looked over, and I couldn't help grinning. Her eyes were so serious. She gave me another once-over, then turned away swiftly and fumbled with her collar. She got up now and hurried over to the front window and stood looking out.

I sat there. Kind of cute, this dame. A saint, all right, with a big fire blazing inside her. And she had this stop signal in her eyes. Whenever you began to get an idea she turned off the go signal. It intrigued me.

I got up and moved over to the window beside her. She pointed.

"You see there—that's the reason why Reverend Gossin and I insisted on this particular location. Directly across from the Army Hospital."

I guess I'd been thinking about other things when we drove around the corner. I hadn't seen the rows and rows of buildings.

"The hospital is up there on the hill," she said. "If we can assist these men, give them a helping hand, a word of praise—"

"Yeah."

"If God will give us aid and strength to help them, then we will truly have fulfilled our mission."

"That's great," I said. And I meant it.

"Oh, the church isn't pretentious. But wait until the sign is out front: Welcome All. And the interior is newly redecorated and—"

"You're planning on fixing it over?"

"Oh, yes. The roof must be repaired first. And we must have carpeting on the floor. And a small organ." She smiled. "Imagine a church without an organ."

"I sure can't."

I wondered if Lynn was home by now. And about Jeff and Natalie and the old woman—who was winning the first bout. I'd put my dough on the old lady any time.

I turned to Elise. "Thanks for the sermons. I got to be getting back to the house."

"I might as well ride back with you," she said shyly. "That is, if you don't mind."

So we both went outside. She locked the church door and then we got in the Pontiac again. We were off, cruising back up Wilshire Boulevard.

Pretty soon she said: "The Reverend is having a difficult time employing labor."

"Yeah, labor's—"

"I was just thinking, Curt—if you'd like to contribute your services, you could come out and help. We'll all pitch in and start cleaning."

Was she kidding? "Well," I said, "I sort of have a steady job there with the old lady."

"Perhaps next Sunday then?"

"Sure, next Sunday."

She laughed. "Tomorrow is Sunday," she said.

"Oh, it is?"

We reached Beverly Hills. I took Santa Monica down to Lilac Drive. When we reached the house I took the side street and pulled in the garage. The Packard was gone. That meant that the old lady wasn't home. It also meant she knew I had her Pontiac out.

Elise and I went around on the sidewalk and up to the front of the house. I slid my key in the lock and opened the door.

"Thanks so much," Elise said. "And I'll expect you out some time tomorrow."

"Oh, sure."

She hurried up the stairway. I went into the living room. Jeff and Natalie were both seated on the divan by the fire. Jeff looked up. He rose to his feet and eyed me suspiciously.

"Where's Mother?"

I told him I didn't know where in the hell Mother was.

He said: "I can't understand why she'd leave without—"

"You understand perfectly well, dear," Natalie interposed. "She went out early this morning to avoid us. It's going to be interesting to see who can outwait who."

They started arguing again. I went into my bedroom wondering about Mrs. Block. She must've skipped out early, afraid to face Jeff and Natalie. Well, that was her business. I had business of my own to attend to. I had thinking to do. The right way to approach the old woman now—whether to wait and see if Jeff and Natalie were going to leave. Maybe it would be best to wait until they were out of the way, get the old woman to myself again.

I'd come right out with it. No dilly-dallying. I'd tell her if she didn't want cops on the scene she'd better be forking over. No small change. Fifty grand! Why be cheap about it! One lump sum—I'd be fat as a goose!

I'd spend my summers in California, winters in Florida. Fall in New York. The best hotels. First I'd buy a big shiny Cad. Sure. Didn't I have an alert brain? Elise noticed that.

The picture of Henry flashed again in my mind. *Couldn't I ever forget him?* How do you forget something like that?

I stood thinking about Henry. And then I felt the arms sliding around my waist from behind. I jumped a foot before I whirled around.

It was Lynn—all dressed up in her new outfit. A frilly blouse. Her hat was flaming magenta flowers. Her lipstick and gloves were the same color. Gray pumps. A bright pink suit.

"For Christ's sake!" I said after I found my breath. "What's the idea—creeping in on me like that?"

She laughed and twirled around. "How do I look?"

"Swell." I was lying. The outfit was too loud. She really looked better in those old clothes of hers.

"You like the suit?"

"Nifty."

She put her arms up around my neck and started kissing me a mile a minute. When she let up I went over to the dresser mirror and rubbed off the lipstick. Next thing I knew she was at me again.

"Take it easy," I said. "I got a sore mouth."

"Oh, *darling*—" She examined my lip. "How did you do it?"

"Fell in a sewer."

She stood back from me again, admiring herself in the mirror.

"You really like it?"

"Yeah."

"They had the same suit in blue, darling. But I like the shocking pink better."

"It's real nice."

"The two pieces cost seventy-five dollars. The blouse was twelve-fifty extra."

"Nice blouse."

"The hat was sixteen dollars."

I whistled.

"The gloves were eight-fifty and the shoes eighteen. I always wanted to buy a pair of eighteen-dollar shoes. That leaves me fifty dollars to start dramatic school." She gave me a look. "Thanks, pal." She picked up a cigarette from the dresser, stuck it in her mouth. "Got a match?"

I lit her cigarette.

"You're a lovely guy," she said. "Have I told you?"

"It sounds good to hear somebody say it," I said.

"I wish I didn't have to start work tonight. I wish we could go out and get drunk and celebrate and show off my new clothes."

"You're nuts."

She had her arms around me again. "Too bad I have to start work. I'll get in late and have to sleep late. And in the afternoons I'll be over at Creighton Hall. We won't get to see much of each other."

"We'll see each other, all right."

"I'm going to study hard and become a famous actress, darling."

"No doubt about that."

"Way up the ladder, that's where I'm going."

"I'm sure of it."

She kissed me again. "Oh, hell," she said abruptly, "maybe I'm only kidding myself. I'll probably never get clear up the ladder."

"So what if you don't? You shouldn't seek so far," I said. "Sometimes it's best to let a star be just a star—"

She leaned back and looked at me. "That's Elise's poem—"

"Yeah."

"Has she been quoting it to you, too?"
"Yeah."
"That's the silliest damn poem!"
"Think so?"
"Oh, you like it?"
"I thought it was kind of good."
"Sometimes I think you stink," she said.
"Thanks."

She sighed. "I have to go up and take these Cinderella clothes off. And get ready. You ought to see the costume I have to wear selling cigarettes. Like this." She pulled up her skirt—high. She looked down at her legs. "I ought to be a big success at that." She dropped the skirt.

"Make sure it's only cigarettes you peddle," I said.

"Don't worry. You make sure your interest in poems is—purely an interest in poems."

"I will," I said.

She kissed me again and left.

A few minutes later I heard the Packard pull in. The back door opened. It was the old woman. When her footsteps hit the living room, I heard Jeff's voice:

"Mother!"

Then you could hear them talking. I didn't bother to get up and listen. The phonograph was playing upstairs.

I'm a little on the lonely,
A little on the lonely side.

Chapter Fourteen

The next morning I didn't wake up until ten. I stretched out in bed like a fat old tycoon. It took time to get used to being a man of leisure. When I swung the final deal with the old woman I'd stay in bed every day till noon. I'd get me a little Filipino boy to cook up my meals and drive me around in my light green Cad. And I'd sit in the back, like the old lady.

I could just picture myself sailing off to Tahiti or to the Hawaiian Islands. Deck chairs on a big steamer—dressing up in a tux for dinner every night—monogrammed cigarettes—blondes draped all around me!

I stared up at the old dingy ceiling and suddenly felt depressed again. Something in my stomach, and in my head. I can't describe it.

The damnedest feeling! What was wrong? Suddenly I knew.

Henry. Why did that guy have to haunt me? When everything was going so pretty. Why did he have to pop up? Couldn't he just lie there quiet? He's dead, I told myself, the blood's on the old woman's hands, not yours. The blood's—

There was the sound of footsteps in the kitchen, the rattle of dishes. Natalie's voice. She was fixing breakfast. Jeff was in there with her. The two of them—they sure cramped my style. Say that I wanted to fix myself a bite to eat!

I threw off the bed covers and got up and went into the bathroom. I turned on the shower. Stayed under the water a long time. I wondered how Lynn made out on her new job last night, what time she got in. She was sleeping now. It dawned on me that today was Sunday. Elise was expecting me out at the church. Well, she'd have a long wait.

How did you figure a dame like that? She was really one for the books. Kind of pathetic, though in a way. Two years is a long time. She sure was nervous. A saint, eh? How would a saint be in bed? I laughed like hell.

I got out of the tub and dried off. I felt gloomy again. I couldn't stick around this joint today. I'd get in the Pontiac, grab me a bite of breakfast at the corner hash house, and go on out to the church. Hell, it was Sunday, wasn't it?

"I'm going to church," I said. I laughed again. And I felt better.

The sun was shining bright when I reached San Clemente Boulevard. I parked out in front of the church and sauntered up the steps. The door was open. I walked in.

Elise was standing up on the platform—only she wasn't alone. She was talking to an old gray-haired gent. He wasn't much taller than she. He had watery eyes, a roundish strawberry nose and a long sad face. He was wearing a dark suit which needed pressing around the edges. In one hand he held a battered felt hat, in the other an old-fashioned umbrella.

Elise saw me now and motioned me over.

"Curt," she said, "I'm so glad you could come. And I want you to know Reverend Gossin." She turned to the old boy. "This is Mr. Blair."

He walked over to me, held one limp paw out, down over the platform. I reached up and shook his hand. He turned back to Elise. Then the two of them were talking again.

"Don't worry," she said sympathetically. "Something will happen. God knows our need. He will aid us."

The old boy nodded, looking down-in-the-mouth. "The decorating will cost around eight hundred." His eyes flickered up. "The collection basket brought only sixty dollars this morning."

Reverend Gossin rubbed his nose. He shook my hand again and then jabbed his hat on his head. He marched down the steps to the aisle and out the door. Elise watched him leave. When he was gone she turned to me.

"Poor dear, he's tried so hard. But if worst comes to worst, we'll simply have to forget the decoration." She looked around the room and shuddered. "Everything is so run-down, and we *do* need a small organ."

"You sure do."

She had a cloth in one hand. Now she began dusting off the pulpit. She was wearing a little starched peasant outfit. The full skirt and low-necked blouse. There was a locket around her throat tied with a ribbon. And her skin was white behind it.

"There's the soap," she said, "over there, Curt."

"The what?"

"The soap and bucket."

I didn't get it.

"You can start scrubbing the platform if you like."

I wondered if I'd heard right. Her face was serious. I grinned. "Why not?"

So I scrubbed the floor—G.I. style—and it looked good when I was through. I saw her down in the aisle, looking up at the cracks in the wall. I went through the door up on the platform to the back, and looked around, thinking maybe there'd be an extra room around here. But there wasn't. Just old brooms sitting around, scrub brushes, and a bunch of hymn books.

I went back inside and moved down the steps to where she was. She stood surveying the walls.

"Everything is in such chaos," she said.

I looked up at the cracks. "I could fix those. If I had some plaster-of-Paris. You just fill them in with that stuff and paint over."

She turned to me swiftly. "Curt, you don't mean it! You know how to fix them? You can paint them?"

"Sure." I was so close to her I could see down the neck of her blouse.

"Would you—would you, Curt?"

"I sure would, lady."

She uttered a moan of incredulity. "It'd save no end of expense!"

"I sure would be glad to help you."

She was all enthusiasm. "I'll have the paint here in the morning. And let's see, you'll need brushes."

"Brushes? Oh, yeah. Sure. Brushes."

So you see how I roped myself in on that deal—that for-free stuff. The next day I was out there working. And when I painted one side wall, the rest of the room looked muddy. It took the next day after that to complete the interior of the church.

But I was glad to do it. It kept my mind busy. No time to think of Henry or the old woman. I figured that Lynn was all wrapped up in those dramatic lessons, so I had time on my hands.

As for Elise, I was the sucker, sure. Nobody had to tell me that. She still had this stop signal in her eyes. Hell, don't think I didn't get ideas while I was working out there. And once in a while she'd let down her guard—when I touched her arm, for instance, helping her into the car. Things like that. She liked me, I knew by the way she got so nervous when I touched her. For one second I'd think it was maybe time to put up the sails. Then something in her eyes would stop me.

The saint look? Maybe. Your guess is as good as mine. I couldn't figure it out. And it about drove me nuts. Something would stop me. I'd go numb all over looking into those big blue eyes. What the hell caused it?

I tried to figure it out. Alone at night I'd try to figure it out. Why didn't I just grab her and—she'd forget the boyfriend, all right.

It was an idea. It was an idea that stuck in my mind.

Anyway, I painted the church interior. The night I finished that job I drove Elise down to the beach, to Santa Monica. We had dinner together at a little seafood joint with a jukebox playing. I ordered us both champagne cocktails.

Music—food—wine! That was how they did it in the movies. And I sure needed a new approach.

She smiled over from across the table. She was wearing a little white fluffy coat and a white tam with her hair curling out at the sides. She looked cute as hell.

"I don't know what I'd have done without your wonderful assistance," she said.

"Forget it."

"But even with your help, the rest of the decoration is going to cost eight hundred dollars. The roof has to be repaired, new carpeting, and we must have an organ."

"Yeah."

"About fifteen hundred dollars. That is—to tide us over. The redecoration, the rent on my flat, and, of course, Reverend Gossin must live."

"Oh, sure."

"He spent his last money buying the church."

"He bought it?"

"Yes. We tried to lease the building, but the landlord had made up his mind to sell. The Reverend made a five-thousand-dollar down payment."

"Five grand, eh?"

"It was all the money he had."

The waiter brought the food.

Elise smiled. "We need an angel. It simply amounts to that."

My mind started ticking. "I think I know where I can raise the dough."

She set down her fork and stared. I thought: somebody ought to give me the grand prize. Number One Sucker. Why did dames do that to me anyway? But then what the hell was the difference. I'd have a lot left over. So I *give* Elise fifteen hundred dollars. It was a drop in the bucket compared to the fifty grand I was going to collect from the old woman. Fifteen hundred bucks—a mere bagatelle! Didn't I have almost *eight* hundred in my pocket right now! A big shot like me could afford to be philanthropic. This kid was struggling along.

"Curt, you don't mean that *you*—"

I sipped on the champagne and nodded—as if I was made of dough. Suddenly her eyes darkened. "Oh, Curt—*not* like the overcoat."

I looked insulted. "Strictly on the up-and-up. I'm going to proposition old lady Block."

She thought for a moment. Her eyes lighted. "Do you think she'll—"

"I'm sure of it," I lied. "Especially when she finds out it's for your church."

"It's a splendid idea."

"Yeah."

"She has so much; she wouldn't miss the money!"

"No."

"It would help so tremendously!"

"Yeah."

"It's for such a *worthy* cause."

"It sure is."

"Ask her, Curt. Why not?"

"Yeah. Why not?"

So I put my foot in it again. When we got back to the house that night I went straight to Mrs. Block. I found her in the sunroom, with a little garden sprinkler in one hand, watering the plants.

"Look," I said, "I need next week's salary in advance. One thousand bucks." I figured I'd give Elise the extra five hundred out of my pocket.

The old woman straightened. "You're not going to get it!" She bent over again, ready to sprinkle a little group of cacti. Then: "What do you want it for?"

"A good cause," I told her. "For that church of Elise's. She's short on decoration dough. I want you to help her out."

"Humph!" Her voice was a hissing whisper. "Are you going to keep this up? Are you going to continue pirating thousands of dollars from me in *advance?*"

"No, Virginia. It's only this special occasion."

She kept glancing at the door that led into the living room. Her lips twitched. "There's nothing else I can do—except give you the money."

"You won't even miss it."

"Miss it? All the cash I have to my name is one thousand dollars! The very last cash on hand. That's every penny I have in this house." Her voice broke. "My very last penny."

"I need that dough, Virginia."

She glared. "Very well." With shoulders dejected, she left. I went into my bedroom. In a few minutes she came in. She counted each bill and handed me a thousand dollars.

"Remember," she said with vehemence, "this is next week's salary. I'm not paying you one cent over a thousand a week." She looked longingly at the money in my hand, then turned abruptly and left the room.

I was hiding the dough behind a picture when I felt the presence of somebody else. Through the dresser mirror I saw Lynn, behind me in the doorway. I stuffed the bills in my pocket quick. I turned around.

Lynn hurried over to me and put both her arms up around my neck. And the light was in her eyes again. I pushed her away.

"Beat it," I said. "The old lady's home."

"But, darling, this is my night off. I thought we could go to a bar or something."

"Not tonight, baby. You'd better beat it."

"I want to talk to you."

"Well, I—"

"I'll meet you down in the cellar."

"No, Christ, no!" *I was thinking of Henry!*

Her eyes were puzzled. "What's come over you?"

"That damned cellar's too damp."

She stiffened. "It was never too damp before."

"It's—it's different now."

Tears welled in her eyes. "It's all right. I understand."

"What the hell do you—"

"It's Elise, isn't it? You're in love with that goddamn Salvation Nell!"

"Now where do you get an idea like that?"

"I don't need a house to fall on me. You're out with her every day. She told me. Tonight she said—she told me you're going to contribute fifteen hundred dollars to her church."

"She's nuts."

Lynn clung to me closer. "What's come over you, darling?"

"Look," I said evenly, "the old woman might come in here any minute—" I blew up. "Okay, okay—it's the cellar!"

"You're not in love with Elise?"

"You know I'm not."

"She isn't for you. Why, you two are in entirely different worlds."

"Think so?"

"It isn't—*us* anymore, is it, darling? You're in love with Elise. You can deny it all night. But it's in your eyes—I can see it!"

"Then why did I deck you out in those new duds?"

"That's easy. You think those goddamn clothes make up for everything, for the fast shuffle you're giving me. The only reason you've even got your arms around me now is because you're trying to let me down easy." Her voice wavered. "You're that kind of a guy. You're getting money from the old woman somehow, and you're giving Elise fifteen hundred dollars."

I didn't say anything, and finally she asked:

"Everything I said is true, isn't it, Curt?"

"Yeah."

She was crying, and I was feeling like crawling back into the apple. She rose quickly and ran out the door, up the cellar steps. I hurried out after her, into the house, through the kitchen, the sunroom. I stopped before I hit the living room. Because you could hear the free-for-all inside. Natalie and Jeff and the old lady.

So I turned around and went back into my room, figuring that was best maybe, after all. And in a moment you could hear the phonograph, playing louder than ever before:

> *I'm a little on the lonely,*
> *A little on the lonely side.*

It became a house divided. With Lynn and Elise sleeping in the same room and Lynn not speaking. And Lynn turning her eyes away every time she saw me. And the old lady giving me dagger stares every time she ran across me. And Jeff and Natalie eyeing me suspiciously. And the old lady trying to avoid them and having nothing to do with the girls.

Anyway, I'd given Elise the fifteen hundred. She spent three hundred of it on the organ, and got the roof repaired, carpets in and new drapery in back of the pulpit. Everything was fixed up spic and span. And on that next Thursday I was relieved to get Elise moved out of the house. I drove her over to her new flat and carried her luggage up.

That was when we had our big scene.

Chapter Fifteen

The flat was about a half mile from the church. Elise showed me all through. It had a little kitchen with a Victory stove and red-and-white woodwork and a living room with a tan rug and a fern. It had a small bedroom with one double bed and fluffy white curtains at the windows and a snow-white bedspread with yellow-and-blue embroidered flowers. It was nice all right.

I wonder if I ever really explained about Elise. I wonder if you can find words to describe something like her. When you go to sleep feeling lonely and dreaming about her, and you wake up in the morning with her on your mind—a saint on your mind. But underneath those reverential robes, what kind of dame was she?

A woman? I wondered. She was human, wasn't she? You touch her arm and it's warm, isn't it? And that night, driving her home from the beach, the champagne loosened her up a little. She sat over a little closer in the seat. She relaxed just once. She was herself for one moment—a lonely kid, slowly starving to death. She could pretend all she wanted that the church was her only interest, but she didn't fool anybody. And from that look in her eyes, you can tell she'd rather melt in your arms than anything else. But she's afraid. She freezes up quick and flashes that stop signal. But some day you'll catch her with it down. If you hang around long enough.

That was what I was doing this Thursday afternoon—hanging around. We were sitting on the couch in her flat when she said:

"Curt, I—I don't think we'd better see each other anymore."

My heart skipped a beat. "Why not?"

She was flustered. "I'm really terribly fond of you—you know that. And of course you know I'm engaged."

I looked over quick.

"Oh, yes, to Philip."

"The Chaplain, the one that's—"

"Oh, yes."

The words spouted from my mouth: "For Christ's sake—he's *dead!*"

She flinched. "You don't understand. That doesn't matter—even if he is."

"What d'ya—"

Her voice trembled. "He's with me every day. In everything I do, he's with me. Even when I preach, he's standing there beside me, guiding me. Giving me strength. He's—" Her voice ended in a sudden sob.

"I'm confused," I said.

Tears sprang into her eyes. "If I didn't love him quite so much! If I could *only* put him out of my mind. But I've tried and I can't! You see—" Her body crumpled. She began to sob, violently, with her face buried in the couch pillows.

I reached over and started to put my arms around her. She flung back her head.

"Don't touch me!"

I cringed, wondering what the hell had come over her.

"Can't you understand?" she said slowly, painfully, "I feel that Philip is watching. It's no use—he won't let me fall in love with anyone else!"

I felt the blood creeping up hot in my face. I managed to laugh. I got to my feet and paced up and down, spouting off words like some goddamn philosopher:

"Okay, okay! So he says nix every time I touch you. You have to realize that it's all in your mind. He isn't actually watching, you see; he's dead. He's over there plowed under. And the sooner you realize it the better off you'll be!"

She only cried harder.

"So what are you going to do—spend the rest of your life pretending?" I stopped and looked at her. "Is that what you intend to do?"

"You don't understand," she sobbed. "There's still a chance. Maybe he isn't—" Her voice trailed off.

I lifted her gently to her feet. "Look, baby—you got the letter from the War Department, didn't you? If I were you, I'd believe it. They don't send out those letters by mistake. He isn't coming back. You'd better let that sink in."

She wiped the tears away. "Maybe you're right, but—"

"Of course, I'm right." I grabbed her up close. Her lips were beautiful and trembling. I pressed my mouth hard against hers. Just for a second she relaxed, then she was pushing me away with all her strength. When I released her, her hand flew up to her lips. She rubbed the kiss off.

"*Please go!*" Her face was crimson.

I held her again, tight. "What do you say—is it us, or isn't it?"

"*Please*, Curt. Give me time to think!"

"Okay. You can tell me tomorrow." I was still shaking. I sat down on the couch. I could feel the blood draining from my face. "We'll get married, honey. If you like, if that's the way you want it. I'll get a good job. It'll work out. I mean business—the whole works!"

"I—I'll let you know."

"Tomorrow?"

"No, Curt. A few days."

"That's Sunday. You'll let me know Sunday?"

"Yes. You'll be at the opening of the church on Sunday, of course. You promised to play the organ."

"Well, I—"

"Oh, yes, Curt. Please do. Just this once. That's all I ask. For the opening. I haven't located an organist, and you play so beautifully."

"But I never touched an organ."

"It's *simple!* This is a small, four-octave Estey—the same keyboard as a piano. The only difference is the pump pedals. You have to keep your feet going while you play."

"Kind of like swimming, eh? I can't swim. And I never played a church hymn in my life. I might mix everything up for you."

"You can read the music. That's all that's necessary."

"Yeah. Okay, honey." I got to my feet. "I'll see you Sunday—bright and early."

"You'll definitely show up, won't you, Curt? You won't fail me."

"No." I paused. "And then you'll let me know about us?"

"Yes," she answered solemnly.

"All right, honey."

She smiled stiffly. I turned and walked away from her and out the door. I sailed down the steps and got back in the Pontiac. I started the motor and prayed to God to keep me away from her until Sunday.

I drove back down Wilshire. A wind was brewing, blowing leaves and papers across the street. I went straight to the house.

Inside, I found the old lady in the kitchen. She had an apron on, puttering around, washing silverware and singing. When she saw me you'd think I was an old lost friend. She almost hugged me. I tried to figure it out—this sudden change.

"Curt," she said buoyantly, "I want you to know I'm not angry about that advance I gave you. It's for such a worthwhile cause. Just think—I've contributed to a church!"

"I knew you'd feel that way," I lied.

She came closer and whispered confidentially:

"I think I'm wearing Jeff and Natalie out. They're talking of leaving."

"Yeah?"

"I think they've had a terrible tiff between them. Jeff left this afternoon and went out to play some golf. He loves the game so, and he found his old clubs in his room. And she's upstairs brooding."

"That right?"

"Yes, and I think the York girl is leaving."

"Leaving?"

"I heard her call up and cancel those dramatic lessons she was taking. She mentioned something about a new job she has somewhere."

"Oh, she has?"

There was a silence.

"Had your dinner yet?"

I shook my head.

"Smell something good?"

I sniffed in the air. My eyes went over to the stove.

"If you had your choice, Curt, what would you like for dinner?"

"Something simple," I said. "A small shark under glass with cranberries."

She poked her elbow at me and chuckled as if it were a good joke between us. She lifted her eyebrows. "How about good beef stew?"

"Swell."

She cackled a laugh. She went over to the stove, lifted the pan lid and peered inside. "That's what we're having. Yes, indeed. Natalie and Jeff—and I've invited the York girl—and you and me."

I grinned. "When do we eat?"

"Just as soon as Jeff comes home from his golf game."

"You mean we're burying the hatchet, Virginia?"

She laughed. It was a hollow laugh—without mirth. "Yes, Curt, we're burying the hatchet. We're going to have a party!"

Chapter Sixteen

At seven o'clock we all sat down at the table. Dinner à la ritz. Candle light—a lace table cloth with an elaborate centerpiece of purple bougainvillea. The old lady even dragged out her best silverware and lace napkins. She'd set up the table in the sunroom, looking out to the patio. Outside the palms swayed to and fro and the tall shrubs near the house kept touching the panes, making scraping sounds.

Mrs. Block sat at the head of the table, Jeff at the other end. Natalie next to him, all dressed up in a red velvet dinner gown, with pearls around her throat and a lot of bracelets on one arm. Lynn sat beside her, wearing her new pink suit. I sat opposite Lynn. She was all ice as far as I was concerned. Every time our eyes met she'd turn quick to Natalie and start talking, putting it on thick with the phony patter again.

Jeff wasn't in much of a conversational mood. Besides, I could tell he hated my guts. I knew he was wondering why the old lady had to invite the hired hand. And I sure was deliberating the same question myself. It was Mrs. Block who was the chatterbox. She kept up the chit-chat like a veteran windbag while she opened a new bottle of wine. She brought a tray over from the buffet with five goblets on it.

"Curt," she said sweetly, "would you mind pouring the wine?"

I got up. "Sure thing." I poured four glasses and came to the fifth.

"None for me, please," Lynn said. "I have to be at work at eight."

Natalie turned to her. "Isn't it dreadful—night work? I *know*. I used to be in show business. I was with—"

Jeff coughed and interrupted: "What kind of wine is that, Blair?"

I looked at the bottle. "Sparkling burgundy." I passed the glasses. When I sat down at my place, Natalie kept glancing my way.

"Have you been a gardener long, Mr. Blair?" she asked.

I sipped on my wine. "Yeah. I come from a long line of gardeners."

"You scarcely seem the type," she said.

I smiled. "I'm a great lover of nature."

"How interesting." She set down her glass. "Then perhaps you could tell me something. Why in the world do they use dichondra for lawns? It's so unattractive, don't you think?"

(Dichondra? What the hell was she talking about!)

"Don't you agree with me, Mr. Blair?"

"Very definitely. It's—"

"I hate to interrupt," Lynn said, "but really, I'll have to be leaving in a few minutes. If I'm to have dinner with you I'll have to be—"

"Well, of course," Mrs. Block said, rising to her feet. "Here we are sitting here talking as if this young lady had all night. I'll bring the stew and salads in. We're all ready, aren't we?"

"I certainly am," Jeff said. "I'm starving, mother."

Lynn left the room with the old lady. You could hear them talking in the kitchen. Mrs. Block telling Lynn to go right back in and sit down, that she needed no help whatever. So Lynn brought in the plates filled with salad and took her seat. Mrs. Block dragged in the dinner plates with beef stew. Then she sat down, as merry as Disney's mice, and kept gushing on about nothing.

I nibbled around on my salad, still trying to figure this thing out. *Why* had the old woman switched to such high spirits? Something was behind it. The picture of Henry flashed in my mind. How had she killed him? Poison? She had easy access to it—the lead arsenate out at her ranch. Maybe that was the stuff she put in the old man's food. Jesus! I looked down at that beef and felt sick. Why hadn't the old lady wanted Lynn to bring in the dinner plates? Could she have a special formula in my stew?

"Curt," Mrs. Block said with a quick little gesture, "you're not eating. Here—have some string beans." She held out her hand for my plate. I lifted it up and she gave me a scoop of the vegetables.

I looked over at Natalie and Jeff. Their eyes were on their food. I glanced back at the old lady. She was sipping on her wine. I gave my plate a little twist before I let it fall from my hand. At that moment I saw Lynn's gaze: she'd seen me deliberately dump my plate over. She looked puzzled.

Mrs. Block jumped up. "Goodness, Curt—that'll stain the table cloth! How in heaven's name did you—"

"I'm sorry, ma'am. My hand must have slipped."

"Oh, my! On my good lace table cloth!" She hurried out into the kitchen and came back in carrying a dish towel.

Lynn was beside me now, with a spoon, dishing the garbage back on my plate. Jeff looked over in disgust, while the old lady kept sopping up the debris. I noticed a thoughtful glint in her eyes.

"I'll get you another plate," she said.

I kicked Lynn—under the table. She gave me a look. Then she was making tracks into the kitchen.

"I'll do it, Mrs. Block," Lynn said.

"Stay where you are!" the old lady commanded. She ran out after Lynn.

You could hear them again in the kitchen, Mrs. Block telling Lynn to go right back in and sit down. But it was Lynn who came in with my new plate of stew. She put it down in front of me and took the spilled plate out into the kitchen.

Mrs. Block came in and took her place at the table. She looked worn out all of a sudden. She sat sullenly, staring at her plate. She picked up her glass of wine and downed the contents in one gulp. Then:

"I don't feel so well," she said. "I think I'll go up to my room."

Jeff bounced to his feet and assisted her through the door. When they were gone, Lynn came in.

"I gave the spilled stew to Blackie," she said.

I threw my napkin down and jumped to my feet. I went out the back door and over to the dog house. It was too late. Blackie'd already lapped up the beef. I hurried into the back porch, hauled out a quart of milk from the ice box and dug out a pan. In case there was poison in the stew the milk might counteract it. I took the pan out to Blackie. He only sniffed at the milk. I wondered if I should take him to a dog hospital.

I could be wrong, I told myself. *I could be wrong!* Maybe the stew was okay. But *why* was the old woman in such a gay mood before dinner—before I spilled my plate? Then when Lynn had fixed me another, she'd suddenly grown ill and gone upstairs without finishing her dinner!

I didn't go back to the dinner table. I went into my room and sweated it out.

It was in the middle of the night that I woke up with a start. I turned over and closed my eyes again. All of a sudden I heard somebody breathing. Close to me! I leaped up, still half asleep, and squinted through the darkness. The door opened and closed.

Somebody had been in my room.

I switched on the light. I went out into the kitchen and stood there motionless, with questions streaming at me.

Who was it—in my bedroom in the middle of the night? What the hell was up? Was it the old lady or Jeff or Natalie or Lynn?

The rest of that night was a sitting-up marathon. Vigilant till daylight. I sat in a chair by the door, waiting. Whoever it was didn't return.

It wasn't until around eight the next morning—when I went out to feed Blackie—that I put the whole puzzle together. There was no use giving him any breakfast, because he was lying stiff with his legs straight out.

Blackie was dead.

Chapter Seventeen

It didn't take any mastermind to piece the thing together, to know it'd been the beef stew that killed the dog. Filled with some deadly concoction. Probably the lead arsenate from her ranch.

Probably the same poison she'd given Henry.

How long did it take for that stuff to work? *Was she crazy?* What if I'd keeled over at the dinner table? They'd have had to call in a doctor—Lynn would have seen to that. My autopsy would prove I'd been poisoned. How did the old woman figure she'd get by with it? Unless—

Unless after I'd taken a few bites last night she'd gotten me away from the table, back into my room, on some pretext or other—or sent me down in the cellar for something while I was still kicking. That was it. She would have found some excuse to get me down in the cellar.

Then locked me in—while the arsenate took hold. Then later, maybe in the middle of the night she'd come down and—

One gulp of that beef and I'd be Henry's new bunk partner.

I stood there looking down at the lifeless form of Blackie and thinking until my brain ached, figuring out my own murder plot from the old woman's viewpoint. Even the next day when Jeff or Natalie or Lynn asked about me, she'd have told them that I'd quit my job, or skipped out. Or she'd fired me. It was that simple.

The dinner party last night had been all for my benefit. And I knew why she'd gone up to bed without finishing her dinner. After my plate had spilled, Plan 2 was ruined. I thought of how she'd hurried into the kitchen ahead of Lynn to fix me up a new helping.

Then last night, in the middle of the night, it was the old lady—trying to complete her job. *But I woke up in time!*

Blood drummed sickeningly in my ears. I looked back down at Blackie.

"Poor dog. Poor dead pup."

I picked him up and carried him around in back of the garage. I gave him a decent burial.

Just as I was going into the house I saw her—the old lady—on the porch, peering out the back screen. I opened the door. She stood there with a book in her hand. She viewed me defiantly.

"You killed Blackie," she said impassively.

I brushed past her, into my bedroom. She came in with the book in her hand and stood staring at me steadily with loathing in her eyes.

"I haven't slept all night."

I reached into my shirt pocket for a cigarette. "I can understand that, all right."

"But this morning," she said with alacrity, "this morning it's all quite clear to me." Her face twitched. "You thought you were clever, didn't you, blackmailing an old defenseless woman? You had a good thing, didn't you? You had the gall to keep squeezing thousands of dollars from me. You thought you could do it for the rest of my life!"

I lit the cigarette and took a deep drag. "What's on your mind, Virginia?"

Her lips pursed tight. She snapped them open. "I've been stupid! Stupid!"

"That makes two of us."

She leaned forward, studying me intently. "It was you who discovered the body of my husband in the cellar, you who buried him the second time, you who nailed the boards back up." A smile flickered across her face. "Why didn't you report it to the police. Why *didn't* you?"

"Yeah. Why didn't I?"

"Humph. We both know the answer to that. You wanted money." Her voice came up on the word money. "Even if you did report it now to the police, you too would be implicated."

"That right?"

She brought one arm up in a dramatic gesture. "Oh, yes, they'd know I killed my husband. I'm an old woman. I haven't much to lose. But you, Mister Curtis Blair, you—they'd be interested to know that you're an accessory—"

"I'm an accessory, eh?" I laughed.

She flipped the book open. I saw that it was the one from the living room shelf: *Penal Code of California, 1941*.

"I've been devoting a great deal of time and study this morning to our little pact," she said. "It says here in Section 32, page 15—" Nervously she began to read:

"Every person who, after a felony has been committed, harbors, conceals, or aids a principal in such felony is an accessory to such felony. An accessory is punishable by imprisonment not exceeding—"

"Trying to scare me, eh? Is that it?"

Her head came up triumphantly. She turned a few pages. "And here—Section 257, a very serious crime, indeed. *Blackmail*. It says—"

I stubbed out the cigarette. "Tell me, Virginia, who's going to prove blackmail, since you paid me in cash? Course," I went on, "you can tell the cops all about it. If that's what you want I'll call them up right now. Is it a confession you want to make?" I took a step toward the door.

"Curt!" In the next second she flung herself in the doorway, blocking my exit. Her hands gripped the side panels. Her voice came in spasms. "Don't—go—near—the telephone!"

"Okay," I said. "But when and if you do want to talk to cops invite them in to see me." I lowered my voice. "I ought to have you arrested for attempted murder. I haven't forgotten how you tried to hack my skull in two that night in the cellar. And as for that elegant dinner seasoned with arsenate—"

"You have no proof," she rasped.

"That's where you're wrong, lady. An autopsy on a poor dead pup named Blackie would be proof, his belly full of poison. Remember it was Lynn who gave that plate intended for me to the dog. Lynn's a pretty nice kid. She likes the way I part my hair. She might testify in court about that dog, that you—"

"You *can't* go to the police!" she whined. "You're an accomplice. It says so right here in the book. Don't you realize the seriousness of this!"

"Sure. I understand. You haven't a leg to stand on. As for Henry, I'll expect that grand per week to keep my trap shut. And I want you to lay off. You tried to kill me twice and—"

Her eyes gleamed threateningly. "The third time's the charm."

"No, Virginia. You're wrong again. There'll never be a third time."

"I ought to have Jeff throttle you to death!"

I grinned. "Don't scare me like that."

Her eyes went to the floor. She stood for a long moment. I heard her heavy breathing. Now her eyes came up.

"Henry put me up to all this," she said.

"Henry?"

She sniffled and nodded. "Every night when I'm talking to him, he—he whispers all sorts of horrible things to me."

A shiver zagged up my spine. "You talk to him—at night?"

"Oh, yes," she mumbled. "He won't let me be. He keeps tormenting me, standing there by my bed, asking me to give Jeff that money." She clenched her fist. "I hate him! I've always despised him!" She smiled cagily, her eyes shifting. "He never knew it. I worked along with him and slaved and scrimped and raised his son. And he showed his appreciation by wanting to squander thousands of dollars on the fool brat! And that night—that night two years ago—that night I thought I was rid of him. But he came back. You were right, Curt. He never did leave at all."

I kept staring.

Her eyes shone. "You see—I don't want to kill you. It's because Henry keeps putting me up to it. He's driving me to it! He doesn't want you to have any of Jeff's money."

Slowly she turned and left the room. The door clicked shut.

I sank down on the bed and exhaled a deep breath. The old woman's words kept drumming in my ears: "*I don't want to kill you! Henry keeps putting me up to it!*"

Christ! Maybe the shock of all this was driving her nuts. Maybe she was just pretending. Maybe it was a new approach, trying to play on my sympathy. It didn't work, but it got on my nerves plenty. I felt almost sick. What happens, I asked myself, if she really does lose her mind? What happens to me then? God damn it—always some new worry. Nothing in life ever goes in a straight line. Not even a deal like this one. I felt spooky. I was going to go out and talk to the old girl some more. I had to hear more of that dialogue. But suddenly the closet door of my bedroom was opening.

Lynn stepped out.

Chapter Eighteen

Lynn's eyes met mine. She looked at me for a long second, then moved toward the door. She put her hand on the knob. When I didn't say anything, she turned around slowly.

I said: "Why in hell don't you set up a grandstand in my room?"

Her voice was higher than usual:

"I—didn't mean to hear anything. I woke up early this morning. I came down here because I—I wanted to talk to you. I'd stepped inside your bedroom when I heard Mrs. Block come in the kitchen." She gestured to the closet. "I hid in there. And the next thing I knew both of you came in and started talking. I couldn't help overhearing."

"This is swell," I said. "Great."

"Yes, isn't it?"

I sat there on the edge of the bed, fumbling. "Go on," I said. "Keep on talking. Go on. Tell me what kind of a louse I am."

She didn't answer—only said: "Is Blackie really dead?"

"Yeah."

"Such a cute, funny, sweet little dog."

"I liked him, too," I said.

Her eyes came up slow. "There was poison in that stew I fed him?"

"One hundred percent."

"Intended for you?"

I nodded again. "The wrong dog got it."

She shuddered. "And the old woman, she—she murdered her husband."

"Yeah."

"And he—he's in the cellar—right now?"

"For Christ's sake—" I pointed to the closet. "You heard it, didn't you?"

"Yes," she said quickly. "It's hard to believe." Her face was pale. "I couldn't have stayed down in the cellar with you if I'd known he was there. Oh, my God," she moaned, "to think he was right there next to us!"

"I don't think he was watching," I said.

"And you've been blackmailing the old lady," she went on quietly. "That money you gave me was part of it."

"Yeah."

"And you gave Elise fifteen hundred dollars for the church."

"Yeah."

Her eyes flashed. "Aren't you ashamed of yourself—shaking down a crazy old woman?"

"I don't think about it."

"Perhaps Elise would like to know."

"What?"

"About what a nice guy you are." Her tone was brittle. "Maybe there's still time—" She laughed deep in her throat. "—to save your soul!"

I got up from the bed. "You tell Elise one thing about that dough and I'll—"

She moved over closer. "I won't tell her anything. You know that."

"You better not."

Her arms slid around my neck. "Let's get out of here."

"Nuts," I said.

Panic shone in her eyes. "You heard the old woman, all that crazy talk about Henry telling her to kill you. She's tried it twice. Oh, darling, please—let's both get out of this dirty, bloodstained house!"

"Sure. And where to? And what'll we use for dough? Answer that one."

"Don't you have any money left?"

"Not to spend on hotel rooms—if you can find one. No, baby, I need all the dough I can rake up for future use."

Her head jerked back. "You mean for you and Elise."

"I didn't say that."

"You didn't have to say it."

"Don't start that again."

"No," she said, "I won't start that again."

There was an awkward silence. Through it the house creaked. A cricket in the corner chirped noisily. Lynn's arms dropped from around my shoulders. She laughed—that sarcastic way she had of laughing.

"It's really a riot! You do make a striking couple. The Chiseler and the Preacher. Tell me—how long do you think it'll last?"

I didn't answer.

Lynn walked over to the dresser, picked up a cigarette and lighted it. "She must be terrific in bed."

"Shut up!"

She blew out a thick stream of smoke. "She can have you. All of you. I don't want any part." She paused, laughed again, and there were sudden tears in her eyes. "I'm not *good* enough. The hell I'm not! I'll show you about me."

"Listen—"

"I'm glad to be rid of you. Now I can concentrate on one thing, my ambitions."

"Sure, sure."
"Just don't ever look me up in the future."
"No, I won't."
"Just make sure of that."

She looked at me and tried to say more, but couldn't because she was crying now. I don't think I've ever seen a face so streaked with pain—the way she stood there opening her mouth, trying to keep on talking. Now she turned and left.

I sank down on the bed again. My head began to ache, a dull burning throb. I wondered if Lynn would tell Elise the kind of a guy I was.

The kind of a guy I was—

I thought about that while I smoked a cigarette. I thought about that while I smoked a full pack of cigarettes, pacing back and forth in the room. *The kind of a guy I was.* The phrase kept repeating itself in my brain.

I picked up a magazine. Couldn't read. I went into the bathroom. Shaved and took a shower and put on clean clothes. I went outside to the garage. There was a padlock on the door. I wasn't going to use the Pontiac anymore—the old lady had seen to that.

I walked down to Wilshire, to the corner hash house and went inside. Sat up at the counter. A tired little waitress came up and set down a glass of water before me. There was a sign on the wall: *Fried Chicken— 85c.* I pointed to it.

"The lunch goes off at four-thirty," the waitress said. "It's five. I can give you the chicken with the dinner."

"Okay, the dinner."

I couldn't eat the tainted chicken or the greasy stale French fries or the cold squash. I gulped down the coffee, paid my check and went outside again. I ambled back to the house, wondering what my next move should be. I thought about the old woman. You could bamboozle a sly old miser, but a *crazy* sly old miser was something else again. Even I couldn't go for that. Even being *the kind of a guy I was!*

I went to the garage and retraced my steps to the house. There was a light in the kitchen now. Through the open window, I glimpsed Natalie standing over the sink. I was about to put my hand on the door knob when Jeff entered.

"Blair went out the back gate about an hour ago," he said.

Natalie's voice came over: "Why in the world does Virginia keep him around? Have you seen him do one bit of work around here yet? Have you?"

I moved over to the shrubbery, next to the, window, and listened.

"It isn't like Mother to keep a loafer about," he said.

"Stop calling her Mother!" She paused. "I'm fixing spare ribs, dear. Does that suit you?"

"Yes, of course."

There was a silence.

"The old fox is slyer than ever," Natalie said slowly. "We're getting nowhere fast. Are you going to let it go at that?"

"What else can I do?"

"Plenty!"

His voice came hesitantly: "I still hope that Dad might show up one of these days. I wish he hadn't run off like that."

"Who could blame him?"

"Yes, but to leave all his money with her. It isn't like him."

There was the sound of water running and the rattle of silverware.

"Do you think he's really found another woman?" Natalie asked abruptly. "At his age?"

"It's the only solution I can think of. It's simply the old story. He never had a pleasant day with Virginia. When he found this new one, he gave up everything for a chance at happiness. It's worth a great deal more than money, you know. Dad valued it more."

"But he wouldn't leave his only son out in the rain," she said. "I wouldn't be surprised if she'd murdered him."

"Don't be preposterous Natalie. Mother is wicked and queer and scheming, but she isn't capable of—"

"I wouldn't put anything past her!"

"No. Dad made a decision. He isn't the sort who'd stick around bothering to iron out details. He made up his mind to skip out. And I can't help but admire the old boy for it." He paused. "I hope he *has* found happiness."

"Yes, but he should have put your money in your hands before he went off on this romantic spree. He at least could have done that, knowing Virginia the way he did."

"Still, the fact remains he didn't. So now we have to hope and pray that he'll come back. And in the meantime trust that Virginia will—"

"Die?" The word was staccato.

"I wasn't going to say that."

"But you were thinking it."

"I wasn't thinking it, Natalie. It's too damned unpleasant."

Her voice lowered. "Aren't you a pure, trusting soul, though? Why don't you burst into 'The Wishing Song' from *Snow White* dear? Go ahead, sing it. I'll play accompaniment on this spoon and pan."

"Since you're so very clever, my pet, what do you suggest we do?"

"I've told you, dear."

"Oh, God—I'm beginning to think you're serious."

"I *am* serious."

There was another silence. Presently he said:

"You must be terribly bored, supporting me the way you have."

"Frankly, yes. I was always under the childish illusion that a man took a wife. When I married you it didn't occur to me that a woman could take a *husband*—and all my worldly goods to thee endow."

His voiced faded. "You—want to call it quits? Is that what you're getting at?"

"Of course not, stupid," she said calmly. "I'm only saying that my money is evaporating. It isn't fair for the old slut to have so much. She's—"

"Shhhh," he said quickly. "Someone's coming down the stairs."

"It's probably she. Shall I put in an extra rib for *Mother*, dear?"

I went back out to the garage and to the street. I began to walk again. The air was damp. It chilled my bones. My legs ached; my throat felt dry. I noticed the sky: dark, no stars, no moon. I looked all around the heavens. No moon tonight.

I kept on walking and thinking and feeling lousy.

When I got back it was midnight. The house was enclosed in darkness. I went around to the rear, past the empty doghouse and across the patio. A light was burning in the kitchen. I went up the back steps and inside the porch. All at once I heard snoring from upstairs. My throat still felt dry. I went into the kitchen to get a drink of water.

Natalie was there.

She was dressed in a thin black negligee and black satin high-heeled slippers with open toes. Blood-red polish on her toe nails. She'd let down her hair; it hung in long reddish waves down her back, almost touching her waist.

She held a carton of milk in one hand. She emptied it into a pan on the stove. She saw me now, pulled the negligee a little tighter at the neck. I turned my eyes away and picked up a glass and held it under the faucet and turned on the water.

"Just wanted a drink," I said.

When I looked back at her she smiled and tugged on her negligee again and nodded toward the pan on the stove.

"I'm fixing myself some hot milk," she said. "Can't sleep tonight, somehow. I felt—restless."

"I'm restless myself," I said.

She jabbed one long finger into the pan of milk—to test the temperature, I guess. She turned up the fire and sighed. There was a silence. Through it we were both conscious of the snoring from upstairs.

She sighed again. "If my husband would only stop snoring!"

I drank down the rest of the water. "Ever try putting cotton in your ears?"

"Cotton? For what?"

I pointed upstairs.

"No," she said, "I haven't tried that." She poured the milk from the pan into a glass. Then: "You don't like her either, do you?"

"Her?" I paused. "The old woman?"

She nodded slowly.

"No," I said. "I don't like her, either."

She put the glass to her lips but didn't drink. "I think it's terrible the way she treats you—like a common servant."

I was beginning not to know what this was all about. What did this Natalie care how the old lady treated me?

She sipped on the hot milk; her eyes didn't leave mine. "What are you doing around here anyway? It seems that a man like you ought to be able to find a better job than this. And she must pay you in buttons."

"Yeah. Buttons. And I keep the lawn up well, too." She wanted me to be a goof—okay!

She flashed her lovely teeth at me. "You certainly do keep the lawns up. The grounds look so nice." She paused, then slyly: "How much is she paying you?"

"I wouldn't like to tell you, lady."

She laughed lightly. "Of course it isn't much; I could tell you that. She should be paying you at least twenty dollars a week."

It occurred to me suddenly that the whole idea might be that she was so furious with Mrs. Block that she was in effect trying to sic me on the old lady. It was obvious that she didn't think me very bright and felt that she herself was a very smart woman. I was suddenly disgusted with her clumsiness. But I decided to play the game right along with her. She thought I was dumb. Okay. I'd keep on playing dumb. The household idiot.

"Sure," I said. "I always figured this job should pay right around twenty a week."

"Of course it should," she assured me in a cooing little whisper.

"Confidentially," I told her, "what I get is six dollars a week and my bed and board. But that's six dollars *every* week."

"Oh," she gasped, "you poor fellow! Haven't you ever heard of labor laws?"

Arise and Sing, ye workers! I thought: she's working me up to a revolt. All by myself I'm the downtrodden masses!

I said: "That old Mrs. Block is a regular pinch-fist."

"She's worse than that." She moved closer. She was so tall her eyes came level with mine. Her negligee slipped down further off her shoulders. Her mouth was soft and relaxed. Her eyes began flashing an S.O.S. She gave me a look that delineated things clearly. She was so close now her eyelashes brushed my cheek.

"Lady, I—" I broke off, puffing hard.

The snoring went on, undisturbed.

She was bedazzling, *she* thought. The Lady in Black. The Bewitcher. She'd completely enchanted me. I was overpowered—*she* thought.

What did I mean, *she* thought.

It took all my willpower to take that first step away from her. After I reached the door I was okay.

"Nightie-night," I said. "It's past my bedtime."

I went into my room. After all, I was too dumb to know what she'd wanted. I heard her shoes click up the stairs, her footsteps in the hall. I heard the springs squeak with her weight as she got back in bed.

And suddenly Jeff's snoring stopped.

I guess she woke him up.

Chapter Nineteen

Early the next morning I heard the scream from upstairs. High and piercing. I stood motionless. Then all at once I was jabbing my arms into my leather jacket. I ran all the way to the stairway. I bounced up the steps with a nauseating wave all through me. Before I reached the top I heard the scuffle, the scrambled words, and Natalie's moan above the rest:

"*I think she's dead!*"

Then Jeff's frantic command:

"Call Doc Stetson, Natalie. For God's sake, hurry!"

I heard all that before I reached the second floor. I saw Lynn's suitcases sitting in the hall—the ones I'd carried up for her—and her little portable phonograph. Natalie brushed past me, down the stairs. I moved to the old lady's bedroom and looked inside.

Jeff was on his knees by the fireplace, holding the old lady's body, her head in his lap. She was lying very still and her eyes were closed. I saw dark splotches of blood on the sharp corner of the cement hearth, and blood trailing along the hardwood floor.

Lynn was there too, with her hat and coat on. She ran over to me and sobbed out the words:

"I knocked on her door just a few moments ago. I wanted to tell her I was moving out this morning. So I walked in, and—" She pointed to the cement slab in front of the fireplace. "She was lying there. I called Natalie—"

Jeff's voice interrupted. "Come here, Blair!"

I hurried to him.

"I can't tell if she has a heartbeat," he panted. "Would you please—"

I kneeled down beside him. With sweat pouring down my face, I pressed my fingers against the old woman's pulse. All I could feel was my own heartbeat, thumping like crazy.

"Christ!" I blurted. "I can't tell."

We all waited there for what seemed an eternity. Finally Natalie came back up, ushering in a little bald-headed guy with a shiny black satchel and a sickening odor of sweet cologne. He felt the old woman's pulse and shook his head. He got out a stethoscope from his bag and knelt beside her.

"She's departed from this world," he finally announced in a high, saccharine voice.

Natalie groaned, deep in her throat. Jeff whispered: "Oh, my God!" Then he was on his feet, talking to the doctor. "This young lady," Jeff said, pointing to Lynn, "found Mother here. Evidently she'd had another fainting spell. Her head hit the cement—"

Doc nodded, but his eyes were roaming over to the trail of blood. He stared at it for several seconds, then at the old lady. He bent over her again. His eyes squinted at the side of her face.

"Has she fallen before—recently?" he asked.

Jeff looked at me.

"Not that I know of," I managed.

"There are two wounds," Doc said. "One at the base of her skull where she hit as she fell. But this here—on her face. A second injury—a wound as fresh as the other."

"Then she did fall previously," Jeff said quickly.

"Possibly," Doc said. His eyes came up. "But I'm inclined to believe it's a matter for investigation."

"Investigation?" The four of us—Lynn, Natalie, Jeff and I—echoed that word.

Doc got up and went over to the telephone by the bed and dialed, his eyes shifting suspiciously from one to the other of us.

Chapter Twenty

"I've never seen so much junk."

It was this detective talking. This impatient, droopy-eyed, hollow-cheeked, anemic Beverly Hills cop, who kept sucking on his unlit pipe. Lefty Mason, he said his name was.

I'd walked around the grounds with him, out in back of the house, for a good half hour while cops turned the house inside out. The fingerprint man was there, and the coroner, and a guy who kept measuring things with a metal tape. Another cop was powdering woodwork for fingerprints.

But I was in the cellar now—with this detective. He was ogling around everywhere, poking his feet around, lifting up stuff. Suddenly his eyes rested on the cellar partition. My pulse quickened. I expected any minute for him to notice that the new wood had been put up. I held my breath, and he was about to speak when a uniformed cop hurried down the steps and over to us.

"Say, Mason," this cop said, "here's something." He held up a broken stick, charcoal burned. "I found this in the incinerator."

The detective took it and rolled it over in his hands. He ambled up the cellar steps. I followed, and the cop came up after me.

In the sunlight, Mason looked at the burned stick again.

"What d'you think?" the cop asked him.

"Could be," Mason replied. His voice was deep and liquid. He dropped the stick into the cop's hand. "Hold on to it. And dig up the lower half." He started toward the back porch, and, with his large bony hand, beckoned me to follow.

We went into the house.

"You say you've worked here approximately three weeks, Blair?" he asked, while we walked through the kitchen.

"That's right."

We went into the sunroom.

"You burn the trash around here?"

"No sir," I answered.

"Burn any trash last night?"

"No, sir."

"Early this morning?"

I shook my head.

"Play golf?"

"No, sir."

"The burned stick we found is the upper half of a golf club—an old wood putter."

"I wondered what it was," I said.

He gave me a look. "Sit down."

I sat. He'd fixed up office quarters in the sunroom. His notebook and papers were on the table. He'd already questioned Jeff and Natalie and Lynn, and now it was my turn. We'd been talking outside while I'd shown him around, the way he'd asked me to do. I'd told him everything I wanted him to know. But he wouldn't let up.

He sat back, rubbing his chin. "Now, as I was saying—about Mrs. Block—we have a record on her." He rubbed his face, as if he were tired and wanted to wake up. "She came to see me a couple of years ago, soon after her husband disappeared."

"Yeah," I said. "She told me something about that—how the old man had walked out on her."

He scratched his forehead. "It's damn funny what happened to old Henry Block."

"Oh, you knew him?"

He shook his head. "I read about Block in the case file before I came over here today. And I remembered that Mrs. Block came to see me about him. Trying to get me to help her locate him."

"Oh."

He leaned forward. "Now—this stepson of hers, and this daughter-in-law. They came out here from Salt Lake City to try and recover a sum of money from Mrs. Block."

"I wouldn't know about that."

His black eyes squinted. "That's what the son told me, anyway—this Jeff Block." He paused. "Did you ever happen to overhear any conversation at any time—I mean, did you ever hear any quarreling around here?"

"No, sir, I didn't. Except, of course, Miss York and the old woman had a regular brawl about the condition of the room she rented upstairs, the way I told you."

"You don't think either one of these girls—" He peered down at his notebook. "—this Lynn York or Elise Monteith—you don't know any reason why either one of them would want Mrs. Block dead?"

"That's strictly out," I said.

He gestured impatiently. "I figured the same." He smiled. "Then that leaves the stepson and the daughter-in-law."

I knew what he was getting at. So I plunged in before he had a chance to say what was on his mind.

"And me," I said.

"You?" He made a wry face. "Now why would *you* want to do a thing like that?"

I grinned. "I was here in the house when it happened."

He studied me for a long second. "Exactly what are you hanging around here for, chum?"

I felt my heart thumping. "I told you," I managed calmly. "I'm the handyman."

It struck his funny bone; he burst out laughing. "Good Christ," he blurted. "Beautiful and dumb. With those looks it's a wonder you aren't conning a lot of rich dames in this town."

I looked insulted. "I'm not the gigolo type."

"No? Just the same, you're a pretty good looker. If I was a woman I could go for you."

"Thanks."

"Don't get me wrong, chum. I'd just as soon knock you down as look at you. But," he went on, "I don't see anything in this house to hold you." His eyes were on me again. "Unless it's that sexy brunette."

"Miss York?"

He nodded.

"Yeah. Miss York is an eyeful all right."

He put the pipe in his mouth and nodded. "Beautiful and phony."

"Phony? How do you mean?"

"She's too quiet." He tapped a pencil against the notebook. "She only talks when she's questioned. That's unusual for a woman who discovers a body. From my experience you can't keep them quiet. But this girl, she mummies up."

"Maybe it was a shock to her," I said. "Discovering the old woman like that."

"Could be." He paused. "Perhaps you're right. I have nothing on her. I'm letting her go. She told me she's got a new job—out in North Hollywood. She wants to get out there right away."

"She does?"

His eyes came up slow. "You didn't know?"

"I sure didn't."

"Who you kidding now, Blair?"

"What do you—"

"You're telling me you aren't acquainted with that girl?"

"We know each other, only—"

The door opened. A cop came in. He went over to Mason and said: "The York girl is leaving. She wants a few words with Blair here."

Mason perked up. "Show her in."

Then Lynn was standing in the doorway. She was wearing the new suit I'd bought her. She looked tired.

"I—just wanted to say—goodbye to you, Curt," she said awkwardly.

"Goodbye, kid. Good luck."

"Goodbye."

"Be seein' you," I said. I didn't look at her. I had my side to her, hoping she'd catch on that I didn't want to make conversation in front of these cops.

"Yes," she said softly, "I'll be seeing you."

I watched her legs move out the door. When she was gone Mason's voice shot through the air:

"You didn't know her very well, eh?"

"That's right."

He stood up. His voice was suddenly crisp. "You're lying, chum! I can tell in that girl's eyes just how well you knew her."

"It's none of your business!"

"Anything that ever happened in this house is my business." He paused. His tone was suddenly sarcastic. "So you slept with her. How many times?"

"Go to hell!"

"You figure it's something to be ashamed of?"

"Christ, no."

"Okay, then—how many times?"

"Maybe not at all. Maybe once. Maybe ten times, maybe a hundred."

He whistled. "In *three weeks?* Say, you must eat Wheaties for breakfast!"

"You must be nuts!"

He chuckled. "How about this other one—this preacher who used to room in the house?"

I tightened my knuckles. "We can leave her out of it."

"You didn't get very far there, I'll bet. Did you, chum?"

"She's going to be my wife," I said.

He lifted his eyebrows and his lips formed an O. "Now I understand why this York girl is eating her heart out. She's crazy about you, too. How does it feel to have two women in love with you?"

I gave him an exasperated look.

"I get you," he went on. "You take it all in your stride. Me? I was born unlucky. Women always did take one look at me and go back to their husbands. I affect them like that." He laughed again.

But suddenly his face was dead sober.

"Now Jeff Block will inherit the old lady's money," he said. "All of it."

"I didn't know."

"That makes Jeff the logical suspect, wouldn't you say?"

"I sure do. In fact, I was thinking—"

He interrupted: "You don't really think that the two of them came back here to the house and bingo—pop off the old lady—knowing they'd be number one suspects?"

"Unless," I said, "the two of them never intended for it to look like murder. Maybe they intended it to appear accidental, never figured on cops on the scene."

He smiled. "Now you're talking more like it. You have a sharp mind there, Blair. Maybe you learned all that from those *True Detective* magazines piled up in your room."

"Hell, I don't read those. They came with the bed."

"Just the same, you're no dumbbell."

"Thanks."

He sat down again and leaned back. "Do you think this thing was premeditated?"

"Well, it's hard for me to say."

"Somebody tapped the old lady on the head. But it was her skull hitting the cement fireplace that did the trick."

"Oh, it was?"

"It might be a very clever murder, Blair. Somebody might have planned it that way."

"How do you mean?"

"Somebody could have tapped her hard enough to knock her unconscious, then let her body fall so that her head hit the cement."

"Jesus! You think they did that?"

He grinned. "Could be."

"The stepson and the daughter-in-law?"

He nodded. "But even if you think they intended it like that—to appear accidental—I still don't buy it."

"How do you mean?"

He leaned forward. "Sometimes I wish I wasn't a cop. I've got the record on old Mrs. Block. She was a mean, miserable old skinflint. Her heart was of glass. And the world is better off without her. But somebody killed her, and, the law says—"

"Yeah, the law's—"

"I'm going soft, chum. I ought to get me a motorcycle and go back to passing out traffic tickets." The next words came slow: "I hate like hell to arrest you for this murder."

The sun was shining in through the window, beating down hot on my face, but I shivered. "M—" I couldn't get the word out.

"Yes," he said with a funny stare in his eyes, "I think you're my boy."

"You're crazy! You're—"

"We'll get a confession out of you," he went on calmly. "I don't worry about that. But it'll make it a lot easier for you if you'll cough up all that poison in your system right now."

"You're *wrong*, you're—"

"It's in your whole body. You're a hell of an actor. Trying to register shock now, indignation." His voice came up. "The only thing you're putting across is that you're a pretty sick guy—through and through." His tone was all sympathy. "You didn't mean to kill her, did you?"

I opened my mouth. The words still wouldn't come. Because my lips were shaking like a jelly fish. He patted my arm.

"I like you, chum," he said. "I'll get you off on a manslaughter charge. I'll try. Her head hit cement, didn't it?" He paused. "What'd you hit her with?"

"I—didn't go near her—this morning."

His head jerked up. "Who said it was morning! It's the dark I'm interested in. We figure it happened around three A.M."

"I was asleep."

"Sure. Everybody was asleep." He pointed his pipe at me. "Somebody wasn't."

He got to his feet. "You and I had better go on up to the station now. We'll continue our nice little chat sociable-like. I'll pour tea. And then I'll expect you to do some talking."

Chapter Twenty-one

Somehow I found my hat. Mason ushered me to his sedan sitting out front. A few of the neighbors had gathered on the sidewalk. They were talking in excited whispers. I saw Jeff and Natalie coming out the door. Two cops escorted them into the police car across the street. I was relieved to see that. They were coming along, too, and that meant I wasn't the only suspect.

Mason got in the driver's seat beside me and pulled out.

He parked out in front of the City Hall. He got out and walked around to the side, up the steps to the Police Department entrance. He ushered me into a small office.

I'd barely sat down when a cop came in and said that Mason was wanted outside. They both left the room. But several minutes later, Mason came back in.

"We just had a visitor," he said. "A woman who lives on Greenleaf Drive. Funny how fast things happen in murder. Her five-year-old son found the lower half of a golf club in a vacant lot next door. The reason she brought it in to us is because it was covered with blood."

He watched me closely and went on: "Our serologist is typing the blood. No doubt it's the murder weapon."

I cleared my throat. "Where did you say it was found?"

"On Greenleaf Drive. Sound familiar to you, chum?"

"I didn't even know there was a street by that name."

"It leads right up to the Beverly golf course." He pressed a button on his desk. The same cop came back in. Mason said: "Get the laboratory on the phone." He glanced at his watch. "It's Saturday afternoon, but I want a report on that blood."

The cop left. The phone rang. Mason snatched it up. From the conversation I gathered that he was talking to a cop at the Block house. I couldn't get the gist of the talk. But in a minute he put the phone back on its cradle. His eyes darted over at me.

"Our men just found a fragment of wool caught in a splinter on the victim's bed. Do you know whose bathrobe it matches?"

"No, sir."

"Know who owns a purple bathrobe, Blair?"

"Hell, no."

"Jeff Block," he said. He went over to the window and stood looking out. "I couldn't believe it," he said half to himself. "I couldn't believe that Jeff Block would conk the old lady on the jaw with his own golf club." He turned to me. "I thought you had a hand in it, chum."

"Jesus. You don't think—"

"Not anymore. I'm going to have to apologize. I've been making passes at the wrong guy!"

"You sure have."

"Maybe the two of them had a finger in it. This Jeff and Natalie maybe went in to threaten the old lady in the middle of the night. Jeff Block admitted he was hanging around for some dough." He sucked in his breath. "It could have been like you said, Blair. They wanted it to appear accidental." He rubbed his ear. "Course—maybe they didn't intend to kill her."

"Well, I—"

"Maybe Jeff got hot-headed and swung." Mason winced. "He swung hard enough to break that old wood putter in two." He scratched his chin. "But the coroner says it was the blow when her head hit cement that finished her off."

"Yeah."

The cop came back in. "I have a report," he said. "The blood on the golf club is Type A, the same as Mrs. Block's."

Mason nodded. The cop went out.

Mason's voice was high with tension. "Now why would Jeff Block burn *half* of the club. Unless—he was mixed up. He was afraid to attempt burning the lower half, the one with the blood on it. He didn't have time to stand by the incinerator watching it burn. He thought maybe all the blood wouldn't come off the head of that putter—that maybe cops might find a trace. In his excitement he went in a direction *familiar* to him. The golf course. He dropped the club in a vacant lot—"

"It sounds logical, all right," I said.

"Logical?" he grinned. "That's the way it happened." He touched the buzzer again. The cop came in.

"Bring in Jeff and Natalie Block," he said.

Natalie came in first, her long fingers twisting the pearls around her neck. Jeff followed and sat beside me. Natalie took the chair by the window.

"It's all such a ghastly affair," Jeff murmured.

Then Mason was beside him.

"I understand, Mr. Block, that you're quite a golf enthusiast?"

"Yes," Jeff replied. "As I told you, I used to play a great deal. But in the last few years—"

"Have you played a game recently—since you came to visit your stepmother—at the Beverly Green course?"

Jeff hesitated. "Yes, I—yes, I'm acquainted with the chap who runs the place. We—"

"And you were arguing with your stepmother last night, weren't you, Mr. Block? Around three A.M.—in her bedroom?"

"That's ridiculous. I never argued with Mother. And I haven't been in her bedroom this last visit home."

Mason smiled. "You own a purple bathrobe?"

"Why, yes," Jeff replied. "As a matter of fact, I do. What in the deuce has that to do with—"

Mason's eyes hardened. "A fragment of that robe was picked up in Mrs. Block's bedroom. You've never been in there, heh, Block?"

"No, I haven't."

Mason grimaced. "I'm holding you both on suspicion of murder."

Natalie uttered a little cry. Jeff's face paled.

"You're joking, surely," he said.

Natalie faced him in sudden panic. "Say nothing, dear, until we speak to our attorney."

The cop led them out. Mason turned to me.

"Sorry, chum."

"That's okay."

So I left.

I walked back to the house. I turned my key in the lock and went inside. There was only one cop here now. He was sitting in a chair in the living room, reading the copy of *Robinson Crusoe*. I told him I'd come for my clothes. I went into my bedroom and started packing. Then this cop was standing in the doorway.

"You're wanted on the phone, Blair," he said.

"Thanks." I hurried into the front room and picked up the receiver. The cop took his seat and started reading again, paying no attention to me.

"Hello," I said.

"This is Lynn, Curt." Her voice was higher than usual. "Is everything all right?"

"Yeah."

"I've been ringing the house ever since I got here. The policeman there told me they took you—up to the station. So I called Mr. Mason just now. He said I'd find you at the house." She paused. "Jeff and Natalie are under arrest, did you know?"

"Yeah."

"I called you because I thought you'd be leaving."

"Yeah."

"You're going—for good?"

"Yeah."

"Where will you be?"

"Hell, I don't know."

"*I've got to see you!*"

"No can do, baby."

"It's important!"

"I'll be at Wilshire and Lilac Drive in about fifteen minutes."

"I can't make it. I'm in North Hollywood. I'm at work. I can't get off until late. I'll meet you tomorrow morning at—"

"No can do, baby."

"Curt, this is important!"

"I'll be out at the church at ten in the morning."

"Oh." The word was flat. "I didn't want to just say hello, goodbye. I have to talk to you."

"Can't you meet me at the church?"

"All right. But wait for me if I'm late. The buses don't run regular, and—"

"Sure, sure."

"Her church is on San Clemente, isn't it?"

"Yeah."

"Right off Wilshire?"

"Yeah."

"I'll be there."

"Okay."

I put the phone down. The cop was still reading. I went back into my bedroom and picked up the suitcase and my hat. I walked through the kitchen, the sunroom, the living room, and out the door. I stood there for a moment looking up at that old house, knowing I'd never see it again—or the old lady either.

I took a bus on Wilshire out to San Clemente Boulevard. I found a hotel room in Sawtelle that night. I remember it was Saturday. I remember that. And my room was on the first floor, next to the elevator. And every time somebody went up, the windows would rattle.

I threw off my clothes and got in bed, not daring to think of anything except that tomorrow was Sunday and I'd see Elise again. I remember the ringing in my ears and the pounding in my heart, and the ache all through me.

Tomorrow I'd see her again—

Chapter Twenty-two

It was Sunday. I woke up feeling the vibration of the elevator again. There was a broken pattern of sunlight over my bed. I heard a babble of voices in the hall, and then the church bells, ringing sweet and crystal clear. I jumped out of bed, into the shower and out in three minutes flat. I couldn't get my clothes on fast enough.

Outside I stopped at a little hamburger joint and ordered a couple of doughnuts and java. But I could only gulp down the coffee. Then I hurried on down to the church.

In the doorway I stopped. She was standing up on the platform, wearing a little yellow shiny smock, the outfit she preached in. There was a white gardenia pinned on her shoulder. I'd never seen her so beautiful. I stood there for a moment breathing her in. She watched me, smiling, while I moved down the aisle. When I reached her, she took my arm and hurried me over to the organ.

"You're late," she said in that breathless way of hers. "Start now with 'Count Your Blessings.' And when I signal later, go into 'Let the Lower Lights Be Burning.' Then, for the finale, play the 'Battle Hymn of the Republic.' I have the pages marked."

I sat down and looked at the music. Then I was playing—pumping like hell. "Count Your Blessings". I got mixed up, all right, I'd pump and forget to play. Then I'd play and forget to pump. I sure felt foolish.

The room was already half-filled and everybody was ogling me. People of all descriptions: one guy in the front row had one foot all bandaged up, with crutches sitting beside him. There were a couple of women, too. But the crowd was mostly guys. One with a cast on his arm, another with bandages around his hand, showing underneath his overseas cap. And most of them were in uniform. So you could tell they came from the Army hospital across the street.

By the time I got through with "Count Your Blessings" the room was three-quarters filled. And even after she began to preach, guys in uniform kept straggling in and quietly taking a seat in the rear.

This was the first time I'd actually heard her preach. And it was hard for me to believe my ears. She had a magnetic way about her. She must have reached the heart of every person in the room. Because you couldn't hear a pin drop. The audience sat there listening intently while she raved on:

"And you wonderful, gallant soldiers," she said now. "Some of you are sick, wounded. The Lord will help you. Truly He will—if you have faith. If you will only ask Him."

She went on. And I sat there feeling self-conscious. Because once in a while one of the guys would look over at me.

"We all depend on a higher force to guide us," she said. "We call it Fate, Lady Luck. But it is none other than God, even if we do not recognize Him."

I fumbled through the hymn book, trying to find "Let the Lower Lights Be Burning," because I knew I had to play that one next. I found it, and saw that she'd already turned down a corner of the page.

When I looked back out at the congregation, I saw another guy entering the room—in uniform, limping—with the aid of a cane. Elise continued, using words like: The Great Teacher, Divine Presence, God's Viewpoint.

I couldn't begin to tell you half of what she said. But finally: "Let's all stand. We're going to sing! We're going to fill our hearts with music." Her voice rose. "Let the Lower Lights Be Burning." She looked over at me.

I got flustered. How were the guys going to sing if they had no hymn books to read the words. I was trying to tell her that by mental telepathy, but she kept saying: "Page eighty-six, Mr. Blair. 'Let the Lower Lights Be Burning?'"

So I started playing. The screwy part was—the guys knew the words. They didn't need a book. They sang with gusto:

*Let the low-er lights be burn-ing! Send a gleam
across the wave!
Some poor fainting struggling sea-man, you may
res-cue, you may save.*

The room swelled with voices, and hers above all the rest. And I sure was bearing down on that old organ! I was getting pretty good at it by the time I hit the last note. I held it. The room fairly shook. Now the monitors got up and passed the collection baskets. When that was over, Elise uttered a short prayer. Then:

"There's going to be a meeting Wednesday night at eight o'clock. A special message for all of you. But before we leave let's have another song." She turned to me. "The Battle Hymn, Mr. Blair." She faced the congregation. "Let's *all* sing this one!"

I was pumping and playing again, and the voices were even louder than before. When I hit the chorus, the guys really gave:

*Glory, glory, hallelujah, Glory, glory hallelujah.
Glory, glory, hallelujah, His truth is marching on.*

"Amen! Bless you all. Let's see each and every one of you here Wednesday evening!"

So it was over. Church was out.

A couple of soldiers went up on the platform to her and shook her hand and stood talking to her. I sat on the organ bench, waiting for them to go. Then I noticed this guy who'd come in last, in uniform, with the cane, still standing by the aisle in the rear.

I can't tell you exactly how it happened, it was all so fast. I remember the moan from Elise's throat—the look in her eyes, as if she'd seen Christ! It was the same as that light she had in her eyes the first day I saw her, when she came down the stairs at the house and stood by the piano listening to the music: "One Fine Day". And all of a sudden I was hearing the melody again.

This soldier was limping up the aisle. And she was running down the steps. They met halfway. They stared at each other, then she was in his arms. And I was getting up slowly from the bench, with my fist all doubled up.

"Oh, my darling! My dearest!" She was hugging him and saying that and kissing him, with tears streaming down her face and laughing, too, at the same time.

He was grinning—this pale-faced soldier, with the hungry eyes. I saw that he was wearing a half-dozen ribbons, including the Purple

Heart. I guess the guy was handsome. Dark-brown hair, blue eyes—too thin, maybe. The uniform hung loose on his frame. Gold oak leaves on his shoulders. The guy was plenty okay.

He spoke to her now, his voice strained.

"I got in touch with Reverend Gossin. A friend of mine drove me here." He held her close and kissed her hair and her forehead.

"My sweet darling." Her voice was like a prayer. "I *knew!* I *believed!* I knew you'd come back!"

I stood there, weak all over. *This was her guy!* This was Philip! The Chaplain—

He said: "For months in the hospital, here in the States, I was tormented—whether or not to see you. Then I had a long talk with God."

"And He showed you the way to me."

He nodded. His eyes were feverish.

She looked down at his cane. "You're injured, darling. You carry that because—"

"My right leg," he said slowly. "And then, you see, I'm blind."

"Yes, darling," she said. "I thought you were. I wasn't quite—sure." Her voice was even calmer than before.

She pressed her mouth against his, and then she was clinging to him again, laughing with the tears rolling down her face. "I've never stopped loving you, my dearest. I never will! Foolish boy—how *could* you have had any doubt!"

They went into another clinch, and I was making a quick exit up the aisle. Before I reached the door I heard her voice: "Oh, Curt—"

I went on, out the door, down the sidewalk.

Then Lynn was walking beside me.

"I couldn't help hearing," she said. "I was standing in the doorway. Elise's major came back. It—it's wonderful for her, isn't it?"

"Yeah."

"But I know how you must feel."

"I feel fine. I'm okay." I said that, but my insides were burning and there was an ache in my guts shooting out in all directions.

We walked on. I could still hear the organ music. I was all loused up. I couldn't think straight. How could those guys know the words to those hymns? They must've been a bunch of sissies! How come the sun shone on that church? How come that guy walked in when he did? How could he? He was dead!

We reached Wilshire Boulevard. A taxi pulled up at the stop signal. I asked the driver if he was going in to Beverly Hills. He was. I opened the cab door.

"Get in, baby. Get in."

We sat in the back and the taxi rolled out. I looked over at Lynn. She was gazing straight ahead, all forlorn, like she'd lost her last friend.

"I hear you've got a new job," I said.

"Yes."

I couldn't stand it; I wanted to cheer her up. "Looks as if you're on the way up that ladder, kid."

She said: "Don't joke about that ladder. I didn't like my job at the Vanities. I quit. I'm working out in North Hollywood. I—I'm a car hop at Vince's Drive-in."

"How about those dramatic lessons?"

"I never went back. It's the way Elise said once—you've got to want something desperately before you get it. I guess I didn't want that bad enough."

"Yeah?"

"I decided that fame and fortune don't mean so much after all. What the hell good did all those Saks labels do me? After I wore them once they're the same as the twenty-five buck outfits I used to have. No better."

"That right?"

"There's something more important than that. Having the guy you want, and maybe even kids." She broke off and looked down at her fingernails. "But people are always reaching up for something."

"Yeah. Sometimes it's best to let a star be just a star."

She gave me a look. "Don't go quoting *her* poem again! Can't you forget her for even one minute? She's got her major. Besides, she's way over your head. She isn't for you. She isn't perfect, either. She's only perfect in your mind. She has the same faults I do. Nothing is ever perfect!"

"I guess you're right."

"If you knew her, she'd do things wrong. Just the way I do. She'd make my same mistakes."

"Maybe you've got something there."

She was over in my arms now. "I talked big—the big-league baby, that's what I *thought*. But I love you, don't you see? And if you loved me, we'd have everything there is. All you need is to find yourself. You're really a wonderful guy!"

"Yeah, a great big genius."

"Oh, maybe you don't say all the words right. But you've got what it takes, deep inside. I wouldn't be willing to settle for you otherwise. I'd keep on knocking around—looking." She put her arms around me, her face against my chest. "I love you, Curt. I want kids of my own that look like you. Not act like you, but look like you. And that's how you can tell real love."

"That right?"

"I'll *make* you love me. And she never loved you. She *never* did. She's cold and selfish and she doesn't love you." Her head came up. "But I love you." Her voice trembled. Tears welled in her eyes. "Oh, honestly, Curt, I do!"

She loved me! That was great! She loved me. And Elise loved her guy. A triangle of hearts, all cockeyed, all jumbled up! Who made the world so screwed up anyway! Why didn't somebody do something about it some time? Why didn't somebody fix it up?

Then I thought: maybe I'm the guy who should fix it up. Starting with my own life, starting with Lynn's.

I guess Lynn heard it under my breath:

"Let a star be just a star, a woman but a dream."

Tears streaked her face. "I take back everything! That damn poem! I'm no dream, you dope! I'm real flesh and blood and warmth. A woman but a dream—that's the silliest—"

"You're no dream, baby. And I'll forget the poem, all right."

"Promise?"

"Promise."

"Then kiss me. Kiss me the way you used to."

I kissed her—the way I used to. Then she was holding me close.

"This is goodbye," I said.

"What?"

"It's going to be easier if you go in yourself and confess. If you don't the cops are going to arrest you anyway."

"What are you talking about?"

"They're easily as smart as I am," I said. "And if *I* know, they'll know in time. They always find out—in time."

"Know what, Curt?" Her cheeks were crimson.

"You killed her, honey. You killed the old woman. I've known all along. Only I let you play your own game. I owed you that. I, of all people, certainly owed that to you and a lot more, I guess. Anything else you want you can still write your own ticket. If you don't want to tell them, you don't have to. I won't. I guess you know that. Only for your own good, I think you'd better."

"Curt, Curt—" She was sobbing.

"Why don't you tell me about it, honey?"

She looked up at me, brushing at her tears. "How did you know? Tell me how you knew."

"The footsteps."

"Footsteps?"

I nodded. "Everyone has a different pattern. I used to lie awake in bed listening to your footsteps upstairs. I got to know them. I could tell by the sound whether it was you or Elise or Jeff or Natalie or the old lady."

"And you heard mine—in Mrs. Block's room?"

"Yeah. I heard them. I woke up when you came in the front door. I heard you going up the stairs. I got up and went out in the kitchen for a drink of water. I heard the old woman moving around in her room, right over the kitchen. And I kept listening for your footsteps in the hall, for you to go into your room. But you didn't. Then in a few minutes I heard your footsteps directly overhead. I knew you were with the old woman."

"Yes," she whispered. "I'd just come home from work. Mrs. Block was up. She was singing in a thin little voice—a weird garbled tune. Her bedroom door was slightly ajar. I only got a glimpse of her at first—it was a horrible sight."

"Go on," I said.

New tears swelled in her eyes. "The old woman kept singing and jabbering in that little girl voice, with her hair all down over her face." She clutched my arm. "She'd gone—crazy!"

"I was afraid of it," I said.

Lynn went on: "I saw something shiny in her hand. I moved closer to her door, but in the dark hall I bumped into Jeff's golf clubs, sitting at the top of the stairs. Mrs. Block must have heard me. Because the next thing I knew her door opened. I jumped back quick against the wall, by the bag of golf clubs. But she saw me. She had a revolver in her hand, and her fingers were working on the trigger. If you could have seen her eyes!

"I was afraid to scream—for fear she'd fire. So I tried to be as calm as I could. I—I started asking her about some clean sheets for my bed."

"Yeah?"

"Yes. And she only stared at me. Then she motioned me inside. I grabbed one of the golf clubs and went in her bedroom. She—she told me to drop the club. That's when I—I threw it at her."

"I heard it fall," I said.

Lynn covered her face with her hands. "I didn't want to hurt her, Curt. I aimed the club at the revolver in her hand. But it hit her on the side of the head, I think—and she—she fell."

"I heard that thud, too, from downstairs—her head hitting the cement."

Lynn shuddered. "I knew that the police would come. And I made up my mind that I wasn't going to be blamed. I've been through enough. I didn't want to get into anything like that. I knew I had to work fast."

"Yeah," I said. "I'm beginning to understand now how the cops found a thread of Jeff's bathrobe on the old woman's bed. You planted it there."

"No," she breathed. "I didn't. But I remember that Jeff's robe was flung over the cedar chest in the hall—and when I picked up the golf club a thread of it must have pulled off. And that's how it got in Mrs. Block's room."

"I guess so."

"Then," Lynn said, "when I looked at the old woman again, there was blood all around her head, running on the broken club. I picked up the two pieces. The upper part I took outside and put in the incinerator and set it on fire. The other half, the one with the head, I took with me because I thought all the blood wouldn't burn off it. And I started walking. I thought I'd put it in a place where the cops wouldn't find it."

"You did pretty well, baby. But not well enough."

She jerked up her shoulders. "But it *is* good enough. They don't know yet. We have each other, darling. We can go away. We can—"

"And how about Jeff? He's taking the rap for this."

"They'll never convict him. They haven't enough to convict him."

"And when they realize that, they'll be after you, baby. We'll never be able to run far enough away to escape them. Never. Cops are like adding machines. In time they find the right answers."

Her voice was huskier. "Look who's reformed! It's great for you, since you want me to take the rap. What if it was you?"

"Okay," I said. "Do what you want. But if you went in and told the cops your story, just the way you told me—there'd be a chance."

"No. No. Curt! Let's go away!"

"Sure, baby. Maybe you're right. I'll go anywhere in the world with you."

"You're not lying?"

"No."

A shiver went through her. "Only we'd have more of a chance at happiness and—and everything, if we were in the clear."

"It's ourselves we've got to live with. Lynn. And it's ten to one you'll get acquitted."

Her face was white, and she was shaking now. She leaned forward in the cab.

"Driver," she said, "take us to the Beverly Hills police station."

I'd been wrong. It wasn't ten to one. Or even eight to one. But it was acquittal in the end.

She didn't even have to stand trial. The coroner's jury did it. If it'd been only Lynn's story they'd listened to, they'd never have acquitted her. But there came to the witness stand, in view of that old withered body, a host of witnesses testifying to Mrs. Block's character. All the people who had ever hated her—and the world was full of them. It started with Jeff and Natalie, who surprisingly rallied to Lynn's defense, and went on. The junk man she'd gypped. He'd bought an old safe from her, paid her by weight and discovered that she'd filled the thing with cement. There was the gardener who'd worked for her and was never paid. All the laundry companies she owed. The house cleaners, the decorating company, the butcher, the baker, the Eastern Star Furniture Company. She'd bought furniture from them and sold it before it was paid for and defied them to collect, though she had collected well on the resale of the merchandise. Even her cars weren't paid for, and how she avoided having them picked up by the finance company is a miracle of deceit. The coroner's jury wasn't interested in that part, and wouldn't let them finish.

But these people were there because they wanted to be. They couldn't get paid while she was alive. They damn well were going to, now that she was dead!

And it all added up. I guess after everybody was through, the jury felt that Lynn had done no more than protect herself against a woman who, from all evidence, had been on the border of insanity for a very long time. They made it justifiable homicide. Self-defense.

They never did find out about Henry's corpse. They didn't have to. Lynn never told them. For all I know, Henry's still there in the cellar. The place was sold, and maybe some unfortunate tenant of that termite-ridden house will find a skeleton there some day. And that'll be just one more sin uncovered against the old woman, who left so many sins behind her—big and small.

I know that Lynn and I will never see the place again. We're a long way from there. Living in a little town in New Mexico. Don't laugh, but I'm a short-order cook now, and Lynn's a waitress. It isn't so bad, because, you see, we own the place. That is—all except the first and second mortgages. And we're paying them off fast. It seems awfully good not to be worrying about anything except mortgages. Lynn makes a wonderful wife. A girl has a lot of time for that in New Mexico—being a wife. The nights are long—and they're cold. You have to sleep close together to keep warm.

THE END

THE SLEEPING CITY

MARTY HOLLAND

I

It started with rain in the city, with Officer Harris and myself in the plainclothes car. By now it was daily routine. The radio was giving out with a few drunks, a fag molesting somebody, a hit-and-run at Center and Third. There were no earthquakes, no murders, no tidal waves, no invasion from Mars, and no premonition to warn me that on this January night was to start a chain of events that led to love and death and the corrosion of a guy's soul—the kind that could eat your life away.

There was just the same pattern of pedestrians' faces, with their umbrellas and raincoats, scurrying through the downpour. Worrying wives, gumming up downtown traffic, picking up their guys from the office buildings, the same lonesome kids on the corners, hustling to sell their sheets.

I wheeled the squad car on up Tower, fighting through early evening traffic, the windshield wiper working overtime, rain splashing around us, sounding like gentle hail on the steel roof. Harris and I had been working partners for about a month. The guy could talk to horses, but they couldn't talk back. The local race track had opened only a week ago. "Laddie Boy" was all I'd heard all day.

The radio began blasting from the various controls. I listened with half an ear.

"Nineteen-T, Columbus and Whitsett, ambulance traffic. Fourteen-L, call your station. One-four-L, call your station. All units in the vicinity Spruce and Eighth, at the liquor store. Two-eleven there now. Sixteen take the call, Code Three. Eighteen-W, call your station. One-eight-W, call your station."

18-W was our car. I reached over and pulled up the mike, pressed the button, heard the transmitter whir and rogered in. Harris was still on "Laddie Boy." I don't think he even heard the call. I pulled over to the curb at the first drugstore. I ran out through the rain and inside to a phone booth. I dialed the City Hall and asked for our extension. The phone buzzed, then a voice boomed on the other end of the wire:

"Sergeant Jackson—Gangster Squad."

"This is Wade," I said. "What's up?"

It took him a minute to answer. I heard him lay the phone down, heard a rustle of papers, then:

"Yeah, Wade. The old man wants to see you." He paused. "How far out are you?"

"About fifteen minutes."

"Okay. Come on in."

The phone clicked in my ear. I hung up and went back to the car. Harris was sitting there with water spots on his gray hat and coat, and a new *Racing Form*—the first time he'd moved his fanny all day.

Twenty minutes later, Harris and I had checked the hack in, and I was ambling up to the third floor. The robbery office was humming with change of shift and guys shooting the breeze. I checked the keys in, signed Harris and myself off the log book and made our daily report—all the time wondering what the captain had on his mind.

I went into his office.

Captain John Roberts—the old man. He was only six foot three, with Joe Louis shoulders, gray-black hair, a chubby red face. I'd met him first five years ago at briefing for the first Berlin raid. An iron-ass colonel, just in from another group. I'd looked at him and thought, "A retread from the last war! What the hell does he know?"

I flew left seat for him, co-pilot. Everything had gone fine until we turned I. P. on the bomb run. Kraut pilots that day must have been the original Abbeville Kids—the top boys that Goering had once owned. They even had their trainers up, with the engineers and ground crews throwing monkey wrenches!

Roberts had the ship, and the bombardier was flying it with the bomb-sight, going in on the target. I'd been calling fighters to the gunnery crews when I felt the ship lurch, and smelled smoke drifting in from the radio room! A 109 had sewn a nice long ripple in the top of our Fort.

When the nose of the ship dropped I looked over at Roberts. The flak helmet he was wearing hadn't done him too much good. He'd been clipped across the top of the head with a cannon shell. Blood was seeping down the side of his face, onto the beaver collar of his flying jacket. I knew then that he might be a colonel, but he could die just as quick as a lieutenant.

When the fighters stopped coming in, I got hold of the engineer on intercom and had him come up and take care of the colonel.

I started the turn to the rally point, leading the group, with flak laying before us like a black cloud. Our ships were strung out beside me and in the rear, with several spots—ships that had gone down.

We hit home base with only two wounded aboard, and plenty of holes in the skin that covered the plane. Roberts wasn't in too bad shape. Two weeks in the hospital fixed him up. He'd lost a lot of blood and a lot of hair in the flak helmet.

Two weeks later I received notification from General Farmer that I had myself a DFC for leading the group home. It was one medal that I didn't deserve.

It wasn't until after I'd joined the cops, and had worked six months doing foot traffic duty, that I learned that Captain Roberts of the Gangster Squad was the old Colonel Roberts that I'd known in the Eighth Air Force. I went in to see him, introduced myself, and met him all over again.

I had him out to dinner. He met Betty, my future wife. We talked old times and lived them again.

Three days later I was transferred to the Gangster Squad, to work under Captain Roberts. Nobody had to tell me who was responsible for my promotion.

Now he was seated at the old mahogany City Hall desk that looked too small for him. It was cluttered with debris, a model of a B-17 holding down a stack of papers. Roberts sat with his glasses pulled down on the end of his nose, reading a report.

"Hello, Wade." His voice was deep and resilient. His eyes hadn't moved from the report. "I'll be a minute. Sit down."

I got the uncomfortable feeling then that I always got with Roberts. He hadn't looked up when I came in. I might have been the janitor or the chief. The guy always did have eyes in the top of his head.

I sat facing his desk and looked out the window. Night had dropped her curtain on the city. There was the steady downfall of rain, and through it the faint echo of traffic from below, the distant whir of wet automobile tires, and the huge neon sign from across the street flashing on and off, casting its purple shadow in the room.

It was then that I noticed the suitcase on the floor by the desk. Draped over it was a two-hundred-buck houndstooth topcoat and a nice brown felt. I looked back to Roberts.

"How's Betty?" he asked, his eyes still on the report.

"Fine. Fine."

"Tell her hello."

"Sure will. She'll be pleased."

There was a silence, then:

"Harris okay?" He was still reading.

"Horsey," I said, "but okay."

"I'm pulling you off," he said brusquely. Then his voice softened somewhat. "That is, if you'd like working alone."

"Suits me," I said.

Roberts stopped reading. He leaned back in his chair, scratched his head, regarded me, then offered me a cigarette. I took it and lighted up and waited for what was coming.

He lighted his cigarette. "I've grown weary of Eastern hoods coming in here for no good. Jim Cox flew in from Chicago this morning." He reached across his desk and picked up a report. "Here's the dope on Cox, and a mug."

He threw the police photo down on the desk before me. He adjusted his glasses, kept glancing at the paper in his hand.

"Theft from person in the State of New Jersey," he went on. "Also a record of having stolen property. Record of being an enemy of state, and embezzlement of state funds. In Cleveland he was picked up for murder, and released. Known as a jewelry fence in Detroit. Picked up for murder in Miami for the killing of Willie LeMont, and released because of insufficient evidence." His eyes snapped up.

"Never heard of the guy," I said.

"Neither did I"—he smiled grimly—"until I got word from an informer that Cox was coming in and that he was recently a member of the Les Ties gang." He took a breath. "Last week Les Ties was found in the Loop with a lot of holes punched through him." He glanced at the floor. "Somebody worked him over with an ice pick."

"Yeah," I said. "I know. What the hell is Cox doing out here?"

Roberts shrugged. "I planned a little reception for him this morning at the airport. Cox wasn't too talkative at first. It took persuasion. Finally admitted that Ties had arranged for his contact here before he was killed. Cox came on out to take advantage of the deal."

"What sort of deal?"

Roberts sat back, rubbing his five o'clock shadow. "Cox says he doesn't know details. His only instruction from Ties was to see a bartender at the White Lion Club." He paused. "That place ring a bell with you?"

"Louie Thompson's new joint," I said. "On Sixth Street."

He smiled. "And you know who Louie is?"

"Yeah. Got his start back in the Twenties during prohibition. He took a fall for the Wright Act. After he got out of the joint he moved to Miami. Came here last September. Been running bookmaking and narcotics."

Roberts nodded. "What we want is to see that he hits the bucket again—but good. Thompson doesn't know we're wired. Thinks as far as our Department goes he's an honest citizen, running a legitimate café. And to all that meets the eye, he is. A smooth baby." His voice lowered. "Maybe this is my chance to dump him."

I studied Roberts. "What's the pitch on it?"

"Jim Cox is buried. No counsel. No writs. Nothing. Incommunicado. He's never been in contact with Thompson or any of his men." He smiled again, humorlessly. "So what keeps me from sending in a substitute?"

I nodded. "What charge did you hang on Cox?"

"Suspicion of murder." His eyes flickered. "Somebody killed Les Ties. Why not suspect his trigger man? The idea didn't set too well with Jim. He knows I can bury him forever on that charge, and I'll get plenty of help. That's why at four this afternoon he was ready to talk. The beautiful part is, since Les Ties is dead, Thompson won't be able to check on him with Jim Cox. Jim swears everything he's given me is straight. If it isn't you'll find out soon enough."

"I'm beginning to see how I fit in," I said.

He nodded. "Don't worry about Cox. I can hold him as long as it takes to set up our deal."

He leaned forward and gave out with the old spiel about my clean record on the force, said I'd been chosen for this assignment because of my integrity, because I'd kept up to date on the pulse beat of hoodlums, because I had been born and raised in Chicago, and also because I bore somewhat of a resemblance to Cox.

"Get to the White Lion around ten tonight," he continued, and glanced at my brown gabardine. "Cox was wearing a dark business suit, white shirt, red tie. Pack up the clothes you feel will be suitable. This is a job that'll take time. See Al, that bartender. You're to tell him to fix you a Haig and Haig, Silver label. Al will take it from there. Cox swears that's his only instructions."

I took a deep breath. Roberts went on:

"Okay, Jim Cox—" He reached for something in his desk, handed me a ring, a gun and a wallet. "Jim's property. We're borrowing them." He nodded toward the suitcase on the floor. "There's his luggage, his topcoat and his hat."

Jim's gun was a .38 two-inch with a ramp sight—a belly gun. His ring was set with a round green stone with a little snake eye in the center. I jabbed it on my finger. It was tight but not too uncomfortable. I opened the wallet. It obtained the usual cards of identification.

Roberts rose and stuck his hands in his pockets.

"You flew in on American Airlines, arrived at six-fifteen this evening, Flight Four-two-eight." His eyes narrowed. "If it's a bum beef give me a call at the Roxy dining room tonight." He flushed a trifle. "Little birthday party for my mother." His voice shot up. "If there's trouble you can handle it." He looked at me and smiled. "I found that out a long time ago. If Cox has given me the straight goods, sit tight and play. It'll take time to discover what Thompson is up to."

He handed me the report on Cox. "Memorize the record and put it back in the top desk drawer." He went to the closet, pulled out his tan slicker and jabbed his arms into it. "Report to me any way you can. Don't come near the office." He gestured to an envelope on the desk. "There's your expense money. If you need more, yell. Count it. There's three hundred bucks. Sign the receipt. I'll take your gun, your badge, and your I.D. card."

I got up and handed them to him. He put them on a shelf in the closet, then locked up. I signed the receipt for the dough.

"Oh, yes," his voice ground on, "there's been a dame seen regularly with Thompson. See if you can find out who she is." He paused in thought. "She might prove valuable for information."

He started to the door.

"Play it close to your belly, Wade. Keep everything cozy and we'll be all right. Good luck, kid, and don't get hurt!"

II

Roberts left. I shoved the three hundred bucks into Jim's wallet. I sat back down, stuck my feet up on the desk and lighted another cigarette. Slowly and carefully I began to memorize the report, while rain beat its steady tattoo on the windows, and the neon sign flashed on and off, casting its purple shadow.

Suddenly there was the fury of a moth beating its torn wings against the desk light. My eyes stayed on it. Impulsively I reached out and snapped off the lamp. The moth dropped to the desk. It was snow-white, and as beautiful as a butterfly. It lay fluttering, exhausted.

I wondered what screwy quirk of nature attracted them to light—to the point that it killed them.

A half-hour later I was headed for Spruce Street—and Betty—with rain trickling through the cheesecloth roof of my Ford convertible. For eighteen months I'd planned a new top. But with room rent, car payments, and saving up to be married, I'd never got around to it.

I slid into the driveway, pulled up to the double garage, and parked in back of Betty's Chevvy coupe. Looking at it I remembered that I was supposed to put in a set of new plugs. She was going to have to wait for them now.

I hurried up the drive and saw her through the kitchen window, wearing a red-checkered apron, looking like a Norwegian doll, her blonde hair upswept, brown eyes softly luminous. It was the reason I'd first dated Betty—a blonde with brown eyes. My special weakness.

I kept looking at her, feeling my heart take on an extra beat, thinking of the time when I wouldn't be just the guy who had a room in the house next door to her anymore. But, hell, I wasn't complaining. If it hadn't been for that room I'd probably never have met her.

I set Jim Cox's suitcase, topcoat and hat down on the back porch. I went inside and found her putting a roast back into the oven.

"I'm warming things over for the *fifth* time." Her voice was on edge. "You could have telephoned."

I closed the oven door for her and took her arms and put them up tight around my neck. I said something about how terrible it was what future wives were getting by with these days. Not even one kiss for a beef-weary groom-to-be.

Then all of a sudden she smiled and was warm and wonderful until she remembered the biscuits. Then she was opening a can and pulling out dough.

I said, "Just like Mother used to bake."

I peeked into the living room at Betty's sister, Doris, and her husband, Clyde, with his big fanny sprawled all over the piano bench, his right fist diving into the chocolate dish, his left hand strumming, "Don't Cry, Joe."

Why that guy had always irked me, I'll never know! I've tried to get along with him, because Betty lived with them, but I ached for a day—soon—when I could eat dinner with Betty, and visit her, without that guy prying into our affairs.

Doris was seated on the sofa, by the tired Christmas tree, reading a magazine. I did a double-take, seeing my mother seated beside her. Across the room from them sat a forlorn blond boy of ten or eleven years.

"Forgot to tell you," Betty's voice came over my shoulder, "your mother's here. With another potential little Dillinger."

I groaned. And then my mother, having heard my car pull in, was hurrying toward the kitchen. She swung the door open in my face, then hurriedly closed it.

"Wade," she said a little breathlessly, "I've brought Bobbie."

"What's the charge this time?" I asked drily.

"Well," she said, "his mother permitted little Bobbie to run some errands for me this morning. My diamond ring was lying on the sink and—" She took a breath. "His mother returned it, of course, but—"

"Burglary, eh? Send the suspect in."

A minute later, Bobbie, pale and trembling, came into the kitchen. He stood biting his lip, his eyes on Betty as she moved back and forth from sink to stove.

I gave the kid the old pitch on crime not paying, told him the pride I felt in being on the right side, that I saw all the follies of humanity and profited by them. I got a fervent promise that he'd pass up the stealing urge.

Then my mother had the floor. "My son is becoming quite a missionary," she announced to Doris and Clyde. "This is the *seventh* boy he's saved."

"If I saved him," I said.

"Of course you did." She beamed at me. "One look at that police badge does the trick." She looked down at Doris. "Did you know Wade was a gangster himself once? Oh, yes. At the age of fifteen he—"

She went on, reiterating how, as a kid in Chicago, I'd joined a gang and started out my career by swiping fifty crates of lettuce from an old freight car, then peddled the lettuce from door to door, three heads for a penny.

She was still going strong when I left to go over next door to my room to shave.

Crazy, dumb kids! It was the successful lettuce haul that had lit the fuse. The next job was bananas. After that the local soda fountain. The proprietor was near-sighted, senile, had gout in one foot. Between customers he'd limp behind the back partition and rest on his day cot. Even though the register made a loud clanging noise, by the time the old man could hobble in, our gang member could be out of the store.

Since about a hundred kids bought malts and candy in the place, we felt sure that the old man wouldn't possibly be able to identify the thief.

I'd drawn the short straw. Even now as I thought about it I could taste the brassy fear in my mouth that I'd felt as I'd crept along the counter to the register. And then I was grabbing up greenbacks. Hearing the cash register bell, the proprietor let out a bloodcurdling scream. Before I made it out the door I heard an avalanche of falling debris, and the old man's groans.

Next morning's paper told the story. Several five-pound cans of malted milk had fallen from the shelf, pelting the poor old guy on the head. From a hospital bed he'd told how he'd been robbed by a youth of fifteen or sixteen.

The police visited all the punks in the neighborhood. I denied everything and the cops believed me. But I still remembered my mother's eyes, how she cried all night. She knew how I'd suddenly got the brand-new bike and the twenty-five-dollar bank account.

I became an ex-hood—but fast!

Now I could laugh about it, and my mother could tell about it whenever she had somebody to listen.

"Dinner's ready."

Betty had come in while I was shaving, was beside me. I pulled her over and rubbed lather on her face and kissed her warm, full lips.

"Hurry," she said, and left.

I hoped that the house would cave in, or Clyde would break his leg, or I'd slit my throat shaving, so that after dinner I could be with Betty, instead of starting a long assignment on a night like this!

When I got back over, my mother and Bobbie were gone. Then I was seated, facing Clyde, at the dinner table.

"Darling," Betty said, "as soon as we're married I hope we can afford an automatic washer. Doris says they're marvelous."

I yawned. "If I can rake up fifty grand, we'll even have television."

Clyde pointed his fork at me, a potato dangling. "By the way, Wade, I always wanted to ask—" He went on chewing the mouthful of food he was talking through. "What's your average take in a month—side dough, I mean—on a job like you've got?"

I held back an urge to spring at him. He was like some other people I knew, rating a cop in the hood racket. Sure, a dick thinks in the same pattern as a hood, only he has to think faster, and he sure as hell doesn't make the hood's dough!

Betty reached over and patted my hand. "Wade has never taken any juice," she defended. "Why, I remember one time a grocery clerk gave him a dollar too much change. Wade drove five miles, all the way back, to return it."

"Yeah," I said, "be sure my epitaph reads: 'Here Lies A Poor But Honest Jerk.'"

Betty squeezed my hand. "I'm marrying purity and goodness." She added smugly, "He doesn't even chase tall sultry sirens. I think it's because he's so much in love with Florence. If it weren't raining I'd show you the lovely big cage he built in the backyard next door for her yesterday. So she'll have room to hop around. When she first came, he was up two nights nursing her, then he couldn't bear to let her go."

Florence was the sparrow who'd made a forced landing in my backyard. She'd been in really bad shape—bruised, beaten, wings and legs broken. She got well, but couldn't fly again. She could only hop around.

"Poor thing," Betty added. "She tried so hard to fly today. But there was only a quiver of wings."

We talked about things like that, and finally Clyde and Doris took off for a movie. Betty put her arms around me.

"Darling," she said, "you're tired. Would you like to go home to bed?"

I told her then that there was a new assignment. She'd learned long ago not to ask details. But she said what she always did:

"Is it very dangerous?"

"Hell, no. But it may keep me away for a few weeks. I'll call you the first chance I get."

Her eyes were suddenly misty, and she held me closer. "Wade, if anything happened to you, I'd—"

"You'd be rich, honey. Ten thousand bucks insurance. I've already got it in your name. I'm worth a fortune dead. You could even buy that new washer."

"Don't talk like that, please!" Her body moved closer. "Do you know that when you leave me like this something chokes up in my chest and I want to cry and cry and cry?"

"Your chest, eh?" I grabbed her. "Is *this* where you feel the pain?"

Her lips touched mine. "Yes, darling. There and all over. I hope we can be married soon. I despise sleeping alone."

"Me, too."

She'd be a good wife, Betty. Loyal, understanding. No suspicions, no nagging. Soothing to be with after the beefs of the day. With her snuggled beside me, holding me, I wasn't missing much.

Now she was taking off her dress. I looked at her.

"Baby, baby, come here."

"Darling," she said, "turn off the light. We'll go to bed and pretend we're already married."

"The hell of it is," I said, "in about thirty minutes we got to pretend it's morning, and go over to my room and pack a suitcase. Then I catch a cab and go to work ..."

It was still raining when the taxi skidded to a stop in front of the White Lion.

From the outside it didn't look like too big a place. There was a small parking lot to one side, a big gaudy neon sign in front, and a green canvas canopy stretching from the sidewalk to the entrance.

I paid off the driver, got out, shook the rain off my coat and hat, picked up my luggage, and went inside.

There was an entry hall with four steps leading down, a strong smell of burnt wood, the nice aroma of charcoal steaks, and a strong whiff of "Tabu" from the direction of the carrot-haired hat-check girl. She bounced to me and helped me off with my coat.

My eyes went to the planting box, with greenery and a lot of circus poles. Beyond was the club, looking like a typical English pub, with a small bar of ten or twelve stools, tables scattered around, about twenty people in the place. Two at the bar, the rest at the tables pushing conversation, or trying to dance.

Judging from the patronage, the White Lion wasn't doing too good. Waiters were fumbling around, rattling dishes and silverware, filling water glasses and looking busy.

At the far end there was a large fireplace, with blue-fringed flames licking through the grate, casting lights and shadows on the dance floor. On the right side of the room between the bandstand and the fireplace was a dark, smooth-polished door with a big brass knob. An eight-piece orchestra was knocking hell out of some piece; I couldn't remember the name of the tune.

A waiter made a rush at me. I nodded toward the bar and kept walking. I parked the suitcase and slid up at the far end. It made three of us sitting there.

About eight stools up a tall bartender was shooting gab with a customer. A little fat bartender moved up in front of me, stood quietly, and studied me with his little black shoe-button eyes. His hair was greasy-black, slicked down, and under the dim light I saw the scar, no wider than a hair's-breadth. It started at his hairline and ran down along his face, across his mouth to the sharp point of his chin.

"Scotch and water," I said.

He nodded and made the drink. He set it on the counter with a thud. I threw down four bits and sat there sipping the Scotch and watching the room through the reflection of the mirror. The little bartender kept vigil there in front of me.

I wondered if he was Al, but I wasn't too curious just yet. I'd ordered a Scotch on the city's dough—it doesn't happen often—and I wanted to finish it.

"You Al?" I said at last.

He nodded. I squeezed the glass a little and drained the last drop. I asked for Haig & Haig, Silver Label.

He looked at me for a full second, without the flicker of an eyelash. "We got it upstairs," he said. His eyes stayed on me. "Watch the door I take. Don't follow me. I'll meet you at the top of the stairs in five minutes."

He moved over to the tall bartender, whispered something, then ducked under the far side of the bar and up. He walked straight for the door with the big brass knob, opened it, and hurried up the steps.

I played around with my empty glass, smoked a cigarette, and kept my eyes on my watch. In five minutes I got up, ambled across the room, and turned the big brass knob.

III

I carried the suitcase up the green-carpeted stairs with my heart beating against my ribs. Don't let me tell you that I wasn't scared. No cop goes into something like this without wondering if he's going to die young! If there was an inkling of a suspicion that I wasn't Jim Cox there was going to be trouble, and plenty of it!

Al was waiting at the top of the steps. He moved silently down the dimly lighted hall, motioning for me to follow. At the far end, I could see light seeping under a door. Its corrugated upper half was marked:

PRIVATE – OFFICE

Al paused in front of it, glanced at me, and tapped on the glass. There was a grunt from inside. Al turned the knob.

First I saw the gleaming modern furniture, the chrome and mirrors, and green carpeting, red drapes. Then the perfume hit me. It was about the most exotic stuff I'd ever smelled. To my right was a couch, its high back toward me. In front of the couch television was on. To my left was a desk. Thompson was seated behind it.

He was about fifty, with the balloon look that fat men get. He peered around at me, his third chin hanging over his white shirt collar, resting on the diamond stickpin in his purple tie. His face was as round as a ball, loose-skinned, and dead-white against the red drapes behind him. His hair was black, straight, with frontal baldness, the forehead sloping. The nose was pug, his ears small and flat. His mouth was large, thick-lipped, and drooped at the corners, giving him a sulking countenance. There was a mole on his left cheek.

The two-hundred-buck blue flannels he was wearing looked like a burlap sack with the potatoes still in it. I noticed his pudgy right hand, with a big diamond on the pinky, holding a green unlit cigar. He looked at me impatiently, and kept glancing at himself in the wall mirror that faced him.

"This is Jim Cox," Al said in his gravel voice.

Thompson turned fully and studied me. "You took enough time getting here." He had a voice like a toy steam engine, all wheeze and blow. He stuck out his flabby right.

I dropped the suitcase, went over and pumped the hand, and watched his little dark eyes shoot to the door. I followed his gaze and saw a tall, thin guy had entered.

He was a serious-faced man with a sharp nose, thin arched lips, a slim, long neck and long pointed devil-ears. His skin was coarse, with a few pockmarks, his eyes pale blue, sadistic, his hair a curly blond-gray, white at the temples. He was square-shouldered in Oxford tweed. He saw me and cocked one eyebrow. It gave him an air of insolence.

"This is Fieldman, Jim," Thompson's voice came over.

I nodded at Fieldman. He nodded back. My gaze went to Thompson, in time to see him give the nod to Al. In a beehive like this, you watch the angles. When Al started his move for my pocket I spun and caught his arm just above the elbow. I kicked him in the knees, pulled him over my back, and flopped him on the floor. I stood with my foot on his right arm.

"Don't pull that again!" I said quietly. "If you want my gun, ask for it."

I picked him up by the collar and slapped him against the mirrored wall. I held him there and looked down at Thompson. He sat staring, dead-pan, not moving a muscle. Fieldman stood beside him, tight-lipped. Blood was still pounding in my temples. I took Jim's gun from my pocket and threw it on the desk.

That was when Thompson laughed.

First he sneaked an admiring glance in the mirror. He smiled, then he laughed, his fat belly hanging over his pants, shaking and quivering.

"Say!" he said, wiping the tears from his eyes. "You're all right! That'll teach Al." He grinned up at me with admiration. "Jim Cox, eh?" He gestured to the empty chair by his desk. "Okay, Jim, sit down where I can see you."

I sat. Thompson kept looking at me, then shook his head regretfully, "Humm! Isn't it too bad about Les!"

"Yeah."

He leaned closer, pursed his lips, then said in a confidential tone, "Who got him?"

"Cigarette," a voice said. It was low, husky, and feminine. I didn't see the leg until then, outstretched past the arm of the sofa.

On the other side, a dame was lying on the couch, watching television.

"We got our ideas about Les," I said, trying to think calmly and clearly. "He's—"

My voice died out. Thompson wasn't listening. He was on his feet, moving toward the couch, his gold cigarette case open. I watched long, tapered fingers, with blood-red polish, reach up from behind the couch and select a cigarette. Thompson started back.

"Match, Stupid!" the husky voice snapped.

Thompson whirled and bent over the couch. There was the sound of his lighter clinking open and shut. During this, my eyes went back to the leg. It was as good as Grable's, filmed in a sheer black stocking, tapered thin at the ankle. Everything a left leg should be. If the right one matched, the dame had legs!

Thompson came back at the desk. "You figure—" he began.

"Turn off the light," the woman's voice interrupted. "And be quiet!"

Thompson sat down. He spoke no louder than a whisper. "Who you figure got Les?"

It was a hell of a good question. "I've got ideas," I said, and tried to look bright. "But you can't be sure."

"Syd Rearden?" Fieldman asked in a smooth, cultured tone. He was still standing at Thompson's right, and behind him Al was posed against the mirrored wall, exactly the way I'd left him.

I lighted a cigarette, stalling, and blew out a thick stream of smoke. "Could be Syd," I said. "Wouldn't surprise me if—"

This time I was thankful for the interruption. The dame's voice was with us again, this time tinged with a slight snarl:

"I said turn off the light!"

Thompson sprang to his feet again, spry as a cat, and bounced for the switch at the door. He doused the overhead, then came back, sat down again, and lighted the cigar.

In the dim light of the desk lamp he looked grotesque. When he spoke it was so softly I had to lean closer to hear him.

"Les was a crazy bastard," he was saying, "and a nice guy. We had a hell of a beef in Forty-seven, but he shot square with me. That's when we agreed to help each other out. We—" He broke off, a smile jerking up the second chin. "Did he keep on running around with Peggy? Hell, that woman!"

"That woman is right!" I said with significance, and tried to pass it.

Once more hot fear prickled my scalp. There was a lot I knew about Les Ties, but more that I didn't know. I wondered if this was Thompson's way of catching up with me. What if there'd been no Peggy at all! I looked up at the three grim faces with cold sweat beading my forehead.

"You were in on the last jewelry job?" Thompson asked.

"Hell, yes."

He smiled. "Then I've no qualms about you, kid. That was performance! Just keep your nose clean around here and you'll work in fine!"

I sat there nodding. It was like a drama, some scene on a stage or out of a movie. I was part of it! I had lines to speak, and they damned well better not ring phony.

I stubbed out my cigarette. "How long you figure it'll take?"

He shrugged. "A couple weeks maybe." He looked at me. "Any hurry?"

"Have to get back to Chicago," I told him. "I got a deal there that's good. This town stinks! I promised Les, otherwise I wouldn't be here."

I could feel my lips twitching.

The smile left Thompson's face. "You're nervous."

I nodded and tried to grin. "A strange setup like this always gives me the shakes. You wonder if you're not hitching up to a pine box."

The dark eyes narrowed. He pointed the cigar at me. "Look, Buster, you don't trust Louie Thompson?"

"Are you kidding!" I said, hard. Words just came out. "I know you're a right guy. Hell! I remember you from way back, when I was a punk with the Red Fossett outfit. Seems to me he took orders from you, and seems to me you could give 'em!"

He sank back in the chair, nodded in dreamily, and admired himself in the mirror. "Yeah. Those were the days. Dillinger, Baby-Face Nelson—"

My eyes had shifted to the door beside the television set. I got a glimpse of a kitchen sink. To my left was another door, standing open. I could see beyond into a bedroom.

"Sometimes I wish I was back in the old days," Thompson was saying. He puffed thoughtfully on his cigar. "Still working for Capone. With Prohibition and the way Al was running things, a guy could always make a buck." He smiled. "You don't remember much about that, do you?"

"Not much. I've seen Capone a couple times, though, when I was a small-fry selling newspapers."

"I knew him way back," he said with nostalgia. "When he was producer and manager for the Four Deuces. It seems like yesterday. Two-two-two-two South Wabash." He grinned. "I can still see Al outside in the snow, hustlin', his coat collar turned up, sayin', 'Wouldn't you like to drink some beer with a pretty girl?'" He laughed quietly, the fat shaking.

"That was before my time," I said. "But I ran up against Dillinger once."

"Dillinger?" he reminisced. "He was a good heavy, but he was a butterfly! Always flittin' around dames and bright lights. Didn't know enough to sit tight." He paused. "Me? I always played it safe."

"Yeah," I agreed. "You got yourself a reputation." My eyes wandered to Al and Fieldman. "But I never heard of these guys, and I'm curious."

"Counsel here?" Thompson looked up at Fieldman. "Counsel has brains and guts! Spent seven years in the Bastille. Used to be a top-notch attorney in L. A. Took a fall for narcotics." His eyes moved to Al. "Al's no busher. He's been on the grift all his life." His gaze shifted back to me. "You done any time in stir?"

I shook my head, "Played it too smart."

"Good," he said grimly. "Al there's a hell of a box man. All my men are twenty-four karat. Wouldn't be working for me if they wasn't. You'll meet Tex and Monroe in the morning." His eyes wandered over to the couch. "And Madge there is also twenty-four karat. Relax, kid. You're in for some heavy scratch. Tomorrow morning you'll learn the dope. You're—"

His voice trailed off. He was staring at something on the floor by his desk. His eyes went pale. He turned in his chair and looked slowly up at Al. "I told you over a half-hour ago to mail this."

Al gave him a lopsided grin. "Ever hear of a post office bein' open this time of night?"

Thompson's lips narrowed into a thin line. "I told you Madge wants it mailed!"

"But, Boss, if the post office ain't—"

Thompson's voice shot high. "Madge wants it mailed." His lower lip curled. "Tonight!"

Al gave him an ingratiating smile. "Okay, okay, okay." He picked up the box. It was wrapped for mailing. He staggered a little under its weight, and went on out the door.

Thompson relaxed and nodded toward the couch. "Madge here's got a mother complex. Each week a box of foods got to go to the kids in Europe. Madge says—"

"I say," Fieldman interrupted with dignity, "we should permit Europe to care for their own kids."

The feminine voice shot out from behind the couch: "You say that, Counsel, because you're a filthy selfish pig!"

Fieldman sneered and raised his eyebrows. Thompson chuckled heartily from low in his throat.

Fieldman glanced at his polished fingernails. "Madge is playful tonight," he mused. "Cute as a rattler."

Once more all humor vanished front Thompson's face. Fieldman took one look at him, straightened, then hurried over to the couch.

"Sorry, Madge," he apologized. "No offense."

There was soft sobbing from behind the couch. Thompson got up, went over and looked down. "Don't cry," he said tenderly, as if to a child. "You're just bored. Why don't you go down and sing?"

"Nobody wants to hear me," the dame's voice shot out. "Nobody listens. They go on feeding their mouths and talking. Pay more attention to the jukebox than to me. Everybody but you knows I don't have a voice."

"You *have*, Madge," Thompson insisted fervently. "Your voice is beautiful!"

"That's a lie!" she sobbed. "Nobody wants to hear me!"

"*I* do, Madge." Thompson's voice was sickly sweet. "Sing 'My Heart Stood Still', for me."

"You never listen," she whined. "Nobody listens."

Thompson stood tensely, his lips moving in misery, his face red, bloated, his jaw set. Little veins stood out on the side of his face.

"Well, damn it!" he shouted. "You go down there and sing! And if anybody makes one sound I'll tell 'em! I'll say 'Damn it, this girl is *singing!* And you birds listen! You birds listen, or get your asses out of here!'"

He stood panting. An oppressive quiet closed in. The room suddenly lost its heartbeat. The girl cried on, making little sniffling noises.

Thompson's shoulders slumped. He walked back to his desk and looked at me again, as though seeing me for the first time.

"In the morning," he said morosely, "we'll have breakfast at the Dairy Lunch. On Fourth Street, It's between Howser and Broadway. Meet me inside at nine-thirty."

I nodded and got up. I jabbed Jim's gun back in my pocket and carried my luggage to the door.

"There's no dough until the heist," he wheezed, "unless you need— Hell, I'm squeezed myself, but—"

"I got enough to see me through," I said, and started for the door.

"Say, Jim—"

I turned back to him.

"I've checked with the Hotel Brennan," he said. "It's in the next block. They've got a vacancy. Make your quarters there."

I nodded and went out the door, down the hall, down the steps, through the café, and outside.

IV

My knees were feeling weak as I carried Jim's suitcase through the rain in the direction of the Hotel Brennan. It was the damnedest setup I'd ever bumped into! Why the sobbing dame? Why did Thompson humor her, melt when he talked to her?

I hit the corner drugstore and paused, looking at the window display, wondering about calling Roberts. I decided against it. There was plenty of time. The only information so far was that there was definitely going to be a heist, and a hot one if it would take five guys besides myself. In the morning I'd be the man who came to breakfast and meet the rest of the outfit.

I wondered if Thompson was going to check with Red Fossett, and kicked myself for having said I was once with his mob. I'd have to become more tight-lipped, more impatient to get at the job and back to Chicago.

It was then that I saw the shadow. Little Al, hugging the buildings, a half block behind me, sent by Thompson! I felt cold. Why had Thompson sicked Al on me! A suspicion that I wasn't Jim Cox? Holy hell! Maybe Thompson was play-acting, too! Maybe I'd already tipped my hand! Maybe he was just playing around with me, like a mother lion with her cub, until she gets the idea that the kid's lived long enough!

I hurried on up to the Brennan. Registering at the desk I could feel the little black shoe-button eyes peering from outside the window. The desk clerk's eyes were on me, too. He was a little Greek with patches of black fuzz resting on big flabby ears. Nobody had to tell me that he was being paid by Thompson to keep close tabs on me. Calling Roberts from the hotel would be out of the question.

I took the key to 218 and went up. It was a crummy little room. A buck a night. There was a phone, a rug, a rocker, a dresser, a bed, and running water. At least the sheets were clean.

I put the .38 under my pillow, then dug out my bottle of rye from the suitcase. I sat on the bed nursing it, while big splotchy raindrops pelted the windowpane. I listened to the snoring from next door, breathed in the sour, spongy odor of wet must, and watched a big brown spider swing across its web from the ceiling.

I thought about Florence—then about Betty, and how much we both hated sleeping alone. I got undressed. In bed, lights out, I lay awake for a long time wondering about my new business partners. It was disagreeable duty—strictly for the birds! I didn't like it.

There were a lot of things about working for the cops I didn't like. Not that I felt any sympathy for the hardened criminal; I didn't. Thompson was going to get what had been coming to him for a long time. Sure, they were blind mice, trapped before they started, and I was the executioner, but I didn't think too much about that part. I was too busy worrying about my own hide.

It was a job. Perfunctory. With risk and danger—breakers ahead! You damned well swam or sank! It couldn't be over with fast enough to suit me!

The dame—I thought. A dame always slows things up. What the hell kind of a woman did Thompson have, anyway? A hoodess was usually trustful, loyal, a slave to her master—but with a heart of cobblestone, so hard-bitten she couldn't cry at her own mother's funeral.

Thompson's dame was a babe in arms, throwing tantrums ...

In the morning the city was clear and bright after the deluge of rain. I crossed Howser Street and sauntered on up to the Dairy Lunch. It was on an alley facing Fourth—one of those middle-block, deteriorated, ptomaine breeders where each morning some tired chef knocks cockroaches and rat tracks out of the pans and dumps in the soup-du-jour.

I passed the rain- and dirt-streaked windows and went inside. There was a smell of greasy french-fries—big plate side windows, overlooking the garbage cans of the alley. Sunshine streamed in, providing customers with the vitamins boiled out of the chow.

Thompson, Fieldman and Al were already seated off to one side, by the floor-length windows. With them sat a good-looking thug of thirty or so. Black Irish, with an abundance of curly black hair. He was neatly shaved, immaculately dressed in a dark gray suit, white shirt and yellow tie.

To all appearances the four of them might have been business men from any of the nearby office buildings, grabbing a late breakfast. Actually they represented the lowest dregs of humanity, with little left to lose.

Fieldman, a disbarred attorney, seven lost years behind him. Sprung now and ready to risk it all over. Al, too, with a prison record. And Thompson, a coward, a man of false nerve; bestial, swinish, whose career dated back to Capone; who, through conceit, had played the rackets more slowly, more careful of his hide than most of them, drawing luck all the way. Now again he was running loose because of help from shyster lawyers, payoffs, and law technicality.

He'd made enough to retire, but had spent it basking under the Miami sun. Short on dough, and burning with the old greed and fever, he was ready for a new kill. I watched him gulp a pork chop down his fat sloppy throat, grease dripping down on the stick pin and onto his tie. He looked up and saw me, his dark eyes wide-awake and shining. There was a glossy ring surrounding the iris.

"Hello, Cox."

I grunted something, nodded to Fieldman, and dropped in the empty chair.

"This is Monroe, Jim."

"Hello, Monroe," I said and got a close-up.

He was of medium build, his face thin and lined, in his dark brown eyes the look of a fanatic. He sat tensely, thin-lipped, energy suppressed within him. It took a terrible patience for him to sit there quietly lapping up hot cakes and sausage.

"Here's Tex," Thompson said, looking toward the entrance.

A big moose, around six-two, with heavy shoulders, thin hips, red hair and freckles, was moving toward us. There was a slow rhythm in his arms and legs. Now, with the air of a vagabond, he pulled up a chair.

"Tex—meet Jim."

"Howdy." His Southern drawl carried a faint lisp.

A weary waitress made her appearance.

I ordered Number Seven. Tex mumbled, "Coffee." When she left, Thompson said:

"Jim—"

"Yeah."

"These are the men you'll be working with." He looked at Tex, then Monroe. "If either of you are worrying about Jim here, he was with Les Ties. Says enough, don't it?"

Monroe scratched an armpit, smiled slightly, and studied me. Tex drawled, "It sure does. Anybody with—"

"We'll all concentrate on our plates," Thompson broke in. "Because we all know the setup and plans. Except you, Jim." He glanced at his watch, then went on promptly. "You're to look past Fourth, across the alley."

My eyes came up. I looked out the big plate-glass window. At first I saw only the pedestrians—office girls, shoppers, couples, the slow drag of traffic. Across Fourth the alley continued and then, cater-cornered to the Dairy Lunch, I saw the rear of the big Southwest Bank, with its iron grilled windows, its impenetrable steel slab door that could he opened only from the inside.

"Ever hear of Western Money Transport, Incorporated, Jim?"

I felt short of breath. I sat stiffly, trying to keep my face expressionless. "Vaguely," I answered.

Thompson's voice was a purr. "They handle all the dough that goes to the pari-mutuel windows at the track."

I nodded, feeling my heart take on an extra beat. The waitress was back now, setting down my Number Seven, and coffee before Tex.

After she moved off, Thompson sat quietly, his back to the windows. He glanced at his watch again, then his voice dropped to a whisper.

"There's an armored truck pulling up at the rear of the bank."

"Yeah," I breathed, and wondered if he knew the rest!

The truck was turret-topped; glass windows; with a guard alongside the driver. On the rear were small round ports to stick gun barrels through. A second guard was riding the rear.

I watched awkwardly while Thompson took a silk handkerchief from his pocket and wiped his forehead. "What you suppose they're carrying in the way of artillery?" his voice purred.

"Probably pump shotguns and forty-fives," I mumbled. "Or thirty-eights."

His eyes were on his wrist watch. "In a minute the rear guard will go to the back door of the bank. He'll say 'Open Sesame' to the bank guard. The truck driver and a guard from the bank will start loading the dough. The other two are watchdogs." He sank back, his eyes suddenly glassy. "Over a million bucks take!" he wheezed.

I wondered if any of them could hear the hammering of my heart.

Fieldman leaned toward me. His smile was sickly, and he was breathing too hard. "They have such a heavy load that we're going to help them carry it!"

A nervous, ugly little smile twisted Thompson's lips. He held up his coffee cup with the pinky raised, the diamond glittering too bright. "The scratch isn't marked. It's baled in bills. The complete payoff for a day at the races!" His eyes flickered. "We're the guys at the window, with a win ticket for over a million!" He swallowed; his voice trembled so that he could scarcely speak: "Split seven ways it's still a lot of walking-around money!"

I found my voice. "I only count six of us. Who gets the seventh slice?"

Thompson's mouth jumped. "I get two satchels. That's all there is to it." His face and neck got red. "If you don't like it, speak your piece now. It's okay with Tex, and Monroe. We've already talked it over. After all, you're a latecomer. I get two satchels, kid."

"Just thought I'd ask," I said. "It's okay by me."

I was doing some heavy thinking about the seventh satchel. I wondered if there was a voice over Thompson. It was something that Captain Roberts hadn't figured when he briefed me.

"Keep your eye on the ball, Cox."

I looked back out the window.

"Notice," Thompson wheezed, "the driver getting out of the truck and walking over to lean against the wall of the bank building. He's got a bird gun, probably a twelve-gauge. He can't use it because he's spending too much time doing other things. Watch him. You'll see."

"Who does the drill job?" I blurted nervously.

There was a dead silence. They all looked at me.

"What drill job?" Thompson asked with a touch of exasperation.

"The one on the truck," I said. "They—they're like a safe, aren't they?"

Monroe smiled. "No drill job to it." His voice was husky and toneless. "You'll see that when you learn how it's planned."

Thompson leaned forward. "Watch closely. One of the truck bulls is inside the bank signing for the dough. That leaves the two guards, one leaning against the building; the other one is asleep at the front of the truck. They think their job's a pension. We'll catch them flat-footed. They haven't had a knock-over in nine years. Watch Buster there, keeping his eyes peeled for anything in skirts that's coming up Fourth Street. In his mind he can probably undress a woman faster than anybody." He grunted a laugh.

"Yeah."

Thompson relaxed. I picked up my coffee cup, then set it down quick. My hand was shaking like I had palsy.

"Every day the same," Thompson went on softly. "It's a drop-in. Sweetest setup I ever saw." He lighted a half-buck cigar. "Okay, Jim, that's it. Meet me at my place in fifteen minutes. You'll see how the plan goes." He rose abruptly, then hesitated. "Better make it a half hour. I've got business to attend to."

He moved off, Fieldman and Al close behind. I sat there numbly with Monroe and Tex. A dead silence closed in.

"Glad you're with us, Cox," Tex finally said, breaking the gloom.

"Thanks," I managed.

He turned to Monroe. "Heard from Dorothy yet?"

Monroe shook his head grimly.

"You will," Tex assured him.

Monroe rose to his feet. "I will in a pig's eye!" He picked up his coat and moved off toward the entrance.

Tex still sat there, leisurely sipping his coffee. He nodded after Monroe. "His woman left him a couple weeks ago."

"Too bad," I said.

He sighed and gazed thoughtfully at his cup. "Dames are like bees. Buzz around a guy till the honey's gone."

"Yeah," I agreed.

"But Monroe is still hoping. Thinks when this job's over and he's on the plush she'll come running back." He sighed again. "Guess no guy gets in on something as big as this except for a reason." He looked at me. "And the reason's always a dame. Take Fieldman. The guy's lost a bolt. Needs dough to set up a little broad in the dress manufacturing business. She's fetish for a needle."

"How about Thompson?" I said. "I thought he was through."

Tex shrugged. "What do you do when you're stone broke? He's got a bunch of bum paper out. All because of some phony society dame in Miami." He paused in thought. "I'm telling you it's all for dames that guys risk their necks!"

"How about you, Tex?"

"Me?" He grinned. "Let's say I'm doing it for a horse. I'm itchin' to buy back a ranch that a loan outfit stole from old man."

"Well, here's luck," I said.

He nodded. "We'll need it. We'll shore be needin' it." He glanced out the window to the armored truck. "Too big, I'm afraid." He eyed me. "Nothin' had better go wrong."

He left.

I sat there in a cold sweat, watching the truck bulls load the dough—sack after sack. Over a million bucks!

V

When I left the Dairy Lunch the truck was backing out of the alley, heading west on its way to the track. It was then that I glimpsed Al again. He was standing across the street at the corner newsstand. From what I could judge he was the guy to watch—Thompson's stoolie, errand boy, guard, and tail man. Including being the night bartender when there was nothing else for him to do.

I crossed Fourth Street and boarded a streetcar back to the White Lion. I watched Al, in pantomime, still at the corner, screaming for a cab to stop. In a minute he'd be hot on my trail wherever it might lead. Roberts was going to have to sit and sweat until I could find a phone without Al counting the dial clicks.

This time, though, I got to the White Lion before he did, and when I went straight through the bar, opened the door with the big brass knob and hurried upstairs, there was soft masculine humming from inside the door marked "PRIVATE—OFFICE." I cleared my throat and knocked.

Then she stood before me.

The right leg matched the left just fine, and they were even better in a vertical position. She was a babe, all right. Long, shining red hair, past her shoulders. Large gray-greenish eyes with an impudent look, the lids darkened with green shadow, the lashes thick with mascara, skin too white.

Her mouth was full and sensual, glistening with too much brilliant orange paint. A voluptuous body in a white silk dress cut so tight you could see the nipples of her full ripe breasts. If you had the time you could even see the bone structure, and the muscles of her thighs. She wore no bra, and there was no pantie line.

She stared up at me, a little longer than seemed necessary, and I guess I was working overtime myself. She put her hands on her hips and, with grace and arrogance, threw back her head.

Then, with an air of importance she said: "Who are you, may I ask?"

The voice was about five shades too low. One of those sexy tough voices that she'd copied out of some movie. I'd seen her kind before—when the Vice Squad rooted a nest of them out of their rooms and checked them into the wagon while their madame screeched like a parrot. Evidently she hadn't been aware of my presence last night, didn't know that I'd already seen her or, that is, part of her. She didn't know that I already had her tabbed.

"I'm Jim Cox," I said. "Thompson wants to see me."

Her expression changed. "You—you're Jim Cox?" She preened before me, showing off her wares. "Oh, yes, come in. Louie did speak of you, the new—drummer—from Chicago. I'm Madge Morton, and this"—she gestured to a little guy sitting on a chair by the couch—"is Dr. Sloan."

The little man was somewhere in his late forties, with a weak face, a mean, loose mouth; and the eyes were brown and sensitive and shone too bright. I pegged him—a snowbird. The tan suit he was wearing was unpressed and baggy, knees worn thin, shoulder pads hanging. A beat-up brown felt that he must have had in college was smashed down over his hair.

He looked dirty, inefficient, the kind of a doctor I wouldn't let cut my toe-nails. He sat there quietly, humming softly and sucking on his long upper lip, drumming his fingers against the small black satchel he held in his lap.

"Ili," he said, and went on humming.

She gestured impatiently. "Sit down, Jim. Louie won't be long. Take a load off your feet." She looked me over. "Quite a load at that. My guess is two hundred."

"Two twenty," I said drily.

She picked up a cigarette from the desk and lighted it. She kept looking at me. Her eyes came up slowly—with meaning behind them. "I always say the bigger they come the harder they fall."

I met her gaze. "I don't trip easily."

She laughed low in her throat. Her eyelids glistened. "I'll bet you don't trip easy, Jim," she said in her slow, hard, phony voice. "I'll bet all a girl's got to do is wink."

I pulled my eyes off her, and saw that the doc was taking it all in. I walked away from her and went over to a chair by the window. "I'll wait for Thompson," I said.

She moved closer. "I really don't know when to expect him," she said sweetly. "I know nothing of Louie's affairs." She smiled coyly. "You see, I just sing here." She struck a prima donna pose. "I'm the new singer."

A torrent of laughter shook the room. "Ha—ha—ha!" The little doc held his sides. "That's a hot one! The new singer, eh? If you're a singer I'm an acrobat team."

She winced, turned slowly and stared at him, blood draining from her face. "I am!" she cried with vehemence, "I'm a singer! I once sang with a twenty-piece band!"

"Salvation Army?" Doc said, and went into another convulsion of laughter.

She waved her arms furiously; little darts of fire flew from her eyes. "I'm a *singer!*" she panted. Her breasts quivered. "Dammit, I am! I even sang at the Roxy! You two-bit ex-abortionist, what would you know about singing!"

The doc sobered fast. He paled, then shrugged.

"Hell," he said, "maybe you sang in a church choir if you feel any better."

She kept staring at him, still panting, with tears of fury in her eyes. "I'm asking you!" she shouted. "Tell me what you know about singing!"

"I—" he swallowed hard—"I used to sing in a choir myself."

She whirled to me. "Somebody ought to tell him what a son-of-a-bitch he is!" She tried to smile. "Knows all about music, Doc here. Hatched in Harlem. Used to have his own mob of hijackers, thieves and narcotic peddlers." She laughed a little hysterically. "How many patients now, Doc?"

"Go to hell," he said.

She bristled; words gushed out: "Quite a clientele, haven't you? People begging and stealing for your morphine." She turned to me, her voice deeply sarcastic. "The doctor is a specialist now. In plastic surgery and bullet extraction."

He shot to his feet and hurried to the door. "You got too much energy, kid!" He slammed the door behind him.

There was a dead silence. Through it I heard the sound of heavy footsteps in the hall, growing closer. When she spoke again her voice was hard and bitter:

"I know why you're here, Jim. To join our lovely little family." A deep sob escaped her lips, shaking her body. "Don't mind me. I cry at least once a day."

She left the room just as Thompson came in, with Fieldman and the little doc trailing in behind him.

Fieldman pulled off his topcoat. Thompson threw his hat on a chair and grinned at me. "Sit tight for a second, Jim. Got to get my Vitamin-B shot." He turned to the doc. "Hurry it up. I got business on hand."

I watched the doc open his satchel and fumble for a second. He brought out a hypodermic needle and hurried over to Thompson.

"Don't point that thing at me," Thompson told him.

The doc sighed with weary patience. "Take down your pants."

Thompson unbuckled his belt while casting uneasy glances at the needle in Doc's hand. He pulled down his trousers and bent over. "How do I know that thing ain't got germ warfare in it instead of Vitamin-B," he whined.

Doc laughed and advanced with the needle.

"Go easy—watch it—careful," Thompson kept saying, and then yelled like a woman as the doc stuck the needle into his fat right buttock.

In a minute the needle was pulled out, and Thompson was brushing the thin film of sweat off his upper lip and buttoning up his trousers. The doc looked at me and chuckled.

"A good man, Thompson," he said. His voice lowered. "But he squeals like a pig when he's stuck." He looked back at his victim. "Got something big in the fire, haven't you, Louie?"

"Nuts," Thompson told him.

Doc was packing his needle. "Oh, yeah. I can always tell by your eyes when something's stewing." He slammed the satchel shut. "Don't worry. I want no part of it. I'm glad you tossed me out."

Thompson pulled up his zipper. "You proved your worth last time. As I remember, just as I needed you, you were caught in a snowstorm."

Doc looked at him uneasily. "That was five years ago. Now I've grown up."

Thompson's eyes contracted to pin-points. "You'll never grow up, Doc. You like your own needle too well."

Doc laughed. "Someday you'll want a favor from me. You'll want me to remodel your features—like I did with Bobbie Altman."

"I like my looks," Thompson told him. He rubbed his chin in thought, then grinned. "You ought to have heard Johnny Dillinger tell how the butchers almost killed him." He gestured with his cigar. "In the middle of the facelift his pumper stopped!" He looked at me, the grin spreading. "Honest to God. A good five seconds before he died one of the docs had sense to grab his tongue and jab an elbow in his ribs. They told Johnny about it after the operation. It cost him five grand."

"Where he is now," the little doc chimed in, "he don't have to worry about it." He marched to the door, saluted, said, "See you next week,

Louie. Prepare to turn the other cheek."

He made his exit, the black satchel bumping his knees.

Thompson looked after him. "I've known that little croaker for ten years," he said slowly. "And I still don't trust him." He shrugged it off and grinned again at me. "Maybe it's the needle. Come on over here, Jim." He rubbed his right buttock and sat at his desk in contemplation.

I got up and sat down facing him. Fieldman stood quietly.

"Okay," Thompson said, "here's the deal. It's going to take sweat and a lot of work, but it's worth it. Nobody's in the middle. It's a frolic for all."

He clapped his fat hands together, and got up. He opened a small wall safe, concealed behind the red drapes, brought out a paper, and slapped it down on the desk facing me. I saw that it was a crudely drawn map, showing the area around the Southwest Bank, the alley, buildings and streets. He picked up a pencil, squinted, and dropped its tip on the building marked "B."

"Here's the bank," he explained. "Here, across the alley, is the rear of the Coolidge Building, its arcade running through from Fifth Street—"

His voice ground on. I listened to the whole fantastic plan, the setup, what each of us was to do, how it timed out, the precision of it. The more he talked the less fantastic it became. For a million bucks those guys could do a lot of planning. I sat here, thinking about the energy that they were spending on the thing. If they'd put it into legitimate work they'd all be rich.

"Fieldman will drive," he was saying in short, clipped tones. "He'll drop Tex on Howser. Tex will walk down the alley to the rear of the bank, a two-minute walk. Monroe will get out here, across the street from the alley. You'll get out in front of the Arcade—use two minutes in getting through to the alley. In that time Fieldman will drive on, turn down to the bank and wait to follow the truck out. Tex will drive the truck down to the Bank of America, three blocks down. Corner of Sixth and Oak. You'll unload the truck there. Right in front of the public. That way it ain't gonna cause any comment. Average people will think they're delivering money to the bank. You go it straight?"

"Yeah, yeah." I was sweating. "I hope the keys are in the truck."

He nodded confidently. "Tex checked it careful. The keys have been in the ignition every morning so far. All Tex does is drive it out." He went on, "Fieldman will have suitcases in the car. Also some G.I. coveralls for you guys to slip on over your Brownie outfits."

"Brownie outfits?"

"Hell, yes. You guys'll be outfitted just like the truck guards. By the way, I want your shirt and trouser measurements so's Fieldman can pick up your uniform this afternoon. We get 'em at the Union Outfitting Company; they carry a big stock."

"Thirty-seven-trouser length," I said. "Sixteen shirt. Thirty-four sleeves."

He wrote it down, then looked up thoughtfully. "At the Bank of America Fieldman will pull up in back of the truck and you'll load. Then he'll bring you guys and the dough to me at a little motel I've picked out."

VI

There was a sudden loud buzzing in the room. Thompson got up and walked over to a table. He picked up the cream-colored house phone. He listened for a second, grunted something about a shortage on the liquor order. He slammed down the receiver, then turned back to me.

"Study the map, Jim. If you get any good ideas, let me know. I'll be downstairs for a minute."

Fieldman left with him.

Then she came back in. I could feel her, I didn't look up, but I could hear her. She tore out a match from a book and lighted a cigarette. Then her voice came:

"I don't know why I said I was a singer here."

"That's all right," I said.

There was a dead silence. I could hear her breathing.

"You know I'm Louie's girl, don't you?"

I nodded.

She straightened. "Well, he's a nice guy. Don't make 'em any better than Louie Thompson." She went over to the window and stood quietly. "I got nothing to be ashamed of." She paused. "I'm proud of it." There was another silence. I could feel energy burning inside her. "This job's got to go right, Jim."

"Yeah."

She took a quick breath. "When it's over, Louie's taking me on a Caribbean cruise. Then we're going to come back and start living. We might even get married, I don't know." She shrugged, with a heave of her chest. "He wants to bad enough. I guess a girl could do worse. He— he's a nice enough guy." She looked at me for assurance.

"A nice guy," I said.

She nodded and tried to believe it. "I guess having kids by him wouldn't be so bad." She paused in thought; her eyes lost their light. "Sometimes kids are real cute even when the old man is a pot-bellied freak and a creep." She wet her lips. "You—you think kids by Louie might be okay?"

"Hell, yes. He's a swell guy."

Her voice dropped. "He's a little man who must feel important. Now he's playing second fiddle, and doesn't like it."

I nodded and took a chance. "I know—there's a big boss. In New York, eh?"

"No," she said. "He's right here in town." She walked over to the wall mirror. "Louie wants just this one final chance at big-time. Says he's learned not to blow his dough. He'll save it and try to invest right." She studied herself in the mirror. "Maybe this *isn't* all a pipe dream. Maybe I'm the kind of dame that *should* marry a walrus. Hell, maybe marriage is in the cards."

There was the sound of a door clicking shut down the hall, and now Thompson's voice in the hall.

"I always wanted to get married," she said. "I guess any girl does." She crushed out her cigarette in the desk tray and moved slowly to the bedroom door. She turned to me.

"I even know how to make bread," she said.

She left. I just sat there. And then the door opened and Thompson came in.

His eyes shone. "Any questions?"

"Yeah. When does it come off?"

He flopped down behind the desk. "You'll know in plenty of time. In the morning I want you guys to meet and time the distance from all points."

"Rehearsal, eh?"

He nodded. "We can use it. It's got to work like Swiss movement. No bloomers. None of my boys are winding up on the cold meat cart! We don't want this to curdle. Fieldman will pick you up in front of your hotel at nine in the morning." He cleared his throat. "Check in with me when you're through...."

That night I called Roberts at his home. He answered the phone.

"This is Wade, Captain."

"Where the hell are you?"

"A little drugstore on First Street. I've spent two hours going 'round in circles to ditch my tail."

"Yeah, Wade?" he said anxiously. "What are the developments?"

"It's a bank job. A honey. Hold on to your hat! A million bucks involved!" I could hear him let out his breath. "Six in on the take, plus a dame on the outside but in on the know." I hurried on, "A big boss we never figured. I'll have the finger on him soon. Do I make myself clear?"

"Perfectly."

"If Louie's running stuff," I went on, "I've got the little doc that's probably supplying it."

"When do we close?" he asked calmly.

"Time's not set. Sit tight and wait. I'm sitting on a pin myself." I paused. "The dame's poison. But it's from her that I'll get the brains."

"A little soft talk," he said, "and a woman comes through. When can I expect the dope?"

"Won't be long now."

"Good work, boy. Be careful."

"Thanks. If I can't see you personally, I'll drop a report in the mail. They're watching me close. If you don't hear from me for a couple days don't worry. You'll know the date in advance."

"Okay," he said.

"You still got Jim Cox—I hope?"

He laughed. "Yeah. Don't worry."

"You'll be hearing from me," I said.

I hung the receiver up, then lifted it and dialed again.

"Darling!" Betty said. "Are you all right?"

"Yeah. I can't talk long. Stop worrying."

"I'm not worrying. Dearest?"

"Yeah."

"I miss you so."

"I'm glad, honey."

"Think you'll be home soon?"

"A week at the most should see me through."

"Are you taking care of yourself?"

"Of course, Betty, I'm fine."

"Oh, Wade—Florence almost flew today. She's trying again."

"Give her my congratulations."

"She seems to have new courage."

"Swell. I'll call you again first chance."

"Good night sweetheart."

"Good night, sweetheart," I said....

At nine the next morning Fieldman pulled up to the curb outside the Hotel Brennan. I made a mental note of the license plates, and threw open the door of the black Chrysler sedan.

He pulled out, saying that we'd first pick up Tex and Monroe. We turned right, and traveled east on Fletcher Drive until he stopped in front of a modern green-and-white apartment building—the Fletcher

Arms.

Monroe was waiting outside. He hurried over and hopped in the back seat. Fieldman drove on, turning left on Main Street. He stopped a few doors from the corner, then parked in front of the hotel while Monroe went inside and got Tex.

Next the four of us were parked across the street from the Coolidge Building. Fieldman was off on a tangent about nerves—said anything was possible if a guy kept his guts. He went on about the artillery we'd be carrying, and finally glanced at his watch. Then he looked at me.

"Let's get a time back," he said. "It's nine-thirty-five. In five seconds it'll be nine thirty-six. Set your watches." He looked at me. "Jim, you go first. At exactly nine forty-seven you get out and walk leisurely through the Arcade. You'll see how it's timed so that you'll all meet in the alley."

He kept looking at his watch. Then he gave me the signal.

"Okay," he said softly. "Get going."

I got out. He started the car and drove off. I went across Fourth Street and entered the Arcade. I passed a liquor store at the entrance, a dress shop, a barber shop—people. It was easy, because it wasn't real.

The armored truck was in the alley. Tex was coming down the alley to my right, Monroe closing in to my left. We ignored each other. Tex passed close to the truck, glancing in at the ignition.

I retraced my steps, back through the Coolidge Building Arcade. In a minute Fieldman pulled up, with Tex and Monroe in the back seat.

I climbed in.

"The key was there," Tex said. "It's always there."

"About the right timing, wasn't it?" Monroe put in.

"I got there a fraction too soon," I told him. "I can stall a few seconds longer until Tex moves in closer."

"It'll work," Tex said uncertainly. "We'd better not go through it again. All we need now is for some smart cookie to get wise."

"I'll drop you guys back," Fieldman said. "Then I've got things to do." He looked at me. "Check in with Thompson. He's waiting for you."

I got out and caught a streetcar back down Fourth Street.

I found Thompson alone, his face neatly shaved, shining, and stinking of heavy cologne. He was seated behind his desk, sipping coffee and holding a green panatela. He was wearing a red-and-green striped, brocaded satin robe.

"How'd it go?" He looked sleepy, but his voice was wide-awake.

I sat down facing him. "It's clocked as far as I'm concerned. I made it through the Arcade a little before Tex and Monroe made their debut." I lighted a cigarette. "I've got to take it slower on the approach."

He blinked up. "Anything bothering you?"

I shrugged. "This is one of those luck pieces. If we make it it's got to run like oil."

His voice lost its sharpness. "What's the main worry?"

"Bank guards," I told him. "If we don't make a fast getaway we'll have them piggy-back. Besides that, they shoot—and their guns have got real bullets."

His eyes burned bright. "That's why the timing's got to go right." He sucked on his cigar. "We don't want anybody killed. It costs money for flowers."

"Yeah. Stiffs look funny, don't they? They always powder their faces." I crushed out my cigarette in the tray. "It's not for me." I licked my dry lips. "If we don't have to use heat at all it's best."

He scratched his chin in thought. "What about a plainclothes car that might screw up the party?"

I looked at him, feeling a muscle moving in my cheek.

"A lot of dicks eat at the Dairy Lunch," he said.

"Oh," I said, and let out my breath.

"I want you to hang around the alley for a few mornings checking on that."

My voice was weak. "How could I tell dicks from the citizens?"

"It's easy," he wheezed. "They usually work in pairs with their eyes open at the scenery. Hell, you can smell 'em." He thought for a moment. "Tell you what—there's a little shoe repair shop and shine parlor across the alley from the bank. You can get a shine there for a few mornings at nine forty-five and keep your gims open for bulls—any variety. A few days' watch ought to put us straight."

I nodded.

"Another thing," he said, "we've got to have suitcases." He stood up and threw two sawbucks on the desk. "Get a couple made of cheap press paper with snaps on 'em. They have to be at least two and a half, feet long and eighteen inches deep, with a ten-inch fold. That should take care of transportation of the take from the truck."

There was a silence.

"That's all, Jim."

I picked up the sawbucks.

"Bring back the change," he said.

I started for the door.

"Say, Cox—"

I turned back.

He bit his lower lip in thought. "I've got things that have to be attended to. Al's busy, too. Madge wants to do a little shopping. So you drive her."

He saw my expression. "You can't start checking until tomorrow morning." He gave me one of his sickly sloppy smiles, and handed me a car key. "Wait for her down in back. She'll show you where my car is."

I waited in the alley in rear of the White Lion. In about a half-hour she came strutting down the back stairs, heels too high. She wore a little piece of mink hat. Her dress was red, too tight. A three-quarter mink was flying behind her.

Miss Rich Bitch, or something.

VII

She still had on too much makeup, and she had the too-important air again. She looked at me as if I'd just been hatched out.

"Why haven't you got the car out?" she said. "It's in the first garage."

I lifted the garage door, backed out, leaned across the seat and let her in. It was a hell of a nice Cad; it drove like a baby buggy down the bumpy alley.

I turned and took Fifth, and felt suffocated with her perfume.

"My first stop," she said, "is a little glove shop. Six-two-three Sixth Street."

I nodded and drove on, weaving in and out of noontime traffic. When I made the turn over to Sixth, I could feel her eyes on me.

"How'd a nice guy like you ever get mixed up with this outfit?"

"I might ask you the same question," I said.

She gave a short harsh laugh. "Concentration. Hard work. Something I set my heart on. A calling. At five years old every other little girl in my block wanted to be a nun, a teacher, or an actress. Not me. I wanted to be Dillinger's girlfriend."

I glanced at her. "Is it an effort to he so sarcastic—or does it come easy?"

She glanced at her fire-engine-red polished nails. "I got mixed up a long time ago. It began the usual way." Her voice was matter-of-fact. "The usual no-good guy that a sixteen-year-old falls in love with and believed it when he said he made his money gambling. I went away with him and when I woke up it was too late." She looked at me. "Same old story, isn't it? Right out of a prostitute's Bible. You've heard it before." She shrugged. "Only this time it's true. If you don't believe it, go to hell."

"Why didn't you get out?"

"I was in love," she said.

"Continue," I said. "It's touching."

She laughed again; it cracked. "If you cry, use the street. Louie wouldn't like his car all wet up."

"I'll control it," I said.

Her voice dropped lower. "The man I loved was killed. A gun battle. And it wasn't the war. It was a cheap little clothing store stickup off Broadway."

"I see," I said. "And now Thompson lets you cry on his shoulder?"

Her voice was brittle. "After Don, I went farther downhill. And one night there was Louie—begging to buy me mink."

"A nice guy," I said, and pulled up before 623.

"Yeah," she said faintly. "A nice guy."

She opened the car door and got out. "I'll be only a minute." She went inside the shop.

I sat behind the wheel waiting—the longest minute I'd ever spent. I wondered how I was going to learn the identity of the brains. And then I thought about the curve of her legs, the way her hair shone red-gold in the sunlight, and the body underneath that red dress. I tried to stop, but my subconscious took over and got down to real hard thinking.

She came out carrying a small pink sack. Like a good chauffeur, I jumped out and opened the door for her. She accepted it with a tilt of her nose, and when I was back around in the driver's seat, she said:

"Now my dress shop. It's on Eighth, near Princeton. I have some suits ordered."

The shop was across the street from Lakeside Park. She got out again. I sat watching the lake, the people, the frowns they had, until she came back out.

"We'll have to wait," she informed me. "My suits aren't quite ready. It'll he half an hour."

I helped her back in, and gestured toward the park. "Then we got time to drive over there and look at the water and the pheasants."

She didn't say anything, so I started the motor and turned in the driveway. I pulled close to the lake. There wasn't a swan in sight—just a few canoes going by, early afternoon sun on the lake, a blue sky, and a warm breeze shuffling the palms. Directly beyond us were a lot of cat-tails, and old people who were busy reading their papers and poetry.

I cut off the motor and sat there a moment, morosely, wondering how old I'd get to be.

"What are you worried about?" she said.

I heaved a sigh. "The voice. I don't like poking around in the dark." I brought it out casually. "Who is he?"

"I can't tell you."

"Why not?"

"Louie doesn't want it known."

I slid down a little lower under the wheel and stretched out my arms. My right rested on the back of the seat behind her. It surprised her.

"What's that for?" she said.

I'd done it without thinking—I guess. But now it seemed a good idea. A little buttering up, Roberts had said. And with one look at her breasts I didn't have to strain to do it.

"Madge Morton," I said dreamily. "That's a pretty name."

"I hated it when I was a kid," she said without smiling. "I've used half a dozen others, and then I went back to the original—I don't know why."

"I like you," I said.

She straightened. "Don't let it show."

"Why not?" I smiled at her. "When I like something I want to hold it."

She wet her lips; they glistened. "You're just an unhappy lonesome guy."

"Yeah," I breathed, and rested my head back on the seat. "When I'm alone in my room I think too much about you."

"Me?"

I had a feeling that I was six speeds ahead of myself, but words just came out. "I like your straight-forward answers. Anything I hate is a deceitful dame." I caught the curve of her ankle. "There's a lot of things I like about you."

"Don't get ideas," she said harshly.

I shook my head. "You're too nice a kid for that. It's just that—oh hell, sometimes a guy gets to thinking that he's a long time gone. Funerals are permanent."

Her eyes darkened. "Why do you say that?"

I tapped my fingers on the wheel and tried to look like a guy haunted with fear. "This deal I'm in, this job. Just a funny feeling you get in the pit of your stomach that there's a deadfall ahead. Just something that tells you. It's a whisper."

She turned in the seat and looked at me. Her eyes were wide. "I—I've felt it, too. A hunch. I told Louie and he laughed at me, but I—I feel it, too!" A shiver went through her.

"Yeah. Well, I guess nobody lives forever."

She was breathing a little harder. "Then why don't you get out of it, Jim?"

I grunted a laugh. "And leave all of those swell guys in the dark? Louie—Tex—Monroe. Ever hear of honor among thieves?"

"There's no such thing," she said quietly. "If I were you I'd get out." Her voice dropped. "You don't belong in the forest. You'll get lost."

I wondered what she meant about the forest. She leaned closer. "Louie told me about your past. It's hard to believe. But then I guess looks are deceiving."

"Thanks, honey."

Her voice was toneless. "You better get out while you can."

I rubbed my hand down over my face and tried to look worried again. "Some guys can. But my old man's dead, and my old lady's never had a home. She's always lived in a joint and had to take in washings. My main object is to buy her a house—pay cash for it. That way she's got no worries." I took a breath. "In that forest you mentioned, there's still a lot of wood to be chopped. I plan on cutting a few chips."

She was very sober. "And it's for *her* that—"

I nodded and looked grim. "For her. Those chips will buy her a lot of things."

There was a dead silence, an awkward silence. I could feel her pitying me. Then her voice said quietly:

"Put your arm back around me, Jim."

I had got it half-way there when she kissed me—full on the mouth. Her lips were warm and soft and vibrant. I felt the blood pounding up in my ears. And then she was close beside me, her voice a little desperate.

"Why do you think I decided to go shopping today? I knew Louie and Al were busy. I knew you'd be there. I asked Louie to have you drive me."

"I'm glad, honey."

Her eyes shone. "Think I haven't thought about *you?* How clean and nice you are? How fine and strong your shoulders are? Thinking of you alone up there in your room. I *hate* being alone."

"Yeah."

"It's like being in a cavern, with no light or air, your own voice echoing in your ears."

"Yeah. You hit it just right."

She kissed me again, then she laughed, a warm young lovely laugh. Then suddenly she sobered; her voice was low and hard again.

"You think Thompson's my answer?" She drew a quick breath. "Think I'm not sick of his thick sloppy lips stinking of garlic and cigars? Think it's ecstasy when he grabs me, his eyes all lit up? Think my flesh don't crawl at his touch? Think I'm not sick of making up excuses night after night?" She laughed a little hysterically.

I said, "You just need the right guy. Your nerves are all shot."

She nodded and sank back in the seat and closed her eyes. "Why don't you ask me why *I* don't get out? Why don't I?"

"Okay," I said, "why don't you?"

"I guess I'm just sick, Jim," she said wearily. "I haven't got the guts to go out and get an honest job and fight the world alone. I haven't got the ambition. I don't care enough, I guess,"

I looked at her. "Haven't you got folks? Why don't you go home?" "I got folks," she said wearily. "In Cheyenne. The old man's a hard-headed Irishman, thinks I've disgraced the family and I'm not fit to be around them anymore. I wrote a couple times and asked him." Her eyes opened slowly. "And if he'd let me—then what? I can't cry on my mother's bosom and tell her that the world she brought me into is a cold, unhealthy place, and that I'm afraid of the dark." She shook her head. "I'm a big girl now."

"You sure are."

She pressed my hand. "I wake up in the night feeling depressed. I get up, turn on a light, smoke, go crazy, get bent out of shape—all the while afraid of the sounds of the night and its darkness. I get back in bed and die all over again."

I pulled her close. I rubbed her hair and kissed her again. Her lips were on fire.

"Last night," she said softly, "I wanted to come to your hotel room. I tried to think of some excuse that I had to talk to you about something."

I swallowed hard. "You—you did?"

"Yes. But I didn't know the number of your room. And I couldn't pass Pete."

"The Greek night clerk?"

"Yes. He calls in a report to Louie on you every morning."

I felt cold. "Why? Doesn't Louie trust me?"

"He doesn't trust anybody, except me. That's because love is awful blind. He says there's always a chance of a guy losing his nerve in a big deal. He—he had Al watching you, too. But now he's called Al off. What is your room number, Jim? Isn't there a back stairs?"

"Look, baby, you don't want to do that! Risk everything you've got with Louie, a swell guy like that—to—to— You *can't* come to my room! It's impossible! It's not only impossible, it's fantastic, it's— Come to think about it, there is a fire escape. You have to climb three flights because the joint is built on the side of a hill and—" I was breathing too hard—"come in the third floor. I'm four doors from the rear, to the right from the fire escape. Two eighteen."

"I'll remember," she said. "And now we better pick up my suits and get back and check in to Louie."

"Yeah," I said. "Or I'm going to look awfully funny with my throat slit."

VIII

Dark had come when I hit my room, swearing. I was in about eight fathoms too deep. That's forty-eight feet of cold, black, murky water you can't breathe in! There was such a thing as getting information, and there was a way to do it—but who in the hell wanted to drown getting it!

I felt lousy and light-headed. Hell! It was that bright red dress and the body inside it! Something I shouldn't want from a poor sick lonesome kid—afraid of the dark!

I looked up.

She stood there, framed in the doorway.

She closed the door behind her and took off her mink coat and moved slowly toward me. Her lips sank into my neck, and then she was holding me, drowning, too.

I was gone.

I tried to think of Roberts and Thompson and my purpose. "The purpose is to get information!" I reminded myself. "Learn the identity of the voice! That's the purpose!" I kept repeating it and shifted my eyes from her neck.

I had to stop wondering how silky smooth her breasts would feel without that red dress between us! I had to stop licking my lips sunk on hers! I had to stop seeing the hurricane of passion raging in those gray-green eyes. I had to keep my eyes off the perfect symmetry of her thighs, the way they protruded, the classic bone structure.

I had to get her out or have her!

There was no time to draw straws.

I had to have her or suffocate!

I almost suffocated anyway!

You can say all you want to about a Beethoven symphony. Love by a fireside. The exotic breathless quiet of a tropical night. The Isle of Capri. Stromboli. April in Paris. That night brought all of those things to that slovenly hotel room....

"Hello, Betty."

"Wade, darling! Is anything wrong? You sound so all down in the dumps. Are you ill?"

"I'm fine. Fine."

"Sleeping well? Eating well?"

"Sure, sure."

"Coming home?"

"Not for a few days."

Her voice dropped. "Oh." Then she brightened. "I must tell you about Florence, dear. She's been singing like crazy all day! It's really heartening to hear her, gives you a warm feeling all through. She seems so happy. Do you think I could let her out on the back lawn?"

"Why, I—"

"I was wondering, maybe it's the confinement that keeps her from learning to fly again. I'll watch her closely, dear, and let her practice."

"Yeah. Sure, sure,"

"Darling, you must take care of yourself."

"Yeah. You do the same. Be seeing you."

With an uneasy feeling I hung up the phone in the little shoe repair shop. There was little sense in calling Roberts until the definite time of the heist was set. Then he could start the fireworks.

I went out to the Negro shine boy, blinked at the sunshine and hopped up on the bench. I watched the Western Transport truck pull into the alley; I watched the dough being loaded and kept my eyes peeled for cops and any snoopers that might screw the works. Then I finished the shine and walked over to Fifth.

I picked up the suitcase at a little luggage shop on Collins Street. I got nine dollars and forty cents change and a sales ticket. I stuck them in my coat to give to Thompson. He was a hell of a hood when he worried about nine bucks and forty cents!

Then I was seated before Thompson, reporting that everything went smooth at the bank—no cops, no interference that I could see. He said that it would be only a short time before the deal would be set. I nodded, breathing in the staleness of the room, and her perfume.

She wasn't there, and I was glad of that. I was afraid she'd come in and look at me in that hard, bitter way again. But then I knew that we both realized that last night couldn't be repeated. To go on meant hanging onto a straw in mid-ocean.

I didn't want to see her again, and I was pretty sure that she felt the same way. It had been one of those impromptu crazy things where somehow the fuse got lighted and there was damn little you could do about it, except let it explode. What an explosion!

I got back to my hotel room and dug out the rye and put a nipple on it. I wondered if she'd been in one of the bedrooms crying while I'd checked in with Thompson. I began to get scared. I imagined a hundred things that might have happened to her.

I tried not to think. I picked up the morning paper and sat on the bed trying to read. When that didn't work, I went down and got some magazines and brought them back up. I read them all, but it didn't stop me from thinking about her. Hell, the smart thing for me to do was to go down to the restaurant next door and eat and forget it.

I did, then went back up to my room, afraid she wouldn't be there. And she wasn't. By six o'clock I was pacing the rug, all twisted up inside, screwy, fit to be tied. I was afraid I'd never see her again! I wanted to hold her all over; I kept wondering what she was doing. I didn't think there was a chance in hell of her coming back, but I showered and shaved and put on all my clean clothes.

I'd started to tie my tie when she came in.

She wore a light blue dress and gold sandals. Her hair was tied back from her face, and there was a soft light in her eyes—a new shyness. The hard war paint had vanished. She wore just a soft touch of make-up. She was more beautiful than any woman I'd ever seen.

I just stood there, feeling weaker, and holding her. Then we were both giggling like a couple of school kids—until her lips came close to my ear.

"Jim—Jim—"

I kissed her.

"I think I love you," she said.

My heart knocked loud.

She snuggled closer. The perfume she was wearing was like a Garden of Paradise.

"I haven't been able to think of anything but you all day," she whispered. "I felt like dancing on a cloud, or something." She held me closer. "I think last night I died and went to heaven."

"Me, too," I said hoarsely. "But how in the hell did Thompson get up there?"

"You worried about him?"

"I'll break his fat back."

"You're wonderful," she said.

"You're pretty wonderful yourself."

"Do you love me?" she whispered.

"If I don't I got a fever of a hundred and five."

"How *do* you feel about me?"

"Something I haven't felt in years."

"Can you explain it?"

"No. Except that you get me all flustered. See? I can't even tie my tie."

"There's no need of it now," she said. She took off my shirt and kissed my shoulders. "You're so lovely."

Her dress slipped off easy-like. All I had to do was slide down the zipper. All it left was a little blue puddle in the middle of the floor.

She held me tight. "Darling," she said, "I'm so afraid."

"Of what, Madge?"

"Tomorrow—and the day after—and Louie."

"Don't, be scared, Madge. Louie doesn't scare me." I laughed and picked her up in my arms. I tossed her on the bed and climbed in beside her. "We might as well go to hell together...."

I wish I could say it stopped there. That the second night blew out the fuse. But it was only the beginning. I spent my mornings nosing around the shoeshine shop, my nights with her. In those four days I got to waiting for the sound of her footsteps coming up the fire escape, or pacing the rug, unable to wait to grab her in my arms.

Then there was the night she sat, naked, on the edge of the bed, talking quietly.

"I did sing once at the Roxy," she was saying. "Amateur night." She smiled. "I never was a singer, though I always wanted to take lessons when I was a kid. I used to dream of singing in a big important place like the Met. I'd see the beautiful red velvet curtain ringing down and usher carrying big bouquets of flowers up the aisle—to me. I was crazy about the music conductor. He looked like Johnny Weissmuller—only he couldn't swim. I'd smile down at him while I sang, and he was madly in love with me, I suppose. Everybody was."

She laughed. "Bet you think I'm crazy, pretending things like that." She smiled wanly. "I don't dream about stuff like that anymore. Don used to say it's a waste of time to daydream." She looked at me. "Don is the guy I told you about that was killed. Don used to say, 'There sure as hell ain't no Santa Claus! You got to make it the hard way.'" She sighed. "Don used to say things like that."

"Too bad you ever got mixed up with him."

She nodded. "The easiest way is more often the hardest. I guess I liked the bright lights, furs and diamonds, things that only money can buy."

"Yeah," I said. "But Freud would say it all happened in your childhood. The other little girls had fur mittens, while your little fingers froze blue."

She wet her lips. "I can't complain about my childhood. I wasn't chained in an attic, or beaten. I starved a little, that's all."

"That's all, eh?"

She nodded. "Lunchtime in high school is one of those sour things I remember. Sometimes there wasn't even bread in the house to take for lunch. The old man had a bad habit; he was a fanatic on religion. About everything he made went to the church." She smiled. "I had a time trying to hide our poverty from my friends. At lunchtime I simply said I wasn't hungry. But then I couldn't stand to watch them eat, so I'd go off somewhere alone, to the library mostly, and pretend I was looking up something, or read. I began to hate books and learning." Her eyes shone. "And yet something told me that without an education I'd never get away from being poor." She paused. "At that age a body can take such punishment."

She leaned over and inhaled from my cigarette. She blew out a long thin stream of smoke, then continued:

"I wanted to finish high school. I thought a diploma meant something, and I guess it does. I wanted desperately to go on to college. But I couldn't. At thirteen I got a job at the neighborhood theatre, as an usherette. I worked until ten-thirty or eleven each night, and slept through study periods and bluffed my way through." She smiled again softly. "I used to stand at the curtain in the movie house while the glamour of the picture ground on. I'd look at the wonderful clothes and sophistication of the movie stars and feel like dying. Because in my heart I knew I'd never be anything higher than Madge Morton from Poverty Row."

She looked at me. "I don't know why I'm telling you all this. I've never told anyone."

"Maybe I have a sympathetic face."

"But, too," she went on, "there were nice things about my childhood. I remember once my father took me to the High Sierras. I had to hold onto his hand when I saw how tall and majestic the trees were. I never forgot it—how clean the air smelled, with the clouds soft and white and fluffy and so close to me. I've often thought how nice it would be to live there—with the man I love. It was like—like all the poems that Blanding has ever written."

She took a breath, "He's wonderful, isn't he? You get such a clean feeling from all his poetry." She sighed. "I'd give anything if I could think the way he does. Just write poetry and travel." She paused. "But I suppose there's more to it than that."

I studied her and thought of something. Something that was suddenly tearing at my insides. "Madge," I said, "if this job doesn't make the grade it's going to go badly with you. You're an accomplice to the fact. That means you'll go up the same as any of us."

"I know," she said simply, "but if you don't make out, I—I don't want to either."

IX

On my feet I was smoking nervously, and pacing the rug again.

"I'll make out all right!" I assured Madge with more certainty than I felt. "But you've got to go—get out of it. I'll make out!"

"That's what Don said the night he was killed." She looked up slowly, with fear in her eyes. "You can say all you want to about honesty being for the suckers, but you live longer taking the long straight road."

I crushed out my cigarette. "That's why you've got to clear out before the job is on."

She shook her head.

I looked at her. I wanted to kneel before her and cry and tell her that I was betraying her. "I love you, Madge," I said. "You're so beautiful, so lovely."

"Why, darling!" she said in surprise. "That's music!" She rushed into my arms and buried her face in my chest. "I'm so sick of being hard and ugly, hiding under a shell of brittle dialogue. Jim, I—I feel cleansed. With you, everything is so different. It's *us*, darling! It's just got to be!"

I held her.

"There for so very long I was lost," she said. "I never thought anything good would *ever* happen. And then you came along, just when I was choking to death." She looked up; there were tears in her eyes. "Darling, let's both go away."

I felt cold. "Where to?"

"Anywhere. We'll hide out. Louie will never find us." Her eyes shone brightly. "Don stayed, don't you see?"

My voice dropped. "I've got a job to finish."

She shook her head. "Not anymore. We're getting out. To hell with money. I know a place in the Sierras. Nobody'd ever find us. It's beautiful there, and there's peace, Jim." Her eyes shone. "Peace!" She held me closer. "I don't care what you've been, just as my past means nothing to you! Because we've both been so lost!"

She was crying softly. "I love you so! We'll have more than money. Money means so little! We'll both get jobs. I have six hundred dollars in cash and we can start on that. Oh, darling, I've spent my life in the shadows, always aching to walk in the sun!"

"I—" I felt choked.

"I want us to be respectable citizens. A little house. I want to make curtains, and cook for you, and sew buttons on your shirts. I want a dog and a cat, neighbors yelling good morning across the fence; nothing to fear, peace in our hearts!" She was crying harder. "We've both been so wrong. So *wrong!* This is our chance! Now! Before it's too late! Go someplace! Send for me! It'll be just the two of us. My God, don't you see it, Jim? A great blinding wonderful light is shining for us!"

"Madge—" There was nothing but misery all through me.

"You love me," she sobbed. "You just said that you love me. Then save my life—and yours! Please, darling! If you don't, I'm dead, I know. The forest is ugly and black and we'll never get through it!"

Her voice rushed on: "We're comparative strangers, I know. Adam and Eve took a chance and built a world. Darling, we love each other. That's all we need." Her eyes grew brighter, her voice more desperate. "Jim, listen! Open your heart. I'm pleading for my life and yours. Don't go through with it! Come away with me. I'll take your hand and lead you. Maybe the blind leading the blind, but I've been over the path before!"

I kept looking at her. Blood was pounding in my temples. "I—I'll have to think about it, Madge."

"Thank you, darling." She smiled radiantly. "Now I can hope. Tomorrow you'll see it my way, I know. A feeling inside me. Just know that I'm right. Tomorrow it will be clear before you, all doubt gone."

She stood before me, a shining white goddess.

"It's us, darling," she said. "*Us, us!* The rest never happened! We were born today!"

No use kidding myself after that. The water had looked fine, but some damned undertow had dragged me halfway across the Pacific! No use saying I wasn't in love with Madge. I had no other ambition than to hold her in my arms and protect her. I wondered how she'd look at me when Roberts closed in and she knew that I was the hangman. It about drove me nuts!

There was only one thing to do and that was to get her out. Betty? I didn't think about her. Betty was just a face and a dim voice. Betty was a million years ago.

I didn't sleep much that night. My head was too full of a jumble of torturing thoughts. The next day was cold and gloomy, with a tight vacuum in the air. I went downstairs and drank a cup of coffee. I bought a bottle of rye and took it back up. I guess it was about noon when she came in.

She tried to act confident; she tried to smile, but when she saw my eyes she knew—and you could tell that she was scared inside. She spoke lightly.

"I'm all packed. We—we can leave today."

I poured half a tumbler of rye and drank it. "I'm not running out."

"Oh?" There was panic in her eyes. "Sure, you'll beat the cops for maybe another year. If you're lucky. But look at you. Look how crazy you are today, your eyes all wild, nerves jittery, unshaved, drinking too much—all because of this job." Her voice trembled. "That's how you'll spend the rest of your life. Afraid. Afraid of a tap on the shoulder. Afraid of somebody recognizing you. Some day you might want to know decent people, and you won't be able to tell them about your past."

"Shut up!" I said. "Shut off the record! I've heard enough of that fancy preaching." There was a desperate excitement all through me. "It's *you* you should be worrying about! What if I suddenly do see the light and turn the whole bunch of you over to the cops!"

"You?" Her eyes darkened. "I'm not worried."

I whirled to her. "Then you better damn well start getting worried! You've got one of two chances. Get out now—if you don't you'll have to turn state's evidence."

Her lips tightened. "I'd burn first!"

I grabbed a cigarette and lighted it. "Then you'll probably burn, baby. 'Cause I don't like the feel of things. I don't trust the brains, either." I looked at her. "Who the hell is he?"

"Neil Flint," she said. "Owns the stock brokerage on Seventh, as a front."

"Get out of town, baby," I said. "You're all packed, you say. Scram until this deal's over."

Her eyes softened. "We can go together."

"Huh-uh." I was pacing the rug again. "I like the feel of dough." My breath was coming faster. "No dame's going to preach me out of it." I tried to laugh. "Where would we wind up, broke? The whole damn setup stinks! So we leave now and go to the Sierras?" My head throbbed. I rubbed my temples. "The Sierras, eh? A couple of damn refugees on the county? Or do we pan for gold?"

She stared, lips paling. I sank down on the bed. My head was throbbing so violently I couldn't think straight.

"Might as well know, baby, I got no dough, or we'd hit the Sierras all right!" My voice was strange to me. "The important thing is this haul—it may hit the rocks. I don't want you involved. I'm telling you, Madge—like a father, I'm telling you—get out!"

Her mouth quivered. "You don't love me enough, that's it."

"I do love you, Madge. My God, if I didn't love you, I—" My voice choked. "Listen carefully, baby. Write to me in care of the Netherlands Hotel here. I know the desk clerk. He'll send a letter to me wherever I am. Please, baby, for *me* you've got to go. I don't want you in this! I want us to see each other again!"

She kept staring. "You don't make sense. Why aren't you afraid for yourself? If the haul comes off we'll both be all right."

"Madge, will you go—for me?"

"All right," she said. A sob escaped her throat. "You're just like Don and all the rest! You poor, blind fool! You'll never get out; you're too weak!"

She slammed the door behind her.

She didn't come back that night.

Next morning I got the word before I was out of bed—a phone call from Thompson:

"Get over here!"

There was urgency in his voice. I knew that the deal was about to be closed.

I dressed hurriedly, left the hotel without shaving, and started the two-block walk to the White Lion. The city was bathed in sunshine; I could feel its warmth on my back and shoulders, but inside I was icy cold and all knotted up.

I went in the back door of the café, up the stairs, and into Thompson's office.

Fieldman and Monroe were there. Thompson sat behind his desk, with his shirt collar open at the neck and his sleeves rolled up a couple of turns. The room was hot and smelled of his cigar. There was a bottle of brandy by his elbow.

"We'll wait for Tex," he said. His face was gleaming with little beads of moisture.

Nobody said anything. We sat there, waiting. I could hear the soft purr of the electric clock on the far side of the room, the faraway hum of traffic from Sixth Street, and a fly buzzing aimlessly across the room. It landed on Thompson's head. He brushed at it, poured himself a shot of brandy, looked at us, and motioned to the bottle.

"Have one." His voice was hollow.

Fieldman got up, poured three drinks, and handed them to us. The clock ticked off fourteen minutes before Tex came in. He looked at Thompson and grinned sheepishly.

"Sorry I'm late. The damned cab driver had to pick himself up a ticket for speeding and then argue with the slob that gave it to him. I never saw so many spies riding motors. I—"

"Shut up," Louie said, "and sit down."

He rubbed a hand across his face. When he spoke again I knew how scared he was. He looked and sounded like a bullfrog.

"We're going to have a last get-together, go over the whole thing." He paused to swat at the fly. "You all know what you're to do. We'll go over it, the timing, and the things you can expect." He poured himself another drink, and wiped his face with his hand. "I've decided on the Chrysler sedan." He turned to Fieldman. "See that it's serviced. I've got a set of Ohio plates, registered to a Chevvy in Cleveland, off a schoolteacher's car. Put 'em on for cover."

He got up and waddled over to the corner closet, his shirt-tail hanging out, his suspenders dragging behind him. He pulled out a Browning automatic and threw it to Monroe.

"Be sure it's loaded," he sneered. "It's short enough that you can do a lot of damage with it. I had ten inches taken off the barrel."

He wasn't kidding when he said he'd had the barrel shortened. From the right distance it would put out a pattern of shot as big as a bushel basket!

"Look it over," he barked at Monroe, "Get the feel of it. Be sure you know how it works. There's a box of shells in the closet." He turned to me. "Cox," he said, "you got your belly gun. If the going's rough, you can use it." He spoke to Tex. "You got your forty-five. That's all you'll need."

Fieldman drank his brandy, then lighted the cigarette he'd been holding. "Where does Al fit in?"

Thompson blew and wheezed and rubbed his hand down over his face. "I'm not using him. He's good as gold, but he scares easy on something big as this. But we'll still have to cut him in."

He poured himself another drink, then wiped his mouth with his hand.

"I want you guys not to leave home base. You'll get the call, you'll come here." His eyes turned to a big cardboard box by the couch. "I got G.I. coveralls from War Surplus; you'll all wear 'em over your uniforms." He gestured to the closet. "Uniforms are here."

He gasped for breath. "Everything's ready." His eyes hardened. "Remember on the ride to the motel you're to slip on the coveralls again. Won't be time to get off the Brownie outfits on the way to the motel. Fieldman will bring you. It's outside a little burg I picked out. We'll meet there, split the dough, and you guys blow. I got to stay because I'm legitimate. Fieldman will stay because he's manager of the club. We can't have anybody missing us. You guys go your way—Chicago's a good cooling-off town. But get in touch with me in a couple weeks." He grinned. "Might have something else in the fire."

He walked back to his desk and flopped in the big leather chair. I could hear the soft hiss of air ooze out of the cushion.

"Now you guys beat it. But stick close to home, like I said. I want to be able to get you. Right now it's a question of hours." He blinked.

"That's all there is to it."

Nobody said anything. We just sat and finished our brandy and looked at each other. All of us were nervous and scared.

I don't think any one of the others was more scared than I.

I went back to my hotel room and waited, with a hunch that the fireworks were scheduled for tomorrow morning.

X

By midnight Thompson still hadn't called. I wondered if he'd pull a last-minute fastie—call us in at nine in the morning, to go in on the heist. I broke out in a sweat wondering if I should call Roberts. But then, I reasoned, even if Louie did pull a last-minute call, there'd still be time for me to hit a phone booth on my walk to his office. Al was off my tail now, and Louie trusted me—at least it's what Madge had said.

I wondered if she'd flown the coop. Well, damn it, I'd warned her. There was no time now to think of a dame. There was a job to be done, I told myself that over and over, but it didn't work.

That night I slept a fitful sleep, full of strange dreams. I remember the phone rang, and it was light outside. I couldn't believe it was morning. I looked at my watch. Six. I grabbed up the receiver.

"Cox?" It was Thompson.

"Yeah."

"Tomorrow morning. Thursday." There was no emotion in his voice. "Be here at eight-thirty. I mean eight-thirty!"

"Okay," I said, and broke out in a cold sweat.

Somehow I got my clothes on. I had my hand on the doorknob when the phone rang again.

It was Madge. Her voice was pitched high.

"I just want you to know, Jim, that I'm staying. No matter what. I'm not running out, either."

"Madge, *listen*—"

The phone was dead.

I slammed it down and went out the door.

I hurried downstairs, out onto Sixth Street, and found the little corner drugstore. I looked at the phone booth, then turned and walked slowly outside again.

I must've gone around that block three times and drunk fifteen cups of coffee. I remember seeing the same faces, the same stores, over and over.

Afraid of the dark, was she, eh? She didn't know what darkness was—yet. Not until she spent her nights alone in a prison cell. She'd be rounded up with the rest. She'd be booked, tried, and the least she'd get by with was five years.

Madge—in the Joint. For something she'd wanted to get me out of! I could see her being checked in. She'd look sexy, all right, in her prison uniform. With those busts and legs she had the girls up there'd be crazy about her! Madge—pushing a broom in Tehachapi, working in the laundry—

No way she could find out that I'd been the contact. No use worrying about that. Hell, I could visit her, couldn't I? See her about once a week and—

No, no, I could only write to her. As Jim Cox, she'd have to think I was doing time, too. That could be the only way—just some damn silly, trite word of cheer on paper. Or else—else give it to her straight. Tell her I was a dick, had seen my duty and done it. It was that corny! It would go over big with Madge. I could see her eyes when I told her.

What was it I'd heard about that place? Somebody'd said something only last week about the food. Chicken every Sunday, tainted and greasy, lumpy yellow mashed potatoes, those rocky crinkly peas— She helped feed Europe's starving kids, eh? Well, she wouldn't be going for that, either, after her time in stir.

Everybody in the world should be a cop, I thought wildly! Everybody should know the elation of turning some poor weak bastard over to the law! Or a dame—a dame that somehow had crawled into your blood stream, a dame that was afraid of the dark.

But then sometimes a stretch did some good. Why not use cold common sense? Maybe when she got out she'd lay off guys like Don, and Thompson, and Jim Cox, and find her place in the sun. Sometimes it took a jolt. Hell, if I went around trying to rescue every woman in distress I could make a career of it.

I thought of how tender she was, how unselfish, how she'd said over and over how she loved me. "I want a little house," she'd said. "I want to cook for you and sew buttons on your shirt, and—" The plans she'd wanted, for us. "I've got six hundred dollars, Jim," she'd said. "We can start on that." She'd said, "There for so long I was so lost and then you came along, just when I was choking to death …" She'd said, "Darling, save my life and yours!"

Funny how a guy can't forget things—about a girl. Words kept echoing in my brain, spreading, multiplying.

And then I was back at the cigar store, knowing that this was the real lighting of the fuse, for the final disintegration.

I went inside, to the booth, picked up the phone, and dialed. Emotion had drained me. There was only a feeling of numbness.

"Roberts?" I said.

He hesitated. "Do you know it's six-thirty in the morning?"

"Yeah."

"Got the dope?"

"Set for tomorrow morning," I said. "The Southwest Bank at Fifth and Howser. Time—nine forty-five."

I talked on, giving him the setup on the big boss, telling him details, how we'd be dressed in bank guard outfits, the artillery that would be carried, the time of entrance, how each of us would make our approach in the alley, the plan to take the truck to the Bank of America three blocks away, and then the motel.

"They wouldn't give the name of the motel," I said. "And I didn't want to be too curious."

"No need of that," he said. "We'll get those babies before they make the truck."

"I'm the kid that'll enter from the Arcade," I went in. "So tell the guys to watch for me. I don't want to be killed for my efforts."

"It's good work, Wade!" his voice boomed. "Anything else I should know?"

"Not a damn thing!"

"You sore at somebody?"

"Hell, no," I told him. "I don't even feel anymore."

He laughed. "We'll book you with the rest, then release you at the station."

"Thanks," I said drily. "That's damn nice of you."

He laughed again, and I banged up the receiver.

I hurried out of the drugstore and began to walk.

I crossed streets, passed people, shops. I didn't give a damn where I was going. I just had to walk. I felt all loused up, twisted, and dreamy. Thoughts kept spinning. I thought of the High Sierras, poetry by Blanding, Canadian Club whisky, girls I'd known once and would never know again, a fixed prizefight I'd seen that didn't stay fixed, and the way the blood ran down the face of the loser and onto the ropes, and the way his jaw set as they carried him out—because he was dead. He'd been dead before he fell down, but the crowd didn't know until the next day when they read about it.

I thought of these things, abstractedly, half-remembered moments, and all the aching, the dreary monotony in being a cop. I thought of all the poverty in the world, and a million bucks split seven ways!

I don't know what happened in that half-hour.

Sometimes I think I believed that I was Jim Cox!

I remember how my head ached while I talked to Betty from a little cigar store telephone booth.

"You see," I heard her saying, her voice far-away, "I let her out of the cage, so that she'd have space in the back lawn to practice. I went out and—"

"Betty," I interrupted, "I might be away for some time!" There was a ringing in my ears. "For some time, Betty."

"Oh? I'm sorry. You'll write?"

"Yeah."

"Another one of those long-drawn-out assignments?"

"Yeah. Something like that."

"Wade, what I was trying to tell you was when I went out to get Florence she—she was dead, dear. I think it was the excitement of—" She broke off. "I know you're in a hurry, but *why* must you go out of town?"

"I—"

"I know you can't tell me," she added quickly. "This police work is so lousy. You never know what to expect. It—it won't be dangerous, will it?"

I hesitated, then said, "Yes, Betty. This time it *is* dangerous." My tongue felt swollen. "If I don't come back you—"

"Now, Wade, don't talk like that."

"Got to go, honey."

"Darling, I—you—"

I hung up.

It was just 7:15 when I walked into Thompson's office. He looked just like he had yesterday—the same shirt, the same suspenders, the same brandy. Fieldman was there. Thompson looked at me, his pig eyes glistening. He poured a drink, shoved it across the desk to me.

"What's on your mind?" It was a hoarse croak.

I lighted a cigarette with shaking fingers; my eyes felt sunken in their sockets. I looked up at him, at the brandy, at Fieldman, and began to talk rapidly and nervously.

"Just this. I've been doing some thinking. I—I've got a feeling. Call it a hunch, intuition, fear, or common sense, I— This job won't last till tomorrow."

I heard Thompson breathing. My voice shot up.

"It's the same feeling I had on the jewel job with Les. I talked him into pulling it a day early, just because of a hunch I had. If we'd waited a day longer we wouldn't have made it. The jewelry was supposed to go out that night." I inhaled on my cigarette. "Let's do it now."

"Nuts," Thompson said.

I felt my jaws grinding. "Why let us guys stew until tomorrow? We're all jumping like a bunch of creeps the way it is!"

Louie Thompson kept looking at me. Again I could hear his breath whistle out. Fieldman looked at me, scratched his chin and cleared his throat. He looked at Thompson.

"Maybe the kid's got something, Louie."

"Yeah?" Thompson looked like he'd swallowed something bitter.

"Yeah," Fieldinan told him. "The kid's got good hunches. He never hit the bucket for anything. I think he's right. I think today's the day. Let's get the thing over with!"

Thompson sat there, staring into space, making tents out of his hands. Then he picked up the phone.

He dialed, asked for Room 200, and spoke sharply into the phone.

"Monroe? Louie. Get your ass over here. It's going this morning!" He held the receiver down for a moment then dialed again. "Tex? Louie. Get here. It's going today!"

He put the phone down and made a grab for the brandy. Water was running off his face in little rivers.

We must have sat there five minutes, waiting, when I started to smell her. How long she'd been in the room I don't know. When I turned around she was standing just inside the bedroom door. Her voice came from a well.

"You think today's the day, Louie?"

Thompson took one look at her, stood up, and began beating his fists on the desk, wheezing and blowing. "Shut up!" he said. "You fight me off all night, and now give me a lot of cheap conversation." His nerves were jumping. "I can hear that any time. Shut up or get out!"

She turned and went back into the bedroom.

I got up and, with the excuse of finding the bath, left the room.

I found her in the second bedroom. I grabbed her.

"Look, baby, it's *us* all right." My voice shook. "You still got that six hundred bucks you told me about?"

She nodded.

"And you know where the motel is where we'll meet?"

"Okay. I want you to buy us a car. It's eight o'clock now. You got two hours to get to the first car lot and pick us up anything that runs. Give a phony name."

She stared, expressionless.

I took a breath and went on, "Have it parked near the motel—and you inside it. As soon as the dough's split we'll take off!" I squeezed her. "We'll hit the Sierras all right, and we won't be damned mountain-combers!"

She didn't say anything.

Is it a deal?" I panted.

"Yes, Jim." Her voice carried no emotion. "It's a deal."

I left her. I made tracks back out to Thompson.

It was a two-minute wait before Monroe came in, with Tex following two seconds later.

"Hell, I'm glad," Tex said, unloosening his tie. "I was getting nervous prostration."

"Me, too," Monroe said. With restless weariness he began unbuttoning his shirt.

"Let's get this damn thing over with. I see by the weather reports it'll be raining tomorrow, and you know how traffic gets tied up with the streets wet." He pointed to the uniforms lying on the couch. "You guys get into those." We followed his orders.

Tex was stepping out of his trousers. I took off my suit and calmly hung it over a chair. I pulled on the blue-gray uniform pants and the shirt. They were the usual door-shaker's uniforms; the caps were the same shade of teal gray, with cap pieces already mounted.

Somewhere Thompson had picked up some private patrol badges. Sam Browne belts lay in a pile on Thompson's desk; they were the usual black woven leather. I got mine on, buckled the shoulder strap, and wondered how Tex was going to carry his .45 in a cross-draw holster built for a .38. I buttoned my shirt, stuck my gun in the belt holster.

I glanced at Tex and Monroe, already in their uniforms.

They looked just like they were supposed to—a couple of guards going to work. Tex threw me a pair of the G.I. coveralls, and then I was pulling on khaki, over my uniform.

XI

Fieldman got into his coveralls, then stood up and looked at his watch. He checked it with the electric clock on the wall.

"We'd better get set," he said quietly.

Monroe took the sawed-off shotgun out of the closet, loaded it, and charged it. He set the safety, then swung it up to his shoulder, looked down the barrel, and moved it in circles as if he were tracking an imaginary duck.

Fieldman pulled out the suitcases.

Thompson still sat at his desk, his face sickly, perspiration running down his jowls. "All stroll in and take your stations. I want none of you going lop-eared." He picked up the phone and dialed.

There was a short wait, then he said:

"This is Louie. Tell the boss that escrow is closing today instead of tomorrow. That's all." He hung up and made a grab for the brandy bottle.

We sat facing him, while he went over the plan for the last time.

At nine-thirty, we went out the back door, down the back stairs, Fieldman leading, Tex following, Monroe and myself bringing up the rear. I walked stiffly, loose-legged, the two big suitcases bumping my legs.

We'd reached the alley before I became alive enough to realize that my face was wet, and the sky was heavily overcast; the morning air was too cold, the air too soft, too still.

My legs carried me inside the garage. I climbed in the back seat of the Chrysler, with Monroe. Tex sat in the front with Fieldman.

Fieldman backed out. My throat felt dry. I needed another drink. The uniform was too tight around my stomach, the coveralls too hot.

I kept my eyes on my watch. It took us twelve minutes to reach the Coolidge Building.

We sat there, waiting. I noticed with a start that a fine rain was misting the windshield. Now was the time. It was no longer a million-dollar dream! In a few minutes there was much to be done!

Rain fell on the steel roof of the car.

"Hell!" Monroe blurted. He sat restlessly, sweat on his cheeks. Fieldman was pale, but calm, his eyes fixed to his watch. Tex turned around in the seat and gave me a frightened grin. "You can die only once," he said, his voice cracking. He sat there giggling softly.

I began to peel off the coveralls.

We waited. It was the horrifying wait of condemned men, men who sat in the death house with mute, hopeful faces. I held my cigarette at my side, afraid to reveal the shaking of my hands.

Rain pelted the windshield. Thunder rumbled overhead, then crashed, the sound aching in my eardrums. Pedestrians moved past, stunned by the sudden deluge. I shivered. Monroe began to swear—a volume of obscenities.

We kept waiting.

At last Fieldman gave me the signal.

I climbed out, over the suitcases, feeling that it was the long walk into darkness, the end of the world! Maybe it was.

It was my idea of nothing—a madman's dream!

I was walking again through the Arcade. My first thought was that I couldn't be sick, but my stomach began to retch. I moved on, wondering how anything that had once seemed so easy could be so hard to do.

I kept walking. I had no control over my legs. I passed the liquor store, the dress shop. A little barber, in white apron, who was standing out in front of his shop kept looking at me. I felt wired together. The top button of the uniform trousers snapped at my waist. I jumped. Then my pulse was too quiet, my breath quick and shallow. I wondered if my heart had stopped beating.

I walked on, passing distorted images of people. I was too tired, all energy sapped. Ahead, I saw the glass doors. The shock of realization hit me. In a few seconds I'd be through the Arcade! My heart began to beat fiercely. Fear swelled inside me, knotting in my lungs. I tried to breathe, conscious of my teeth being clenched. I loosened my jaw, and kept walking.

I reached the glass doors. Beyond, rain fell in rivulets. I saw the two bank guards pushing the empty conveyor back to the bank door. I was seconds too soon!

A little Mexican guy was entering the Arcade, his hair and clothes limp, water-soaked. He was holding the door open for me to pass first!

I hesitated, my eyes fixed on his, knowing that I must keep moving. I turned around, sauntered back. I counted to five, then retraced my steps to the glass doors.

The two guards were entering the bank. The steel door closed. To my right, Tex was closing in, whistling. His uniform was wet, shining and black. Water ran down the visor of his cap. His face was quiet, unset, easy-going—no different than if he were doing an honest day's work.

The outside guard was leaning against the bank building under the small canopy, out of the rain, holding his shotgun by its stock. He was a small, stoop-shouldered man with patches of fiery red hair under his cap. At the moment, he was our worry—and he could be a damn big one!

Beyond him, Monroe had made it across the street, threading his way through pedestrians. I watched as he stopped, glanced up at the rain, and lighted a cigarette. The only thing that had changed in Monroe was his right eye. It was bulging more than usual.

He came closer. I could see the panic in his face, lips working, as if he were talking to himself, the thin cruel lines around his mouth that hadn't been there before.

He was moving faster, walking directly up to the guard.

I'd stopped thinking which was why I could stand it. I could feel hope building up in me, a silent, fervent prayer that it would be fast— and then get the hell out! I could see vague flickers of all the guys I had pitched in the bucket. I saw my mother's face.

Pedestrians kept moving past on Fourth Street, hurrying through the downpour, bumping into each other. Each time one of them glanced our way my heart stopped. I heard the whir of traffic on the wet streets, the clanging of streetcars. In the distance a newsie was screeching his dead headlines. Within an hour now he'd have the extras, whether we made it or not!

I turned the knob of the glass door, and stepped out into the alley. My arm didn't belong to me. In another second I'd made four feet, stumbling toward the truck, rain pelting my face.

Monroe was walking directly to the redheaded guard. I heard his voice from far-away:

"Hi, Jo. You're going to get wet." He was grinning cheerfully!

I saw apprehension flicker over the face of the guard. Monroe mumbled something else while Tex, holding his gun flat in his hand, moved up beside them.

Pedestrians hurried past for Fourth Street. Monroe reached out and lifted the shotgun out of the guard's arms. The guard stood for a second staring, his mouth dropping open, the cigarette falling into the wet alleyway. He glanced at Tex, his face turning from a healthy pink to gray-green, his freckles making black spots against his skin. Monroe was smiling, saying something else. The redheaded guard turned around slowly, and faced the bank building.

I staggered to the back of the truck, my eyes on the bank door. It was like stage fright; my legs had turned to rubber; there was cotton in my mouth. Waves of nausea hit the pit of my stomach. Someone had clamped a steel hand around my chest.

I climbed up into the back of the truck.

I looked back to see one of the bank guards who'd entered the back door of the bank. I thought I'd gone out of my mind.

He'd come around the corner, around Fourth Street! He ran past the redheaded guard, over to the open doors of the truck. He'd turned to the guard and started to yell, "The doors!" when Monroe shoved the .45 in his back and moved him up in the truck beside me.

Tex slammed the doors shut.

In another instant he was in the driver's seat. I heard the whir of the electric motor that pulled up the bank door!

The truck lurched forward as Tex raced the engine and jumped the clutch. I heard the dull hollow thud of Monroe's gun against the skull of the guard. He pitched forward on his face. Monroe pushed him over to one side of the bundles of cash.

Through one of the ports I could see the bank door go slowly up, the legs of the guards, the redhead jumping up and down, pushing buttons on the rear of the building, beating on the slowly moving door with clenched fists.

With breath gone, I started opening a suitcase and loading. The air was hot, close, inside the steel body. Sweat was pouring off Monroe's face. He was swearing, scared to death, muttering:

"This bastard *would* jam things up! Tex can't drive worth a damn! I should have killed this guy and left him in the alley!"

I went ahead loading the money. It was all in compact bundles, canvas bags with bull-black lettering:

Southwest Banking Corporation
U. S. Federal Currency

With the amounts of the dough on each sack.

Tex drove on. I glanced out the port, seeing the blur of traffic, rain slanting down, the grinding stop for traffic lights. I ducked my head and helped Monroe load the other suitcase.

The guard moved. Monroe looked at him and kicked him in back of the head. We kept loading the second suitcase.

So far we'd made it! I started to breathe. Everything good. I felt the truck lurch on a right turn.

The second suitcase got filled. There were two bundles left over. I automatically opened the front of my shirt and stuck them inside. Monroe was strapping up the suitcase. I was buttoning my shirt back up when I felt it.

A kick in the head!

Only it wasn't from a foot. I reeled; everything went gray. I fell to my knees and heard the savage snarl from Monroe's throat, felt him spring, heard a blur of voices.

My eyes opened. Through thin streaks of red I saw the two men groping wildly—the guard, sap in hand, wrestling desperately, and Monroe rolling on the floor of the truck.

Without thought, my hand reached down for my .38. It took strength to raise it and bring it down on the bastard's head.

There was silence.

Monroe blinked up at me, still on the floor, panting. He got to his knees. "This son-of-bitch came to—caught you with his sap!"

Blood began trickling down my face. I could feel the truck turn once more, then lurch to a stop.

Then Tex was out of the front seat, opening the back door, his eyes on the suitcases. The smile on his face was tight.

"Last stop for Wells Fargo Express! Let's go!"

Fieldman had pulled up behind us in the Chrysler. To our left was the Bank of America.

Tex and Monroe grabbed up the suitcases and walked leisurely to the door of the Chrysler. I staggered out behind them, following.

The car door was open. The suitcases went in. I dived in after them, with Tex shoving me. Monroe was already in the right front seat.

Fieldman shifted gears, engine roaring, and swung away from the curb. Then the big Chrysler was sliding along through the heavy downpour.

We made the first light before anyone spoke.

"What happened to Cox?" Tex asked softly.

"We forgot little Stanley had a sap," Monroe answered in a flat voice.

Fieldman moved out into traffic, traveling easy. From somewhere in the distance the high-pitched scream of a siren echoed through the valleys of the city. Monroe looked back, white and sweaty. Then Tex was shouting:

"Relax! It's a fire wagon! They're on the next street!"

Monroe was pulling on the coveralls, throwing the other two suits into the back, yelling:

"Put 'em back on! And get that head of his to stop bleeding!"

I began to feel the pain in my head. It was sharp, and zigged down my spine. I rested back on the seat, blood dripping from my forehead. Tex mopped at my face with a handkerchief, and helped me on with the khaki.

Then Fieldman was cruising along like a Sunday driver. I tried to relax, but my muscles and nerves refused to settle down.

We pulled onto 101 Highway, and rolled along to the suburb. Fieldman was braking down, pulling into the wet driveway of the Sphinx Motel.

I remember the rising and falling of my stomach as he turned around swiftly, then backed into a garage. He jumped out and closed the door.

Tex helped me out, carrying one of the suitcases. Monroe took the other and walked ahead, up a short flight of stairs. I stumbled against the side of the car, blood running down my face, making a red mist to see through, the warmness of it flowing inside my shirt collar, running down my neck. Suddenly I was walking in a rush, before collapse overtook me.

Monroe dragged me up the steps, and we were inside the motel room.

XII

Everything was a blur, confusion. Madge was there, Thompson, and Al. There was noise, a terrible ache in my head, and everybody talking at once.

Somehow I'd got on a bed. I was lying on my back trying to see. I heard Madge's voice above the others, saying:

"I'm calling Doc!"

The door opened and closed.

Somebody threw me a towel. I tried to wipe the blood with it. Across the room, Tex, Monroe, Fieldman—all of them—were counting the dough, stacking it. I heard Thompson's voice, gleeful, smirking:

"Gentlemen, our horses have just come in! U.S. Federal currency! You can spend it anywhere!"

Then Tex bellowing: "Louie, Cox is getting blood all over the bed!"

Another towel hit me. I heard the door open and close. Then Madge was beside me. "Doc's on his way," her voice came over. I felt her move away, then felt her back once more, pressing a warm wet towel against my face.

"Jim—Jim!" she whispered softly. "You'll be all right, darling!"

I lay there, with my eyes closed, my head pounding, listening to the post mortem, Thompson's voice, screeching:

"A million dollars! We got it all!"

"All except what Cox has got in his shirt!" Monroe said hoarsely.

I could feel Thompson advancing toward me. I felt the buttons go when he grabbed the front of my shirt. He pulled out the red-stained sacks, his lips shaking like blubber.

"Tryin' to pull a quickie, eh?" he rasped.

I heard Tex's voice, hard. "Lay off, Louie. He couldn't get it all in the suitcases."

I opened my eyes to see Monroe looking out the window, screaming: "Cops! The joint's lousy!"

There was a mad scramble. I sat up, dazed. Tex was shouting:

"We been had! If they close in, we're dead!"

I saw the horror in Thompson's eyes. "It —it isn't possible!" he said in a fierce whisper. "How—" Blind fury seized him. "Get the stuff in the car! Let's try to get out!"

I saw Madge's face, deadly pale as she broke out sobbing.

Then Captain Roberts' amplified voice was booming from outside, from over the portable P.A.:

"Come on out! All of you! The place is completely surrounded! If you don't we'll have to blast!"

I turned my eyes, unable to meet six terror-stricken faces.

There was the tinkle of glass as Thompson broke out the windowpane with his shotgun, then an ear-splitting blast went off, leaving an acrid smell of gunpowder in the room.

Roberts picked it up from there.

"Want to play. Eh, Louie?"

Silence ensued. Silence followed by the chattering of the cops' Reising automatics, the sharp staccato bark of the .38s—little swarms of bees buzzing through the air.

I slid off the bed, and onto the floor. A wet wind seemed to blow through the room, shaking the windows. Everything had turned gray-yellow. I saw the low wooden door panels splinter, little chips of paint drop on the maroon rug beside me.

Monroe had picked up the suitcases and was heading toward the door that led down into the garage. There was another spray of gunfire, and he stopped still, one foot in the air. There was only a blank look on his face as he fell down the short flight of stairs.

Al was beside Thompson at the window, using a .45. He began to laugh—laughter beyond mirth.

I caught a glimpse of Madge. "Get in the bathroom!" I tried to yell. "Flat on your stomach."

She nodded, her eyes dead.

She did as I said and fell flat on the tile floor, out of firing range.

Tex was at the window, crouched, letting go with his .45. Thompson was on the opposite side, with the pump shotgun, pumping and shooting, the ejected shells flipping back over his shoulder. Again there was the tinkling of broken glass, the dull thud of lead embedding itself in the walls, the smell of burnt powder, and blue smoke.

"The car's loaded! Let's go!" Fieldman was at the steps, screaming at the top of his lungs.

The heavy roar of the Chrysler's engine started in the close garage. Al, Thompson and Tex made a run for the steps. The doors opened and closed.

There was a splintering crash as Fieldman rammed the door. I could hear the shrieking of tires as he turned, the rising clatter of gunfire outside. Again the shrieking of tires. Then a crash—steel meeting steel.

Then silence.

I crawled over to the window and looked out.

The Chrysler was piled against another car. Dicks were swarming around in the rain, dragging out what was left of the passengers. Two of them pulled Louie out and put him on the lawn. He lay there. I saw Doc Sloan rushing across the lawn. He paused by Louie, then bent beside him, opening his satchel.

I got to my feet and moved back across the room—to Madge.

She was still on the bathroom floor. Behind me, I heard the door opening, the little doc's voice.

"Let's have a look at you, Cox."

I kept staring at Madge. She lay on her back, her red hair haloed by a redder circle on the floor. Blood was seeping from her stomach, running down her dress. Blood was in her hair.

I kept croaking at the doc. Outside, there was the screaming of a police ambulance.

He stepped over me and went inside to Madge. He bent over her, lifted her eyelids, and ripped her dress at the stomach. Then he stood up and shook his head.

"Belly wound, that's bad," he said. "And one through the head."

"An ambulance," I said hoarsely. "Emergency!"

He shook his head again. "No use. She's dying already." He picked up his satchel and walked to the door. "There's one out here in front," he said over his shoulder. "I'll tell the boys."

I found myself on my knees beside her.

She winced in pain, then opened her eyes and smiled. "I love you," she whispered.

"Madge—listen—" I was feverish. "There isn't much time and there's much to be said. I—I'm not Jim Cox at all. I'm a dick. Jim Cox is in the can. I—I took his place. A cop."

She stared, then closed her eyes.

"A cop," I said unsteadily. "An honest one until today. You've got to understand that it—was a job. A web to catch Louie. I—I began not liking it, then I knew you. I—I never was crooked before—until this morning. Until after I checked in with my captain, told him the setup and— For a half-hour I was wrong, Madge, as wrong as any of the guys because I—I wanted the money—for us. I—"

Her body was shaking with regular tiny tremors. I talked on. I didn't know what I was saying.

"Monroe's dead, here on the floor. Louie, out on the lawn, in the rain, dead, too, I think. They—they've rounded up the rest. Why the little doc is running loose, I don't know. Neil Flint will *wish* he was dead. How Roberts found us here, I don't know either. I—my name isn't Jim Cox, it—it's Wade Reed. I—I'm dead, too."

I don't know why I was talking about death, unless I was trying to tell her that she wasn't the only one that didn't get through the forest.

She moved restlessly, then whispered, "Darling, why don't you put a log on the fire? It—it's turned so—so cold."

I looked down at her, wondering if I'd heard right.

She wet her lips. "Are you disappointed? Please don't be." She shivered, then smiled. "In another month the snow will melt, and the sun will make things warm and lovely, and at night we can sit out on the porch and watch the fireflies light up the trees. The village is only half a mile away. Get our coats. We'll walk there and I'll show you." I stared, feeling my heart thump against my ribs.

"A bullet in her head," the little doc had said.

"Up here with you, Jim." Her voice had no resonance. "Everything that was ugly is gone. I—I'm not afraid anymore."

Something kept gnawing inside me. "Not even of the—dark, Madge?"

Again she looked up at me, trying to focus her eyes. "I need a drink." She fought for breath. "My throat feels so—so—"

I got to my feet and found a glass. I filled it with water and kneeled beside her again. "Here." I lifted her up and put the trembling glass to her lips.

Her eyes were staring straight ahead now, glassy. "Darling, why did you turn off the light?"

She didn't drink the water, because she was suddenly limp in my arms.

Minutes passed. I was still holding her when the guys in white came in, their faces and coats wet with rain. I watched one of the internes bend over her, and probe her. Through the blur of the room I saw the little doc, then saw Madge being lifted onto a stretcher.

I got up and stood at the window.

There were footsteps, dim voices, the door closed, then opened. There were moments of silence, and then Captain Roberts' voice.

"Well, Wade, so they decided to pull it this morning instead of tomorrow."

"I—" Words wouldn't come.

His voice came to me queerly:

"There was no way you could let me know. So you had to go in with them. You had to do that, or it would have meant your life. I know how you figured—that even if the guys made it with the dough you could give me enough dope so that I could pick them all up."

There was another silence, then his voice ground on: "If it hadn't been for Doc Sloan the mob would have got away. Doc has been supplying me information for some time. He knew something was ready to explode, but he couldn't learn details from Thompson. He got the call from the dame that you were wounded. He figured that the job had come off, so he telephoned me before he came here. I'd already received the call, that the bank had been knocked off. I—"

"I persuaded Louie to change his plans, to this morning," I said hollowly. "For a half-hour I went in there slugging—not as a cop, but as one of them. For a half-hour I was drunk with a million bucks—and a woman."

There was a long silence. Then I heard him behind me, walking back and forth in the room.

"I wish you hadn't told me that," he said slowly. "But my ears are bad. So maybe I didn't hear right." He paused, then with sudden decisiveness, "When you resign from the Department and start business as a private dick, I can probably throw some business your way."

"Resign?" I turned and looked at him. "Private dick?" Realization hit me. I'd saved his life once! Now he was saving mine!

He nodded, "Guys go screwy once every so often. Petticoat fever. Guess we all get it sometime in our lives."

I tried to say something. "She—she—"

I wanted to tell him that I'd really only wanted to help her, that, like the sparrow in my backyard, she was bruised, beaten, grounded and I'd only wanted to help her. But it was something that was too hard to explain.

Of course Betty threw a party. A party for a hero. The neighbors all came, and my mother was there. My mother had the little table by the window all decked out with candles, and a flag draped over my photo, in uniform, taken overseas beside a B-17, and my medals pinned on the flag.

She had a kid with her, too, another boy to be straightened out. And I gave him the old pitch about crime not paying. I wasn't feeling too good. Then my mother had the floor, with Doris and Clyde and the neighbors seated in a circle around her.

"The D.F.C.," my mother said proudly. "The Air Medal, the Bronze Star. Oh, yes, Wade was a hero in the war, too, as well as in the Police Department, rounding up all those frightful hoodlums. And not only is my son a double hero, but he's sort of a Father Flanagan, in his own way. I want to announce that tonight he's saved his eighth boy from taking the road to crime. Oh, yes, he's more or less started his own little Boy's Town."

Tears swam in my eyes. The phone was ringing. I hurried to the hall and answered it, thankful for the chance to get out of the room.

It was a wrong number.

I put down the receiver and sat there, staring at the phone, feeling a need to cry. From the hallway, I could hear my mother, still holding the floor:

"Oh, yes, I mean it," she was saying. "My son was almost a gangster once himself. He—"

THE END

Stark House introduces a new series...

FILM NOIR CLASSICS

THE PITFALL Jay Dratler
"Dratler's novel is darker, sleazier and less forgiving than the film it inspired. A brutal portrait of blind lust and self-destruction ... a stellar example of 1940s American noir."
—Cullen Gallagher, *Pulp Serenade*. Filmed in 1948 with Dick Powell, Lizabeth Scott, Jane Wyatt and Raymond Burr.

FALLEN ANGEL Marty Holland
"This story, about a small-time grifter who lands in a central California town and hooks up with a femme fatale, is straight out of the James M. Cain playbook."
—Bill Ott, *Booklist*. Filmed in 1945 with Dana Andrews, Alice Faye and Linda Darnell.

THE VELVET FLEECE
Lois Eby & John C. Fleming
"We guarantee your head will be spinning with double-crosses and you'll be talking out of both sides of your mouth before you finish...."
—*Evening Star*. Filmed as *Larceny* in 1948 starring John Payne, Joan Caulfield and Dan Duryea.

SUDDEN FEAR Edna Sherry
"This is a thoroughly exciting read, with brilliant pacing, which makes you absolutely desperate to know how everything will pan out."
—Kate Jackson. Filmed in 1952 with Joan Crawford, Jack Palance and Gloria Grahame.

HOLLOW TRIUMPH Murray Forbes
"...a disturbed personality done in the noir tradition... an atmospheric and evocative yarn that spans the late 30s to through WWII."
—Amazon reader. Filmed in 1948 with Paul Henreid and Joan Bennett as *The Scar*.

Stark House Press, 1315 H Street, Eureka, CA 95501
greg@starkhousepress.com / www.StarkHousePress.com
Available from your local bookstore, or order direct via our website.

www.ingramcontent.com/pod-product-compliance
Lightning Source LLC
LaVergne TN
LVHW021819060526
838201LV00058B/3443